PRAISE FOR *UNBETRO*

Unbetrothed is an enchanting debut enriched with adventure, love, and a pinch of latin flair. From the start, Yamnitz creates an inviting, magical world that will easily draw readers in. With its poetic prose and engaging plot, *Unbetrothed* is sure to be a favorite for many readers to come.

~V. Romas Burton
Award-winning author of *Heartmender*

Unbetrothed is an enchanting tale full of joy, learning, and intriguing fantasy powers. With a touch of romance and a gripping battle, readers will be caught up in this story and the journey of these characters.

~Jenna Terese
YA author of *Ignite*

In a magical debut tackling themes of love, family, and worth, *Unbetrothed* delights with a vibrant Latin-inspired world, swoony love interest, and plot twists galore. This fast-paced fantasy leaves the reader cheering on Princess Beatriz in both her quest across kingdoms and her inner journey to become the princess she's destined to be. I look forward to reading any future titles Candice Yamnitz has to offer.

~Alyssa Roat
Multi-published author of The Wraithwood Trilogy

Magical. *Unbetrothed* is an action-packed gem with a cast of complex characters that kept me guessing, and the unique twist of Yamintz's world-building, tinted with a Latin flair, captured my heart. A blend of The Selection Series, Hunger Games intensity, and imagination of The Story Peddler, the story takes you on Princess Beatrice's quest for identity, purpose, and love—in a way you won't soon forget.

~Sandra Fernandez Rhoads
Award-winning author of *Mortal Sight*

A princess with a lot to learn, a charming prince with a secret, a fantasy world of powerful abilities and shifting alliances, and a dangerous quest with a handsome, mysterious stranger – *Unbetrothed* holds so much promise for an adventure filled with romance and unexpected twists, and it absolutely delivers! Anyone who's ever struggled with self-confidence will easily relate to Princess Beatriz, and her lovable companions and the vibrant setting make her journey unforgettable. I can't wait to see what Candice Pedraza Yamnitz writes next!

~Laurie Lucking
Award-winning author of *Common*

Unbetrothed is a wonderfully imaginative tale of a princess willing to go on a dangerous quest to receive a gift of magic. Candice Pedraza Yamnitz has crafted a young adult fantasy that helps girls embrace their own self-worth.

~Sharon Rene
Author of *Hesitant Heroes*

Unbetrothed transports readers on a fast-paced and magical journey filled with adventure, romance, and discovery. Impossible to put down, this debut is captivating from beginning to end.

~Chandra Blumburg
Author of *Digging Up Love*

UNBETROTHED

By

CANDICE PEDRAZA YAMNITZ

Unbetrothed

Iron Stream Fiction
An imprint of Iron Stream Media
100 Missionary Ridge
Birmingham, AL 35242
IronStreamMedia.com

Library of Congress Control Number: 2021949046
Cover design by Elaina Lee

ISBN: 978-1-64526-342-5 (paperback)
ISBN: 978-1-64526-343-2 (ebook)
1 2 3 4 5—25 24 23 22 21 22
MANUFACTURED IN THE UNITED STATES OF AMERICA

Map of the Agata Sea Region

PROLOGUE

10 Years Earlier

On my seventh birthday, I stood at the center of the dais and held my breath, gaze fixed on the giant doors across the cavelike room. Papá drummed his fingers on the golden armrest of his throne. Mamá sat beside him, clasping my hand tightly. A half dozen servants waited on each side of us. Ever since I saw Mamá transform my first bloodied knee into smooth tan skin, I had eagerly waited for the day I'd receive my special gifting.

A servant boy dashed into the throne room from a side door and handed Papá a folded piece of paper. Papá opened the note.

"What is the message?" Mamá asked in hushed tones as I nuzzled her shoulder.

"The whyzer of the valley sent a boy in his stead." Papá crumpled the paper into a tight wad. "This whyzer's supposedly the most powerful bestower of magical gifts. Sending a boy? He ought to rot—"

"Ezer," Mamá whispered. She gave Papá her you're-in-trouble look.

Papá cupped my cheek. "Don't worry, Beatriz. The boy can give you a magical touch too. And he brought you a gift. An unusual gift."

Every person in the kingdoms around the Agata Sea received a magical power between their first and fifth birthday. When no whyzer arrived on my fifth birthday, Mamá assured me a whyzer would arrive the next year. And when he didn't come on my sixth birthday, I cried myself to sleep. Now, on my seventh birthday, I would finally get my special gift.

The main door creaked open. Uncle stepped through wearing his royal green doublet. He escorted a young boy—no more than ten years old. I glanced at Mamá. She maintained a steady expression on her perfect face, but there was a tiny wrinkle between her brows.

Uncle and the boy drew near. Their footsteps echoed through the chamber. I could now see the boy's sapphire eyes and something clutched in his left hand.

Uncle bowed his head, and dark strands of hair flopped over his forehead. "Your majesty." He snuck a glance in my direction and offered a comforting wink. "The boy tells the truth." Uncle's deep voice rattled through my bones.

My knees bounced under my yellow dress. *Legs, stay still.*

"Check his story again," Papá said.

Uncle grabbed the boy's wrist and closed his eyes. "What did you bring?"

The boy smiled in return, completely unshaken by the gesture. "Naught but a loaf."

"Is it poison?" The markings on Uncle's palms shone like orange candlelight between the boy's wrist and Uncle's skin.

"No, but it is a special sort of bread," the boy said.

The majordomo stood below the dais, staring at my uncle. The maids stepped closer. Mamá remained motionless. Laude, my playmate, held my governess's dress skirt, stretching her neck to get a better look.

My stomach growled. I pressed my lips tight. The room remained so silent a crumb would have been heard falling to the floor. *What if the boy lied?*

Uncle nodded, bushy eyebrows scrunching together. "It is as he says. He'd like Princess Beatriz to eat."

Papá waved a hand. A stout maid took the boy's small loaf of bread, brown and ordinary, and placed it in my palms. Bubbles of joy danced through my stomach. I hadn't expected needing to eat anything. Dozens of stares fell upon the simple offering, and I sank my teeth into the loaf.

The warm bread melted on my tongue—the best-tasting food I had ever eaten. I took another bite, chewed, and swallowed the piece. What was supposed to happen? I felt no different. I continued eating until the bread was gone and brushed the crumbs from my fingers.

Everyone—guards, servants, and family alike—edged closer, unblinking.

The boy beamed, drawing me into his gaze. He whispered through pressed lips, *You shall come to the ruins in Valle de los Fantasmas. I'll be waiting in the valley.*

I frowned at Mamá. Did the boy just speak?

"What is her gifting?" Papá's words sounded crisp.

The boy bowed his head and said in a small voice, "In due time."

Those three words crushed my heart and wrung my insides into knots. Mamá hugged me, but even her warmth didn't ease my pain. Why wasn't I special enough to get a touch of magic?

CHAPTER 1

Starlight faded, and an orange halo graced the mountain-lined horizon with a promise. *Today everything will change. But not in the way I'd like.*

I rubbed the stone balustrade with my palms and arched my neck back. "If it isn't too much to ask, I'd like a betrothal to a handsome prince. You know the one I speak of—the one I've wanted to marry ever since I found out I should marry." *Would it help if I spoke his name out loud?* I pitched my voice lower. "Prince Lux of Pedroz."

Birds squawked in the tall cypress trees below my balcony. Not a single ancient text washed through my mind even though I had grown up tutored in the old ways.

I begged again, "If you—the Ancient One—care, why let your whyzer withhold my magical gifting from me? If he had done his duty, my life wouldn't be in shambles. And I would be betrothed." I stomped my foot on my balcony floor just as the sun speared the sky.

"Beatriz!" Mamá's voice hushed the curse poised on my lips. "What are you doing out here?"

I steadied my thumping heart in two breaths before turning. "Good day, Mamá. How did you wake?" My lips tightened with the expected smile.

She kissed my cheek in greeting. "Skip the formalities. Today has not yet begun." Her regal tone, so controlled, gave no hint to her emotions. She clutched the front of her silk robe and sat on the settee with perfect posture, slippered feet crossed at the ankles and cocked slightly to the side. Morning light shifted on her high cheekbones, and a tear rolled to her jawline.

"What's wrong?" I asked.

Mamá swiped her cheek. "I yawned." She waved a dismissive hand. "Let's review the Ceremonia Esposal one last time. It is imperative that you choose a suitor by week's end for the sake of your Papá and all of Giddel."

"But, Mamá ..." What could I say? I had agreed to this ridiculous ceremonia on a whim after a particularly bad nightmare and a few convincing words from Papá. I rubbed my hands along my thin chemise while crossing the arm span between us. "In my dream last night, the whyzer sent the boy again. He invited me into Valle de los Fantasmas to retrieve my gifting. I think it is important to take such a calling into account."

"Put going to that valley out of your mind." Mamá pursed her lips. "It will torture you worse than breaking an oath."

"You don't understand." I got on my knees and placed my head on Mamá's lap. "Being seventeen years old and unbetrothed has made me ..." Tears thickened in my throat. I tried to hide them—to be strong.

Mamá tipped my chin up and tucked wayward black hairs behind my ears. "You know my story and my struggle. But you? You are the esteemed Princess Beatriz of Giddel. Anyone who says differently is jealous of your title. You will attend the garden party and the ball, with your head held high." She traced the pale markings on my hands and followed the faint lines up to my shoulder.

I shivered. Those lines were supposed to be a sign of a powerful gifting. But what good did being marked do for me? To the servants, I had become a joke, a name people used behind cupped hands. Even the lowliest maid in the kingdom could light a candle with the touch of a finger or levitate parchment or heal a wound. But not me.

The only good I could do for anyone was to marry well. And for what? As Papá had stated time and time again, to build a stronger alliance with another realm to protect ourselves against Himzo—a kingdom set on our downfall.

A fire boiled in my blood. "All these years, you've told me the whyzers—the ones who hear from the Ancient One and bring to life our gifts—spoke to me in my sleep. Now when it's inconvenient for your plans, am I to ignore him?"

"Calm your tone. Nothing about this predicament is convenient for us." She pressed a glowing finger to my forearm, soothing my agitation with a light touch. "We'll meet before high noon at the garden entrance. I expect you to be amiable. No one likes a snippy princess." She placed a gentle kiss on my forehead and glided out of my bedroom and out of sight. The subtle patter of her shoes faded.

I flew to the balcony doors before she left. "Love you." Every muscle in my body tightened with more words I wished to speak aloud. What could I do to prove my worth to Mamá, Papá, all of Giddel?

"I love you too." She clicked the door shut.

Desperation swam within the turbulent waves in my heart. If I went through with today, I could forget marrying the man of my dreams. I'd need magic for that one. No king in any of the kingdoms along the Agata Sea would let their son marry a giftless princess. I leaned against the doorframe, one foot on the hardwood in my room and the other on the stone balcony.

Wait, what if I took an oath? Yes, that was it. If I used words of power, not even Papá and Mamá could stop me from demanding my gift from the whyzer. My breath caught in my throat.

What else could I do? Marry some lord just because it was expected? I balled my hands into fists, fingernails pressing into my palms. *Do I beg Papá yet again?* But no one besides my uncle could ever change Papá's decisions, and my uncle hadn't been seen for years.

Three words echoed through my mind. Maybe, it was a sign. I had never known anyone who dared to say an oath, but I would do anything to have choices.

"*Saalah kai hizzgezer,*" I called to the Ancient One, evoking a solemn oath. Along both arms, warmth blossomed just under the skin. The faint lines came alive and transformed into golden vines. They lit up for the first time in my life. I drank in the sight—elation tingling up my spine. *It worked.*

What am I doing? This is madness. Intense brightness emanated from my body, and I squinted. Words shifted and crashed into my mouth. "I promise to enter Valle de los Fantasmas in pursuit of my gift, even if I die in my attempt … before my nuptials."

Bolts of light raced from my wrist to my shoulders. *Did the oath take?*

The door to my room cracked open, and the golden glow vanished. I edged onto the hardwood, reciting pleas to Mamá: *Imagine the alliance we could form if I had more to offer in marriage. Truly, we don't know if Uncle went into the valley or if he chose to disappear. A broken oath could mean death.*

"Shh … She's still sleeping," my maid, Laude, whispered in her squeaky voice to someone in the corridor. She carried bundles of clothes in her arms while fiery curls sprung loose from the braid running down her back.

I hid on the balcony near the door. The heavy bed curtains blocked anyone from seeing my empty pillow and covers.

"Prepare the tub for her big day." She giggled. Her excitement clashed with my drumming heartbeat.

The servants scuffled about so loudly it would have wakened me had I been in deep slumber. I rolled my eyes. After the door tapped shut again, I scratched my forearms.

Had my vines really glowed so brightly?

What if I made the wrong promise?

I traced the gifting marks whirling on my cinnamon skin. Nothing seemed to have changed. Should I try another word of power? Would I be struck down if I said the wrong word?

Biri-Biri-Bum-Biri-Biri-Bum.

Rhythmic music drifted from the town below, announcing that the waste collectors had started work. A powerful gust carried a sweet, yeasty aroma, a baker's wind-shifting gift in use—the perfect special ability to garner more customers.

The sun continued its ascent, revealing the interlaced roads and flat-roofed houses throughout my seaside kingdom. Though all else was calm, a riptide churned in my chest.

Saying an oath wasn't a crime. There was plenty of time to plan an excursion into Valle de los Fantasmas. My parents wouldn't expect me to decide on a suitor tonight.

"There you are!" Laude's shrill voice prickled the hairs along my back. "Good morning, Princess Beatriz. Would you like breakfast at your settee or bed?"

I straightened up, trying to subdue a sting of annoyance. "What do you suppose?"

Laude skittered in with the tray and touched the tip of her glowing finger to a candle wick. A tiny flame danced into life. She placed the tray on my side table. "Which gown should I prepare for you: the red, yellow, or blue?"

"Douse the flame." I inhaled sharply, hoping she'd let me enjoy the morning air.

"Sorry, Princess." She blew out the candle. "There are so many gowns for your big day. I'm sure you'll be betrothed once the suitors get a look at you." She sighed with longing and threw her arm out in her expressive fashion, toppling over a cup. Papaya juice drenched my toast.

I massaged my temples.

"Ai-yi-yi! Sorry, Princess." She yanked a white cloth from her arm and mopped the amber liquid. "Did you hear of the letter from the Agata Isles? Everyone is talking about it. Lord Pau cannot make it because his father broke an oath."

An oath?

Laude continued, "They say the land ripped apart beneath his father's feet. The land ate him! Can you believe it?"

I pressed my palms together over my mouth and let out a small gasp. Laude took it as an encouragement to keep talking, though I stopped listening. Her story burned in my ears and twisted terror into my soul. A man was devoured because of a broken oath. And Laude, the queen of gossip, had to tell me. *Why must they send Laude on a day like today?* I pursed my lips to prevent any rash words from slipping out.

"But so many other guests have arrived—very handsome lords indeed." She let out a long whistle. "I ran into a suitor last night. His eyes nearly pierced my heart. And Blanca said she saw one who could turn his skin into scales of gold."

Princesses don't choose their suitor. Princesses are arranged to marry a prince. And what sort of men line up to be chosen? Lowly lords! That's who. I pulled my shoulders back, mimicking Mamá's elegant gestures. "Why would I stoop to choose a beggar for a husband?"

Laude's cheeks flushed, accentuating her freckles. "I meant no offense. All the men were handpicked by your father."

"Set out whatever gown you like. Send Myla to dress me. Now, leave." I forked a wedge of mango in my mouth to chase away the stale taste.

"But, Princess—"

"Leave."

"But . . . I was told not to go back down until you come with me."

My eyes snapped wide open. "On whose word?"

"Your mother's." Laude fidgeted with the corner of her apron.

At least she was not exuding joy anymore. Yet, no amount of correction smothered her perky disposition or impulsive tongue for long.

"Lovely." With a curt flourish of my hand, I dismissed her from the balcony.

Laude's story about Lord Pau's father rang through my mind. She was prone to exaggeration, but there must have been some truth to it. Mamá had mentioned the word *oath* too.

I must tell my parents about what I've done. They could fix it.

But that inner voice that knew how to pour salt over wounds whispered: *You are giftless, choiceless, and utterly trapped.*

CHAPTER 2

Sunlight filtered through the tall windows lining the long corridor at the back of the palace. Laude and I waited beside the garden entrance. My quivering breath fogged a windowpane, obscuring the queens, princesses, and high ladies from the eight Agata Kingdoms who mingled in the manicured garden just beyond the terrace.

Have courage. You will tell Mamá about the oath before the party.

Footfalls rumbled from the stairwell behind me. My older brother, Cosme, laughed with his three fellow Dotados, as they liked to call their little band of friends. As he passed through the sunbeams, the rays illuminated Cosme's darkened skin, drab cloak, and muddied boots.

The other Dotados offered cursory bows and planted themselves next to Laude, gawking at all the ladies outside. Cosme patted my shoulder as if I were a pet dog. I scowled at him, and he chuckled in return.

I pressed my shoulder blades back. "Where have you been?"

"About." He took my braid and tickled my cheek with its end. "Smile, dear sister. Such a sour expression will never get you a husband." Cosme whistled and cocked his head toward another passage. His friends followed.

I rubbed my cheek and glared after him. *Why should I be jealous of Cosme's spy work?* He only got to tramp about the farthest corners of the kingdom without opposition from Mamá and Papá while I begged to leave the palace.

Soon, Cosme would see my abilities and worth. I yanked on my sleeves, stifling a scream in my throat. Bronzed skin peeked from under the sky-blue lace, covering my markings yet revealing all the time I spent out at sea with my best friend, Prince Lux. Some things could not stay hidden.

Laude chirped with joy, observing the guests through the windows. "Princess Alexa's frock is so unbecoming."

Alexa was betrothed to the one suitor I wished I could choose. I pressed my lips into a hard line, so Laude wouldn't see the smile she inspired. Inappropriate comments from lowly servants should not be encouraged.

I flicked my braid back over my shoulder and ran my fingers along my high silk belt. Laude had arranged my hair and finished off my look with a matching wide-brimmed hat, praising my appearance. Yet there was nothing anyone could say to ease the ball of doubt in the pit of my stomach.

Rustling echoed from down the corridor. Mamá appeared with several servants in tow. Her vibrant pink gown swayed, creating the illusion of her gliding across the floor.

I forced merriment into my voice. "That color suits you well."

"You're doing that nervous patting again." Mamá grabbed my hands to stop my fidgeting and pulled me in for a gentle kiss on the cheek.

"Isn't there another way?" My confession about my oath played on my tongue, straining to be exposed.

She cupped my face. "Your papá and I would never put you through this if we didn't think it necessary. The Himzos might back down from their threats if they see a stronger alliance between us and the kingdoms around the Agata Sea. Now, where is my bold young lady?"

I inhaled and settled into a neutral expression. It's best to appear put together when being the center of attention. *I'll tell her about my oath later. The conversation will go better when we're around others and forced to appear civil.*

Mamá waved for her servants to open the doors, and we stepped outside. The women applauded our promenade across the terrace and onto the grassy path. Over the mix of voices, I heard scattered conversations regarding my gown, whom they thought I'd choose, and even the dreaded words: unbetrothed and giftless.

An older woman curtsied in a sparkling white gown. "Princess, are you ready for the ball? I hear it's going to be quite the spectacle." Her bright smile grated against my sensibilities. "It's a shame you and Prince Lux couldn't marry. You two are indeed a pair."

I nodded. *It is amazing how people always find the exact concoction of words that stab a person's heart.*

"You are all kindness, Lady Ressin," Mamá replied. Two smile wrinkles formed on her cheeks, and she led me to our seats under the white tent in the center of our vibrant garden. She leaned close to my ear. "Lady Ressin meant no harm."

"Of course. Did I appear anything but pleased?" I straightened my back.

Mamá raised a smug brow. "I am your Mamá, and you are a poor liar."

Sometimes Lux was even fooled by my polite gestures. How could Mamá see through them?

I scratched at my knuckles. *This is the time to tell her.* My heart quickened.

A servant in royal green livery handed her a cup of coffee and poured her a heavy helping of cream, then he handed me my cup. As I turned to speak to Mamá, Lord Pau's mother approached, golden hair shimmering through the beaded netting at the nape of her neck.

"Your Majesty. Princess. Both of you radiate like flowers among the brambles." Her face crumpled into deep crags. "I am sorry for my son's absence and my quick return to the isles."

"No need to apologize." Sympathy danced in Mamá's deep brown eyes. "I'm sorry for your loss. You should be with your son in this moment. I am sure he needs your support."

The lady's head bent low. "I begged him not to make an oath. And when his marks changed, he paid them no mind." Tiny sobs followed her words. "I'm so sorry. I thought I could ... I must depart." The lady pressed a handkerchief to her chest and stepped away with a tiny curtsy.

I gulped.

Mamá whispered in my ear, "What a foolish man. Look at the pain he caused his family. Only a fool would play with words of power."

I drank deeply from my delicate coffee cup. *Should I even tell Mamá about the oath?* The skin under my sleeves burned like if I rubbed against Maiden Plum.

The afternoon went on with one praise after another as gray clouds eclipsed the sun. Some women brought gifts for me. My favorite was a pocket watch that played a song I'd never heard before. While Mamá stepped away for a moment, a demure young lady handed me the gift and disappeared into the crowd. A sensation of unease wriggled within me, but the gift made up for any oddity in the giver.

A chilling breeze blew through the garden, and I rubbed my lacy sleeves. Several other women complained about the dropping temperature. Princess Alexa raised her marked hands to the sky, moving them in circles while maintaining an elegant curve to her glowing fingers. The clouds dispersed, bringing forth yellow rays of light. I was certain she'd brought the clouds to cast a gloom over our gathering in the first place.

Alexa's sea-foam eyes met mine, and she flashed a haughty grin. "Congratulations on your special day. Best wishes on finding your perfect match. I hope you don't mind my small gesture." She combed back stray curls from her face, lifted a hand, and flicked it, bringing in warm sea air over the garden.

A perfume of flowers wafted among us. Ladies close enough to witness Alexa's exhibition clapped and cheered, "Bravo!"

Alexa grinned with delight, and anger burned in my stomach. Why did she get everything I wanted while I got nothing? I steeled myself against the storm within.

Mamá excused herself from a conversation near the terrace and strolled to the empty space beside me. She lowered her head to mine. "Be glad that you are forced into humility. Arrogance is unbecoming." She continued to sip her coffee and nibbled on a pastry puff.

"Your Majesty." A short, round woman in a fine silken dress curtsied and stole Mamá's attention, talking about her very available gifted son.

I pinched my lips tightly, retreating into my mind. Mamá couldn't understand the hollow place within my ribs. Alexa had a betrothal to Prince Lux, and should the kingdoms go to war, she could fight. I wrestled with the urge to march straight to the valley to get my gift but settled on playing my role by pretending to listen to pointless gossip about this and that suitor.

Magic would become my reality, or I'd die. Promises made in the dark counted, made evident by Lord Pau's father.

I inspected the faint markings on my hands, and a metallic sheen caught my attention. My nail beds had a gold line stretching to my first knuckle where my vines had previously been. The skin under my sleeves itched just as much as my fingers. I should have asked Lord Pau's mother more questions about how long it took for her husband's markings to transform before he met his untimely end. But I didn't want to make myself into the fool who made an oath.

What have I done?

"Princess?" Laude said.

I startled and balled my fingers into fists, hiding my nails.

Laude stepped in front of me with a small, folded parchment on a silver platter.

Mamá cut a look in my direction but proceeded to attend to the round mother who now produced a small portrait of her son—the male version of herself. I plucked the parchment from the platter and flipped the note open. In angular strokes, black letters said: *You look bored. How about a swim?*

I darted a glance over my shoulder at the garden entrance doors. A tall figure with strong shoulders stood on the other side of the window. Sunlight shone on the back of his head, reflecting golden hair. My heart leaped, and I knew what I must do. I twisted the corners of my mouth downward. If anyone were to understand me, it was him. Judging by the concern wrinkled on Laude's forehead, I did an excellent job exuding distress.

"Let Mamá know," I said to Laude in a hushed tone. "I am feeling indisposed. I will retire to my room to … to rest. For tonight's ball."

Laude bobbed her head, quirking an empathetic smile. I slid the note into my sleeve pocket along my forearm, strode at a moderate pace across the grass, and to my favorite escape.

CHAPTER 3

A SERVANT RACED TO the garden entrance ahead of me and held the door open. I looked over my shoulder at all the esteemed guests at my garden party. The women meandered through the grassy paths, chatting, laughing, and oblivious to my whereabouts. Mamá stood in the same place I left her, listening to the same plump lady brag on her son. I spun my attention around toward the marble palace floors within the corridor. The servant shut the door behind me, leaving me alone with the person who sent me the note.

But then I realized that Prince Lux of Pedroz had company. Cosme stood several paces off, a hardened set to his jaw.

"Brother." My voice sounded like a chime.

Cosme furrowed his brow with suspicion. "Aren't you supposed to be attending to your guests?"

"I—I have a headache." My fingernails dug into my palms. I snuck a glance at Lux, whose turquoise eyes widened with meaning. We wouldn't get to sneak off to the royal beach if my brother insisted on keeping either of us company.

Cosme closed the space between him and me, blocking Lux out of the conversation. "I'll accompany you to your room."

Why did my brother need to be so hateful toward Lux? Hadn't we all grown up together? Cosme nudged my back toward the stairs, walking alongside me. I took one last peek at Lux, who mouthed *beach* and pointed toward the sea.

Cosme arched an eyebrow at me. Whatever playfulness had been there a couple hours before had disappeared. I hurried up the staircase beside Cosme. Our footfalls echoed through the spacious stairwell.

Once the main floor disappeared from our view and we started up the next flight to the third floor, Cosme sighed with exasperation. "Why is your friend hanging out at the door? He will ruin your reputation."

"Stop being a wet rag." I lifted my dress skirt higher and marched ahead of Cosme. "You are not Papá."

"Beatriz," he caught up to me, "there's a lot you don't know. If you paid closer attention—"

"I pay attention." My boot stomped onto the top step, and I swirled around to fix a glare on Cosme. "Why do you think I agreed to this *ridiculous* ball?"

"Hush now." Cosme lifted a finger to my lips while his eyes focused behind me.

Footfalls approached. An older woman and a young man descended the staircase. The older woman wore a long, lacy mantilla held up by a tall comb at the top of her head. The young man started to turn his gaze toward me, but I fled, cheeks burning.

"Sis-ter." Cosme elongated each syllable.

I strode around the corner into a dim corridor lined with portraits of the ancient stories. The gifted children passing from the old world into Valle de los Fantasmas. The dispersion of the gifted. The lost relics. The cursed northern kingdoms. The grand alliance. My boots tap-tap-tapped steadily with another set of boots thump-thump-thumping at my tail.

Cosme had been Papá's greatest supporter in keeping me from getting my gift. Had he ulterior motives like Lux supposed? Or was my older brother simply overbearing? I turned the corner and followed the corridor to my room. Only landscape paintings of beaches lined this space.

"Brother," I said tersely. "You've accompanied me. Thank you." I pressed the latch, slid into my room, and pushed the door shut. But

Cosme blocked the door with his muddied boot.

"Listen." His grimace deepened. "You might regret associating with Lux. Don't do anything stupid."

A pang of guilt stabbed into my heart. One part of me needed to rush downstairs to the beach to meet Lux. Another part of me stung with Cosme's expectation that I would do something irrational. I loosened my fists and peeked at my nail beds. The metallic line along my fingers seemed to creep a hairbreadth further along my markings. Cosme's warning about poor decisions had come too late. But his warning about Lux set my blood boiling.

I pursed my lips and steeled my emotions. "If you'd like me to smile and find a suitor tonight, you ought to let me rest."

Cosme stepped back, and I slammed the door with a thud. He was the last person who'd help me fulfill my oath. I stormed around my bed and into my dressing room. Three angled mirrors stood against one wall while trunks and shelves lined the opposite wall. I flipped open a trunk and yanked out my swimming dress.

Peeling my sleeves off, I let the outrage Cosme inspired drop with my blue gown. I set aside my chemise and put on the suffocating swimming material that buttoned at the nape of my neck. How dare Cosme ask me to part from the only person who understood me?

I tied my yellow dress robe tight around my body and sped out my bedroom. This wasn't the first time I'd run off for a swim, but it might be my last. Especially if … I gulped. No, I couldn't choose a suitor by the end of the night. Dark wood paneling lined the corridor outside my bedroom. A discreet door tucked at the end of this wing led to the servants' stairwell. I glanced behind me. Not a soul stirred. As I spun my head forward again, I slammed into someone ahead of me.

"Ai-yi-yi!" Laude screamed.

"What are you doing here?" I demanded. I caught my breath and adjusted my robe.

"Your mother told me to see what was wrong and to tend to you. She couldn't get away and was worried. And Princess," she looked me up and down, "are you going swimming? By yourself? Right now?"

Her eyebrows rose halfway up her forehead.

"I'm not that daft." I clasped my hands and pulled my shoulder blades together. "Have another bath prepared for me. I'll be back shortly."

"Yes, Princess." She stepped to the side to let me pass into the spiral staircase.

"And Laude," I called as I descended, "don't tell anyone where I've gone."

She thumped her palm over her heart and bobbed her head.

I fled downward like an arrow flying toward its target. My robe flapped as I hurried. I shot prayers to the Ancient One. *Please let there be no more servants in this back stairwell. Please give me more time with Lux.*

Perhaps, Cosme had a strange disdain for Lux, but he was right to be concerned about Lux and I being seen alone, especially on the day of my ball. My reputation could be tarnished if anyone got the wrong impression.

I sped into the undercroft. Though voices echoed from the kitchen, I turned left and hurried through the servants' corridor to the back doorway. The moment I made it outside, sunlight poured over my head. No one had seen my escape. I climbed up a set of steps and walked through a rocky path toward the private royal beach below. A rock barrier encircled the beach space along with palm trees.

On the shimmering sand, Lux sat with elbows propped on his knees. Should I tell him about my oath? Could he do anything to help me?

The closer I got, the more my insides twisted into a knot. Would Lux think me a fool for promising to go to Valle de los Fantasmas?

I galloped the last couple of steps and removed my boots to walk on the sand.

Lux caught sight of me. "Bea." He stood and wiped the sand off his pants. "I wasn't sure you'd make it."

"Of course I'd come. I just had to throw Cosme off our trail." I glanced over at the enormous castle above. The only windows to catch our swimming expedition were on the top floor. Only soldiers patrolled the back corridor, ready to ring the enormous bell in the front tower or light the logs in the back tower should an enemy arise. Their mischievous princess taking a swim with a friend wouldn't be anything new, nor would they gossip about it to the suitors.

"Come on, Bea." Lux stepped into the surf, letting the seawater rush around his ankles. "One last swim before you're a nearly married woman."

Why did he have to say something like that? It made this moment feel like the end. I let my robe fall from my shoulders and stepped next to him, hot sun rays kissing my forehead and shoulders. Warm water bubbled at my feet and pulled back into the sea. My eyes instinctively closed, soaking in the moment. This was my happy place.

"Good thing you got away from the party. You looked like you were walking through a living nightmare." Lux's tone held a sort of amusement to it.

"It wasn't as bad as the nightmare I had last night." I squinted at him, needing to gauge his response.

"What was it this time?"

"I had tentacles like an octopus and drained the life out of people from afar."

Lux pressed his lips together. "It's too bad you haven't a gift. You might be a formidable enemy."

But now I'm barely a bargaining chip. Useless. The words poured through my mind, stilling my tongue from speaking about my oath, about the ball, about Cosme's warnings.

"I'll give you a five-second head start," Lux said, snapping me out of my thoughts.

I smiled as a surge of energy rushed over me. I ran into the water and swam. The waves beat against me, but I lifted one arm up and then the other, inhaling every other stroke. The constant drum of my thoughts was swept away in the activity. Adrenaline pumped through my blood. Before I knew it, I reached the rocky barrier between the royal beach and open sea.

Lux laughed, a deep, rich sound. "You almost beat me. Six-second head start?"

"Never." I crouched to dive.

"Wait." Lux pushed himself onto a rock. "It's the redheaded dolt. She's waving."

I lowered onto my bottom and perched on a giant rock next to Lux. "Why so soon?"

Laude's squeaky voice cut through the rumbling of the sea. "Lady Myla's searching for you."

My heart sank a fraction.

"What's that on your fingers?" Lux asked. "Did you paint them?"

The metallic coloring glowed in the brilliant midday light. I splayed my fingers over my lap. This was my chance to tell him about the oath. To ask him if retrieving my gift could change our futures. If I wanted to have more days out swimming and racing and talking to Lux, I'd have to risk his good opinion. Why was this so hard?

"We don't have much time!" Laude's voice cracked. She waved an arm and pointed to the palace with wild enthusiasm.

Lux chuckled. "You better go before she faints from overexerting herself."

"Promise me you'll rescue me at some point during the dance."

He met my gaze, a sober expression sliding into place. "Of course, Bea. You know me."

"Good." I scooted into the water and swam to shore, remaining under the surface for as long as possible. The undercurrents tugged on my swimming dress. Pressure from the water hugged my body from every side, offering its condolence for a lost opportunity. My fingers brushed against the sand, and I righted myself.

"Princess, Lady Myla threatened to tell your mother about your little escapade if you do not come in right now." Laude gnawed on her top lip.

My feet propelled me up the beach, up the rocky path, and to the servant's entrance into the palace. I wrung the bottom of my dress, squeezing out the heavy seawater. My eyes automatically drifted toward where I left Lux, but he was gone. I strained to find him in the shallow water, but no signs of a human could be seen. My gaze darted to the rocky hedge to the east and then to the west. I caught sight of Lux's back, walking over the giant rocks between the royal beach and the rocky shore.

An ache overwhelmed my heart. "Goodbye," I whispered.

CHAPTER 4

I SAT ON MY vanity chair, winding and unwinding the golden chain of my mysterious pocket watch around my arm. Myla, the head lady's maid, droned on about the particulars for tonight. The ball. The suitors. All the details besides the ones I desired.

A shimmer on my hands caught my attention. I stilled, and my eyes widened. The metallic lines reached my second knuckle. A sense of urgency gripped my chest. If I fled the palace grounds at the end of the night, would that give me enough time to fulfill my oath?

Laude scrunched her face in concentration and stabbed pins in the braid that spiraled into a bun at the top of my head. Each tiny jab against my scalp punctuated my thoughts.

Myla clasped my shoulder, jolting me back. "Your father will bow and guide you to his first choice in suitors. Remember, you are expected to send half the suitors away by the end of tonight and announce your top choices. A stronger alliance to a powerful lord will help keep the Himzos from edging onto our territory."

The sandwich I ate at the garden party threatened to make a second appearance. "Do you suppose choosing a suitor tonight could end this whole parade sooner?"

Myla huffed. "This is a matter of great importance. I don't see why your parents don't choose for you. But yes. If you choose tonight, you can be married by the end of the week."

Sweat from my palms slicked the pocket watch in my hand. I

squeezed my fingers along the golden rim and pressed the latch. A melancholy tune rang out of the mechanism, and thoughts clinked through my mind.

Drag the Ceremonia on until a way of escape presents itself. What if there are no opportunities to flee? Perhaps Papá might be more reasonable than Mamá when he hears about what I've done.

The foreign song continued to play and soothed my bristled nerves.

Myla's narrowed eyes suddenly widened. "Where did you get that?"

"It was a gift I received at the garden party." I gnawed on my bottom lip and lifted the golden orb into my line of vision. The jagged grooves circled the cover like a mountain ridge on all sides.

Myla snatched the pocket watch. "I must speak to the queen about this." Deep wrinkles pinched between her brows. Then she fled my bedroom, and the door slammed behind her.

I clenched my teeth. Why did she take my watch? What had gotten her so upset? I should be the one bolting to Mamá's room.

"Your markings look more pronounced." Laude poked another pin against my scalp.

A fluttering panic surged within me. "Are they? I didn't notice." I rubbed my bare forearm, thankful for the long sleeves I'd wear tonight.

Laude tucked yellow and orange flowers into my braid. She pulled out wisps of hair to frame my face and curled them with her finger. "Will this do?" She smiled wide, puffing out her chest. The moment our eyes met in the mirror, she sucked in her cheeks.

"Let's just get the gown on," I said.

Laude arranged the bulk of wool and silk layers, and I stepped through the center. She lifted the fabric and tied the back of my dress. How was I to breathe with so many troubles clawing at me? I could be dead by the end of the week. Whatever benefit I was to the kingdom would be lost.

"Ta-da!" She skipped around to the front.

One glance in the mirror told me she had done well. The red dress accentuated my curves, the puffed sleeves hid my markings, and the gold embellishments sparkled. She had many faults, but also many talents.

Should I praise her even after the terror she inspired this morning? Mamá always said that a leader should respect all their people, including Laude. I held back a groan. "Yes, this will do." I watched disappointment spill into her features and felt I should say more. But I didn't. Nothing kept Laude upset for long, so why exert myself?

Someone knocked at the door, and a servant informed us it was time. We marched through the corridors and down the marble stairway leading to the royal entrance into the grand hall. The most esteemed guests from the Agata Sea kingdoms all waited for me behind the arched doors. There really was no escaping today.

My insides trembled, and a sour taste burned my tongue. So many expectant gazes. It brought me back to my seven-year-old self on the day I failed to receive my magical gift.

Breathe, Beatriz. Breathe. Myla did not say I needed to marry tonight. Today will quiet the gossip about a worthless princess. My chest tightened. I stood tall and nodded to the guards who wore my family's golden sigil on their doublets—the symbol reminding of my role in society.

After I get my gift, I'll have an even greater role.

The towering doors swung open, and the crowd blurred on each side of the walkway they created with their bodies. Candlelight reflected on the lattice designs racing down the marble flooring. At the end of the hall, Papá held my gaze as he sat on his gilded throne, Mamá and Cosme beside him.

I stepped forward. The bottom of my gown skimmed the tops of my feet, setting my nerves on fire. I tightened my facial muscles into an austere expression, a dignified look I'd practiced in the mirror all my life. Each step weighed heavily. Mamá's double strand of pearls choked my neck. To think, they felt elegant only an hour ago.

Halfway to the dais.

Keep moving.

Right foot. Left foot.

My heels clicked on the floor. Hundreds bowed and curtsied on each side, igniting flames of confidence in my gait. This was how it should be.

At the end of my walk, a servant offered his arm to help me up the stairs. I lifted my crimson skirt, ignoring him. *A dignified princess doesn't need help.* But I miscalculated the step, and my foot slipped.

I dropped my skirt, and my hands hit the edge of a stair before my face could. A collective gasp echoed through the cavernous room.

Humiliation layered on humiliation.

I blinked back tears.

The same servant offered a hand, his brow wrinkling. A rush of heat shot to my cheeks. If only I could disappear.

I pulled myself up on my own and climbed the last step. My dear papá and mamá remained seated, but they leaned forward.

Chin up. Shoulders back. I curtsied in front of Papá's golden throne. I took my seat next to Mamá. My vision grew fuzzy until the individual spectators lumped together into one gawking mass. The whine of a violin commenced. Musicians strummed the guiterna, and the tap of drums mingled through the hall.

Facing forward with a serene expression, Mamá whispered from the corner of her mouth, "This will soon be over."

I bobbed my head and attempted to replicate Mamá's calm example. Tears burned in my throat.

"You look stunning." With that compliment, Mamá turned her attention toward the line of suitors and their families.

The procession seemed never-ending. And while the princes lined up to show respect to Papá, the noblemen's sons were the ones to make eye contact with me. Those were the suitors, all dressed in finely patterned doublets. Some prospects I'd seen around court, and others came from distant kingdoms.

I swallowed hard. The thought that each of them wanted to become my husband lurched in my stomach.

Pricks of pain crept up my fingers, followed by the metallic coloring stretching to my third knuckle. This didn't bode well for the time remaining until ... my end.

Papá stood before half of those in line could make the proper greeting. Knowing him, he had had enough of the endless bowing. He strolled over and took my hand, inviting me to dance. We stepped down the dais stairs. This time, I was careful to place my foot mid-step. Stringed instruments trilled the traditional Paso Giddelian as we spun into the dance. I peered up at Papá, calmed by the affectionate gaze.

"Daughter, you've never looked more lovely."

A blush crept up my cheeks. With his high spirits, he appeared ready for me to tell him about the oath.

Papá continued, "I know we've put more pressure on you since Himzo threatened to attack. The Agata Sea alliance isn't as strong as it used to be, and we need other kingdoms to join our fight."

"If you allowed me to visit the valley—"

"No." He firmed his jaw. "We already lost your uncle to that place. How could I bear losing you?"

"Can I benefit anyone without some sort of magic? My markings promise us a great power. If I have half your gifting, we could be an unstoppable force."

Candlelight glimmered in his green-and-brown flecked eyes. "You need no gift to shine."

Warmth blossomed in my heart, and I basked in Papá's protection and acceptance. We continued to step in the same mechanical pattern in perfect synchrony with the music. How easy it would be to accept his words as truth. But an argument continued to form in my head. I needed him to think like the commander of his army rather than a protective tigress with her cubs. It slowly occurred to me that I would have to sneak away. Papá had no intention of letting me go on a dangerous quest.

He lifted my hand high and led me to the first suitor: Marden.

I kept my cheek muscles still, though everything in me recoiled.

Marden was a nobleman—tall, handsome, and everything Papá wanted for me. If only he weren't so ... boring. After he twirled and dipped me a few times, another suitor tapped his shoulder to cut in—thank the Ancient One—and I danced with the new suitor, who sported a strip of beard on his chin. A musky cologne overwhelmed my nose.

This transfer of dance partners continued on and on. One name after another, most of them taller than I was by half a head or more. I rubbed my sore neck, muscles protesting for a lesser angle. My feet complained the most, constrained in pointy shoes. But there was no hope of soothing my poor toes until the night's end.

In the crowd, a group of men stared at me. One round fellow failed to hide a giggle behind his fist. Unease settled deep within me. My lanky dance partner grinned with a twinkle of mischief in his eyes, the color as inviting as shallow seawater. It reminded me of childhood days at the beach, of Cosme and Lux, one-upping each other until someone got hurt.

Lux tapped the man's shoulder, releasing me from having to endure this stranger. I breathed easily, letting Lux embrace my waist and hold up my hand. The tip of my shoe caught on my other heel. I stumbled through a spin and turned into his body—his face so close I could shift up the smallest bit and kiss him. All the watching courtiers and royalty blurred in my peripheral vision.

His eyebrows arched as he scanned my face. "Let's take a walk on the terrace. You need a break." Giving me no room to object, Lux led me off the dance floor. He held one hand high and touched my back with the other. My senses awakened to the warmth and pressure of his fingers.

People parted the way. I should have stayed inside the hall, but I needed time with him. I strode into the corridor and onto the terrace, not stopping until I reached the railing overlooking the garden. "Thank you, Lux."

Lux's smile transformed his face into someone irresistible, even though his big nose didn't pair well with his thin lips. He turned to sit on the low stone railing. Lantern light glistened off his sun-bleached hair. His eyes missed no detail as he caressed me with his gaze. "It's my pleasure, Bea. I hope this evening has fulfilled everything you've dreamed of."

My heart fluttered. Long ago, I overheard his father, King Rodulfo of Pedroz, say to Lux that he would not have the future Queen of Pedroz be a useless, giftless girl like Princess Beatriz. The memory soured in my stomach.

It occurred to me that I needed to tell him about my oath. Maybe he could help me figure out how I could make my escape. He'd always had a way of making complicated plans seem simple. He was unconventional and shrewd. I should tell him everything, including my feelings. *He's a betrothed man, Beatriz.*

I should still say something. What did I have to lose? I squared up to Lux, gathering my courage, and I opened my mouth.

But Lux hissed, "One of your brother's ghouls found us."

CHAPTER 5

SO MUCH FOR A *private conversation.*

Marcoin, one of Cosme's closest advisors, approached Lux and me out on the terrace. "Princess." Marcoin bowed so low his beard almost touched the stone floor.

"Is something the matter, Don Marcoin?" I asked.

"No, dear Princess. Your brother requests an audience with you."

My brother must have seen us exit. I flashed Lux an apologetic smile. Lux nodded in understanding, cheeks dimpling. I reached for his hand but stopped short. Marcoin would tell Papá about my impropriety, yet again.

"Prince Lux," I released every bit of my sentiment into my tone, "will you honor me with your presence? Tomorrow, before you return to Pedroz." I would declare my love before fulfilling my oath. It was my last chance.

"As you wish, Princess." He tipped his head.

I whipped my crimson train behind me and followed Marcoin into the palace, peeking through the windows at Lux. His gaze settled on the palace walls, a brooding expression furrowing on his brow. What ran through his head? At least he was not running to Her Haughtiness, Princess Alexa. Even thinking her name set my blood churning.

We crossed the threshold into the hall. Dancers clapped in rhythm and twirled their partners. Courtiers in bright velvets and silks from every province prattled in tight circles. Marcoin greeted and maneuvered his way past the dancers while I teetered behind him. Pain shot through my pinched feet, and I held my breath, giving curt nods to various suitors. All the formalities tired me to the bone. *Play your role tonight.* When we reached the opposite side of the room, Marcoin bowed to my brother.

Cosme brushed his lips against my cheek in greeting and stepped back, wearing his version of an engaging smile. "Dear sister, I'd like you to meet my friend, Sir Lucas."

Sir Lucas, a taller gentleman, drew in a long breath and bowed. Sandy hair flopped over his forehead. I had danced with him earlier but chose not to converse. He looked like every other suitor with a grin and a styled mustache.

"Princess, it's so good to see you again," Sir Lucas said.

"The pleasure is all mine." I stretched a practiced smile from cheek to cheek and addressed my brother. "What urgent matter do you wish to discuss?"

"Nothing of a serious nature." Cosme sipped a ruby liquid and waved a hand in the air, levitating another flute from a server's platter into my hands.

There he went again, exhibiting his gift. I sniffed the liquid and recoiled—the pungent stench of spirits repulsed me. Must he look so smug after interrupting my time with Lux? Cosme met my fury with a playful raise of his eyebrow and darted a meaningful glance at his friend. I squeezed my glass, knowing I needed to bide my time and be amiable, as Mamá liked to say.

So I turned to Sir Lucas, who downed a fizzy, orange drink. "How do you know my brother?"

"Prince Cosme and I spar. He has quite the jab. But don't worry, Princess, I make him work hard for a win."

I wasn't worried. Lucas fidgeted his hands and blinked. A nervous tic, perhaps? *Be kind, Beatriz. This man has nothing to do with Cosme's scheming.*

I said the first thing that came to mind. "What gifting do you possess?"

"I cast wards."

"Like warding spells to keep the Himzos out of Giddel?"

My brother cut in. "Yes, you should see him cast one some time. It's quite the spectacle."

Sir Lucas gave an embarrassed smile. "It's nothing special, Princess. Mostly, I replace wards that have gone missing."

I glanced at my brother, who nodded and took a gulp from his flute. Unease burned in my stomach. These wards protected all the kingdoms around the Agata Sea from invasions. "I didn't know wards could go missing."

"Yes, wards diminish after a time. As of late, there have been many that have gone missing. It means our enemy is scheming for our land again." He must have seen my agitation because he amended, "So long as I'm around to replace them, our kingdom is safe."

"Brother, did you know about this? No one has told me anything." I tried to conceal the hard edge of my voice. *Another reminder about how useless I am.*

Cosme levitated another glass from a server's tray two arm spans away. "Yes, I did. You already have a lot to consider. We didn't want to worry you. Take heart, I will be out to sea tomorrow, investigating."

"That reminds me." I examined his polished leather shoes and white stockings, such a contrast to his appearance earlier. "Where had you been this morning before the garden party?"

He clicked his tongue and shook his head. "Papá forbids me to share Dotado business."

Of course, I'm not privy to important information.

The air in the room grew stifling, and I plopped my glass on a passing servant's tray. "I'm feeling indisposed. Brother, could you escort me to my room?"

Cosme grinned with a spark in his deep, brown eyes. "I would, but I need to speak to Don Marcoin. I'm sure Sir Lucas will be happy to take you."

Screaming was not an option. I looped my arm through the crook of Sir Lucas's elbow. My hands balled into fists, nails jabbing into my palms.

Heads turned as we strolled past insipid suitors and their mothers. I assumed they thought I had chosen a suitor. Angry tears formed behind my eyelids by the time we arrived at the foot of the royal staircase.

I stopped and pulled away from Sir Lucas. "Thank you for accompanying me, but I can walk myself from here."

"Are you sure?"

He must have noticed how I did, in fact, need his assistance. A blister had formed on my little toe. I wasn't sure if I could make it up the two flights of stairs and keep my dignity.

A servant passed, and I called, "Hello there! Retrieve Laude for me." I turned back toward Sir Lucas and ground out, "You are all kindness. Laude will be here shortly."

Sir Lucas stood by my side while I waited. His boot tapped the marble floor, filling my ears with an uneven beat.

"Will you be staying the week?" I asked.

"Yes, I will. I hope to spend more time with you, Princess."

My eyes widened. I knew he was in the running, but hearing him say it wrung my insides.

Laude's frizzy hair peeked out the servant's door, and tension seeped out my muscles. "Look, there's Laude," I said.

She scampered toward me, wiping her palms on her apron. When she saw Sir Lucas, her jaw dropped, and she maintained a dreamy-eyed stare while striding toward me. Lucas twiddled his fingers and blinked even more.

I tried to shoo him away with a dismissive wave, but he didn't budge. "Laude, could you escort me to my room?"

"Of course, your Highness." She came alongside, and I linked arms with her. When I leaned heavily, she wrapped her arm around my waist instead. Lucas meant nothing to me, so why did this embarrass me? We reached the top of the steps.

Laude dashed a glance at Sir Lucas again. "He's awfully cute. Are you going to choose him?"

I pursed my lips. "Just help me to my quarters, and please stop staring."

CHAPTER 6

The time had finally come. Twirling a pink frilled flower between my fingers, I strolled on a grassy path in the garden with Lux by my side. Last night's coming-of-age ball was just the beginning of my search for a husband. It hadn't been a day yet, and I already needed a break—no, I needed to escape.

I passed a sly glance over at my companion. "What gift do you possess?"

Lux stopped mid-step and cocked his head. "We've known each other since we were born. How do you not know?"

"You've never talked about it. I know it has something to do with the way people see you. You used to have a deep scar down your cheek, and I don't see it anymore." I squinted at him, sun blazing in my face.

He closed his eyes while taking a long breath of sea air. In a blink, a scar stretched from his eye, down his cheek to his jawbone, and disappeared again.

"You can change your appearance any time you want? Can you change your skin color or the length of your nose?"

"Yes, yes, yes. You're right about my gift. I thought I had mentioned it before." He bent over a hibiscus shrub and plucked a giant pink flower. He handed it to me casually and kept walking. "I know you've only had a night to consider your options, but who is the lucky lad you're thinking to marry?"

I tucked the new flower behind my ear, readying myself to hear another speech about the good qualities of such and such suitor.

Laude asked me the same question this morning. Mamá and Papá cut the list in half for me. They all had opinions. Laude swooned over Sir Lucas. Papá thought Duke Marden served our purposes well. Mamá thought I should spend this week getting to know each of the suitors better, though she, too, spoke generously about Duke Marden. My brother laughed about it all and left on his voyage.

I crossed my arms. *How does Lux not see that he's the only man I've ever dreamed of marrying?* A knot formed in my heart. *Should I make my declaration now?* My mouth went dry.

I scuffed my feet along the gravel. "I don't want to marry any of them."

Lux laughed. "You can't remain unbetrothed forever."

"That's easy for you to say. Doesn't Princess Alexa of Aldrin wait for you to set a date?" I said sardonically.

"Touchy, touchy. Why don't you like Princess Alexa?"

"Pshh. What's not to like about a snotty, green-eyed goddess? I love it when she flaunts her gift. Like when she made it rain at my beach party. What a perfect present. All was forgiven, of course. She's got that thing that makes every man's head turn—even on her worst day." A quiver of anger vibrated in my chest at the mere memory of my parents forcing me to accept her apology.

"I sense jealousy." The way Lux wagged his brows made me want to slap him.

Why did I waste my time with him? I started walking back toward the terrace.

He caught my wrist. "Don't be like that. You are the Princess of Giddel. The most esteemed kingdom around the Agata Sea. Every other girl, including Princess Alexa, would love to be in your position."

"No, they wouldn't."

"Yes, they would." He lifted his chin, examining me. "You have your mind set on needing your gift."

A lump formed in the back of my throat. I would not cry. "You would too if everyone constantly reminded you of how useless you were." I looked down at my feet and drew in a deep breath. "Lux, I have something to tell you. I—I made an oath to go visit my whyzer, and I think I'm running out of time. Please tell me there's a way out of this."

Lux's eyes flicked wide open, and then his expression softened with compassion. He drew me in a hug. His warm embrace melted my body. He smelled of sweet flowers, seawater, and sun-warmed skin. I'd be chastised for this hug if any of Papá's advisors saw us. He pulled back a bit. "Why don't you go to Valle de los Fantasmas right now?"

"Is this another one of your jokes?"

"I'm serious." He cocked his head with a gleam of something mischievous. "Didn't the young boy tell you to go to the valley when the time was right?"

"But Lux, no one who goes in comes out. My uncle, for one. Many others have washed up dead on the shores of the river. Are you trying to get rid of me?" I swiped his hands off my shoulders.

"I don't know of any loopholes in making an oath. There may not be any."

"Then what do I do?" I pinched the bridge of my nose.

"You, Beatriz, are stubborn. You should have gone on this expedition years ago. That boy gave you directions on how to get your gift. You tell me you have nightmares about this regularly. You mope and groan about how you need this gift to be happy. Stop your whining and go get it."

I swallowed hard. He was right about me always complaining. Could I go through with such an expedition? Did I even have a choice? "My papá and mamá would never approve of such an excursion."

Lux snorted. "When did you start asking permission? As I recall, your parents told you after our boating incident to make your fanciful ideas less noticeable."

A smile spread across my face. "If you hadn't been so keen on swimming, we wouldn't have gotten caught."

"Exactly! Take a few of your servants and tell your parents you're heading over to picnic in the mountains. They wouldn't be the wiser of your true motives." He pressed his lips together.

"Only if you break your betrothal with Alexa." The words had sprung out of my mouth, and there was no going back. I held my breath and pouted my lips. Feigned confidence was the only way to proceed.

His gaze softened my heart like butter on warm toast as he drew nearer. He leaned into my ear, his breath brushing against my neck. "I'd break the betrothal for you."

A tingle of glee spread from my neck all the way to my toes. I stepped away, searching his turquoise eyes to make sure I had not just imagined this moment. Did he feel the same way about me? A muscle in his jaw tightened, and I followed his gaze toward the terrace doors. Sir Marcoin, in all his pomp and sense of propriety, glared at us.

Bells of warning shrieked in my mind. *Coming out here with Lux may have been a mistake.* My chances of finding an acceptable match were slim, especially if the other suitors took offense to this intimate conversation like Sir Marcoin. Well, that is if I planned to find another suitor.

Taking in the question quirked his eyebrow. I pressed a fist to my lips. Why was I flirting with danger? The markings on my knuckles glistened with a metallic sheen. My stomach clenched.

"I need to go." I whipped around, my heart buzzing louder than bees around a hive.

Lux called out, "Bea, I'll be here when you get back. You deserve more."

I took one last peek at him. He watched me, so refined in his white doublet. I found myself hoping against hope that I would be able to call him more than a friend when I returned from my quest.

"Princess Beatriz, do you need anything?" Laude huffed, racing to catch up to me as I strode to my room from the garden, head spinning from my time with Lux. She shut my bedroom door upon entering.

I paced the hardwood in front of my four-post bed and considered her question for a minute. There was so much I wanted, but could Laude help me? The ripples along my bed canopy reminded me of the many mountains around Giddel. I needed to go before the oath consumed me. Laude could accompany me along with my other maids. Mamá would not oppose a picnic in the mountains. She, of all people, understood the stress of choosing a suitor.

"Yes, I do need something. Could you prepare for a picnic in the mountains tomorrow?" I stopped to study Laude's reaction.

Her head cocked to the side, but no suspicion shone in her gaze. "Of course, Princess. Who will be joining us?"

"Only me and you and a couple other maids and drivers and a coach. No, make that a wagon."

Laude's blue eyes widened. "Should we wait for your brother to come back from his voyage?"

"My brother won't be back for another week or so. Yes, get the drivers, food, and other details arranged. I need a change in scenery."

"Of course." Laude bowed her head and twisted around to exit.

"And Laude," I called before she turned the door handle. "Keep this a private affair. I wouldn't want any of the suitors following us on our trip." I winked.

Laude's playful smile accentuated her freckly cheeks. "Of course, your Highness. One can never be too careful with so many handsome fellows about."

"This has nothing to do with those nobodies." I pressed my fingernails into my palm. Could I trust her? If she didn't understand my need for secrecy, she'd surely slip and tell Mamá. She had to know the truth.

My shoes tapped as they crossed the space between her and me. "Laude, we won't be going on a picnic."

"We won't?"

"No." I exhaled. "I... I sealed an oath to go to Valle de los Fantasmas."

She yelped, chin quivering.

"Shhhh! Now you understand. We can announce to the others our true plans mid-trip or ... you and I can take a walk alone and end up in the valley." Blood pulsed in my temples.

Her face paled, and for good reason.

"You'll wait for me outside the valley while I go in." I swallowed hard, burying doubts threatening to emerge. "We leave before first light. Arrange the details." I flicked a wave of dismissal.

She opened her mouth but snapped it shut. Seconds passed. Then she slipped out of the room, gnawing on her bottom lip.

Could I pull this off? I plopped down on plush white covers. Did I have enough courage to follow through with this plan? I pushed out the air in my lungs to try to calm the knocking against my ribs.

As my plans came together, the vines on my arms loosened their grip, but the metallic coloring spread up to my wrists, twisting my insides. Lux was right. I complained too much about my predicament. If I wanted a life worth living, I needed to pursue my dreams. No matter the risk.

CHAPTER 7

I CLUTCHED A LOAF of bread and a bundle of cheese in one hand and carried my bedside candle holder in the other. Candlelight shifted across the dark corners of the getaway tunnel. Something scurried in the blackness, and I moved backward, my foot catching on my other shoe. My arm shot out, dropping my food, but I righted myself before I fell. The tiny flame dimmed, and I held my breath as the fire danced to life again. Cosme and I hadn't played in the secret passages for years but planning an escape, and hunger pangs, seemed like the best excuse to enter the bowels of the palace.

Scooping my meal back into my arm, I continued toward my room. The stairs into my closet were narrow, and I struggled with the trapdoor. I managed to unclick the latch with two fingers and bump the door over with my head. I slid my trunk in my dressing room over the opening and locked it in place. My plan would work. The ease of tiptoeing around the palace unnoticed almost seemed too easy.

Tap-tap-tap.

I froze. Someone was in my chamber. Had I been caught? I left the food on the trunk and stepped into my room. A headache crept up the back of my head as I searched for the noisemaker. The doors to my balcony were propped open despite me having left them closed.

Mamá stood on the balcony gazing out at the Agata Sea. The waves rippled across the surface, reflecting hues of orange and yellow that matched Mamá's gown. Should I pretend like I just happened to walk out of the bathroom?

"I apologize for missing dinner with our guests. I have a headache." I kept my chin high and sat on the settee, my back straight as a rod.

She twisted around, lips squished together, and worry lines deeply grooved along her forehead. "Beatriz, I have something serious to speak to you about." Her tone was flat, but her look held a secret message. I couldn't decipher it.

Did Laude report my plan to her, or had palace gossip reached her ears already?

"You must understand that we do the ceremonia for your own good." Mamá pulled the tail of her dress out and sat in the armchair across from me, leg touching mine. Her large, brown eyes fixed on my face.

I stared at them, seeing my own thick lashes and round, brown eyes. They were the only features of hers that I inherited. Why couldn't I have inherited her confidence in her weaker gifting and the way she gathered others' esteem?

She continued. "You know our predicament. Word has reached our ear that Himzo has already moved their soldiers to the border. If there were another way, we'd have chosen it. I feel most guilty for your lack of gifting since my own gift is so weak."

"Mamá—"

Her hand lifted. "Your papá and I thought it would be fair to allow you the liberty to choose your husband. But I see that it takes its toll on you. If you would like, we could decide for you or give you more time."

Both options wilted the bud of hope Lux planted. I wove my fingers together and forced lightness into my voice. "Do you think the boy with the loaf was sincere when he said I should go to Valle de los Fantasmas?"

She drew in a deep breath. "Yes, my dear."

"Shouldn't I go there now since it is time for me to wed?" I bit my lip and turned my face toward the choppy sea. Was I too transparent? Mamá always had a way of reading my mind, and I couldn't jeopardize tomorrow if she did not agree.

Mamá shook her head slightly. "The whyzer in those mountains is powerful. He lets no one near the old ruins and has no tolerance for those who test his power. I will not jeopardize your life for something such as an Agata gift. And remember your uncle. He had a duty to serve and protect Giddel and gave it up for what? To be snuffed out by the beasts that roam the valley."

"But Mamá, you see what life is like for me without a gift." My voice cracked. A wave of emotions crashed against my heart. "Every person has a place. Cosme flexes his gifting, and it strikes fear in our enemies. Papá can control other people's movements, scores of people at once. You heal with a touch. But what can I do?"

She tucked wavy strands of hair behind my ear. "You are not a sum of achievements. What would that say about all those who are not born with the gifting mark? Do they not have value?"

"I know. I know. But I am supposed to serve the kingdom with a gift, just as all in our lineage have done. It feels so futile that all I can do is marry someone useful."

She stroked my hand. "You need not marry. It might take more convincing for your papá to approve of you remaining unbetrothed, but I'm sure he will come to understand."

"No! Don't do that. Time. That's what I need." I paused, hearing a wave slap the rocky shore and the slurp when it receded. *This is it. I need to ask right now.* "Could I retreat to the waterfalls of Mount Giddel to get my thoughts in order?"

Mamá thought for a moment. "Yes, but go no further than the river. Himzo soldiers have been spotted patrolling the other side. You will need a group of soldiers to escort you. How would you like retreating to your aunt's chateau in the west instead?"

Aunt Isabelia lived along a path that led to Valle de los Fantasmas. Why didn't I think of that earlier? I focused on keeping each muscle in my face under control. One wrong move, and she would notice. "I could if you called off all the extra soldiers."

"My dear, the soldiers must go. Imagine if you got captured. Himzo would pay a fortune to get the upper hand. Nothing good comes from our enemies, and there is something hidden stirring in the air. I feel it."

"You are gifted in healing, not foretelling. You need not worry."

Mamá patted my head. "Your fanciful ideas will one day lead you into real danger." She stood and walked to the open balcony doors, dragging her gossamer train along the stone floor, before turning back. "You misunderstand my gifting. My whyzer honed my gift, but I've spent my days as queen in the words of the Ancient One. Because of this, I know you are meant to do something great. But the way you are right now, I'm not sure receiving your gift would satisfy your longing." She sighed. Her shoulders dropped a fraction, then she quickly raised them again. Did she know about my plans?

I cleared my throat. "You need not worry about me. I'm sure fresh air and calmness will make me happy."

"I hope so." Mamá pushed her shoulders back and lifted her chin, leaving.

The vines along my arms prickled. A need to prove her wrong burned even deeper under my skin.

Mamá will see how happy I am by this time next week.

CHAPTER 8

LAUDE, CATA, MATTHA, AND I sat on the wagon bed, watching the morning light bathe the stone towers of Giddel Palace. What a strange perspective to see my balcony from afar. We hit a pothole, and I bounced hard. The two male coach drivers offered no apology. They had required more convincing to go on this excursion than the maids. To think, I had to beg the disheveled stablemen to obey me. They finally accepted the bag of coins I offered and tucked the lucrative incentive deep in their tattered pockets before we hit the road.

The crisp air blew stray hairs from my braid. No one would suspect I was the Princess Beatriz since I wore a plain white chemise and a gray overdress. My escorts clothed themselves in their most tattered clothes, extra effort on their part to keep our identity hidden. If I weren't clinging to the rails of the side of the wagon and clenching my teeth to keep them from rattling, I might have even giggled. I was on the quest for magic. The quest I'd dreamt of for so long.

"How far until we reach the fork?" I yelled to the driver.

He grunted. "Princess Beatriz, we will take a different route only used by the common folk. We won't be passing the fork." He gave Cata a sidelong look.

Cata nodded back at him. Wrinkles formed on the outer edges of her tiny eyes when she smiled. She had a stout body, always wore a smirk, and was not my favorite maid. Occasionally, she served me, but her regular duty kept her somewhere else on my floor.

Mattha cackled to herself. Why did Laude choose these two maids to travel with us?

Cata slapped Mattha's shoulder. "Shhh ... don't disgrace us in front of the princess."

Mattha rubbed her shoulder. Her unveiled stare sent a shiver up my back.

Protocol forbade maids to make eye contact with the royal family. I didn't know if my apprehension had spiked because no one other than Laude and Myla looked at me so openly or if something more transpired. Mamá said to trust my gut when it came to people. I broke eye contact first and searched the tree lines that blurred by us on both sides of the gravel trail. Misgivings slithered through my head, but I could do nothing about them.

We needed to outrun my papá's gift and his soldiers. Papá could control another person's body with his thoughts. If we stayed out of his eyesight, his power could not reach us. I willed the wagon to bump along faster, clinging to the side rails. The soldiers were certain to come in a couple of hours—once they'd realized we'd bolted without them. So long as my mamá insisted on soldiers, the chateau would never be an option.

Giddel disappeared behind a verdant mountain. A screeching hawk flew overhead.

After a while, we turned onto a more rustic road. The wagon lurched from side to side. I called to the driver, "Where does this road lead?"

He shouted over a shoulder, "To a special spot with the finest view. Only the best for our princess."

Laude wrapped an arm around the side of the wagon. Her curly red hair sprang from her braid, transforming it into a wild mane. "Princess, is everything all right? Should we change course?"

I swallowed, fears burning my throat. "No, Laude. It's just that I've never been to the east side of the mountains."

Laude clasped my free hand. "We can go back. I overheard Myla arranging a trip to your aunt's chateau."

"No. How would we go to," I widened my eyes, mouthing *Valle de los Fantasmas*. "There would have been too many soldiers and others to allow me to relax." The excuse rang off-key to my ears, but no one else turned in our direction.

Laude nodded with a smile. Did she understand what I meant?

The sun beat on our foreheads. We hadn't made it to the tree cover just yet. Instead, patches of thick grass leaned in front of the path, and rocks lined the road. The wagon swerved and hit a bump that launched us into the air. We plopped back down with a thud, and I rubbed my rear end.

"Should we not stop for water?" I yelled to the driver.

"There's a well up the path. We'll stop once we arrive." He whipped the reins hard over the horses.

With each sway of the wagon, a whisper of Mamá's warning echoed in my mind. *Your fanciful ideas will one day lead you into real danger.* We weren't near Valle de los Fantasmas as far as I knew. Going to my aunt's chateau with soldiers may have been the wiser route.

The horses pressed down the lane. Time stood still as miles slipped past us. The horses pressed on, and the wagon lumbered up the mountain until the narrow path leveled. We stopped. A stone well stood in the middle of a clearing at the summit of the hill.

"Get off for water at the well." The driver handed the reins over to the man next to him. He pulled a pail from the wagon before heading up toward the well, which was overgrown with vines.

Laude passed me a waterskin. The other two maids hopped off the side of the wagon and plodded through the grass to join the driver. Cata touched the driver's bicep while they talked. All three laughed as they dropped the pail into the well, and the driver turned the crank connected to the pail's rope. I sipped my water. Chills prickled the back of my neck despite the humid heat.

The smell of cucumber, jicama, and lime perfumed the air and chased away my apprehension. Laude laid out the rest of the traveling spread: refried beans and cheese over toast, chopped fruit doused with lime and sprinkled with spices.

"Where are the fish and meat?" I asked.

"I—I ... Cook was awake. I couldn't take them without him noticing." Laude tipped her head low.

I guess there was only so much Laude could do without getting caught. I began to eat my meal. I had to admit, the crisp taste of the fruits refreshed my overheated body.

Laude offered a sandwich to the grimy man holding the reins. The fool grunted. He had no decorum.

I dabbed my lips with my napkin. Should I tell the other servants we were headed to Valle de los Fantasmas? Cata and Mattha cranked another bucket, chattering in hushed tones among themselves. Our eyes met, and I averted my gaze. A metallic sheen crept up my forearm along the thin vine-like designs, promising death should I fail.

"Your markings are changing already," Laude said in a chirpy tone. She nibbled a piece of toast. "We might not even have to go to you know where."

I pinched my lips together. She must have mistaken the change for me receiving my gift. Not many Giddelians remember attaining their special power since most people get it so young.

The driver trudged toward us. "Princess Beatriz, we need to check this part of the path to see if it's safe for us to travel. Could you wait for us here at the well? It should take no longer than an hour to get there and back. Cata cooled some water for you girls with her gifting." His scraggly eyebrow lifted as if meaning to remind me of my lack of gifting.

"Yes, sir." Laude hopped up. She pushed our trunk of food to the end of the wagon, leaving the other two trunks.

"Laude," I snapped. The decision to stay should have been mine.

"Do you need help with that?" The driver lifted the trunk with a grunt. "Will our princess not go without some comforts for an hour?"

How dare he! I snapped my mouth shut. *When I get back, I'll make sure he gets discharged.* But for now, this man was our guide and protection. He lugged the trunk over to the well and placed it on the grass. Then he ambled behind Cata and Mattha, who trudged to the wagon. A warm breeze eased the knot of tension between my shoulders. It was only an hour delay.

Cata slapped the driver's back. "You aren't gonna do all the adventuring without us."

"You two will hold us back." The driver spat out the side of his mouth.

"Don't you dare, old man." Mattha shook her head and climbed up the side. Cata heaved herself into the wagon behind her fellow maid.

"We should replenish the water, Princess," Laude called. She filled a cup with some of Cata's cooled water.

The wagon rolled away through the trees, and the plod and bump of the horses and wagon faded. The wind rustled through the leaves. Twigs cracked somewhere in the forested area, setting off my adrenaline. Were there ferocious creatures here? I whipped my head toward Laude. She scrunched her nose in concentration while she poured water into our waterskin. Afterward, she grunted with each turn of the crank, jutting out the side of the well.

I sat on our trunk. "Laude, why did you choose Cata and Mattha and those two men?"

"I asked Blanca, but she didn't think it was a good idea. She also didn't want to lose her position in the palace. So she told me to ask Cata and Mattha since they might be willing to go on a secret trip. Cata said she'd arrange the horses and wagon." Laude's forehead glistened from her efforts.

Sweat trickled down my forehead. Would I see that wagon again? I dabbed the sweat with the back of my hand. They would not take my money and run. Would they?

"Don't worry, Princess. I'm sure they'll be back sooner than a coin flip." Laude pulled the pail to the ledge of the well and beamed with triumph.

Which mountain was Mount Giddel? Trees encircled us as far as the eye could see. "Do you know this area?" I asked.

"Princess, you know I've grown up all my life in the palace. The only places I've visited are palaces, gardens, and chateaus with you."

My stomach plummeted. How had I been such a fool? Laude, though loyal, hadn't any worldly experience. She wouldn't know a trustworthy maid from a swindler since she'd grown up with more privilege than most of the other maids in the palace.

"Naïve. Naïve girl." My harsh tone cut through the air.

"I'm sorry, Princess." Laude's voice rose an octave in shock. "I should have prepared better for our trip, but I didn't have time, and I know it wasn't your fault because you had all those suitors—"

I tipped my head back and grunted. "Enough of the rambling, Laude. The others aren't coming back.

"No, Princess, they'd never do that to you. That would put you in danger if we had no one else. And imagine if a Himzo soldier snuck onto our soil and found you. No, you'll see. They're going to make sure the road ahead is safe." She bobbed her head and slurped water from a cup.

"Did you not notice them whispering among themselves and the greedy way they eyed the coin bags?"

"That's just Cata and Mattha's way. I'll put three pennies on their good names." She searched her skirt pockets.

I scratched my arms. "Pennies? Have we come so low?"

A strangled chirp escaped her throat. "Forget the pennies—I left those back home—but you will declare me your greatest friend once the wagon returns." Hope danced in her smiling eyes as she stared down at the road.

I let out an exasperated breath. What else was there to do than hope?

CHAPTER 9

"I DON'T THINK THEY'RE coming back, Your Highness," Laude admitted after hours of denial.

The starlit sky domed over us. We used our trunk as a bench. I massaged my temples. Why did I let them take all our clothes and money? On the positive side, they left us the food, waterskins, and dishes.

"Princess? Do we sleep on the grass or take turns sleeping on the trunk?" Laude's voice trembled.

"I don't know." I scratched at my forearm, and moonlight caught the metallic color stretching further along the spiral designs. I unfolded my rolled-up sleeves.

"If you don't mind, Princess, you can sleep on the picnic blanket, and I'll sleep on this old thing." She bounced off the trunk and lifted a glowing finger to see the latch. "The grass is fairly springy, and Princess Beatriz of Giddel—"

I shot to my feet. "Laude, please don't use my name."

"Why is that?" She flipped the trunk open.

"Call me by any other name but my own." Shadows shifted in an oscillating motion, reminding me of a snake, so I slid closer to Laude. She grappled with whatever she had packed in the trunk, sending clinks and clanks ringing through the air.

"Like a secret name?" She squeaked as she rose with the blanket in hand. The cringe-inducing noise she made was, most likely, accompanied by an exuberant expression. At least her face remained in shadow.

"Yes, a name that does not include princess or Beatriz."

"Won't people notice your clothes?"

My sleeves felt petal soft against my fingertips. Then I reached for Laude's dress skirt. Hers scratched against my skin. "My outfit could pass for one worn by a townsperson, so long as no one touches it."

"Your Highness, I'm not too sure about that." She whipped the blanket, spreading it over the grass.

I rolled my eyes. "We don't have a choice. And call me something like Serilda or Vera or Aldanca or anything but my real name and title." I sat on the blanket, holding my knees tight to my body while Laude rummaged through the trunk.

Between Laude shuffling items, cricket chirps filled my ears, and the hoot of an owl sounded nearby. Just as I began to enjoy nature's waltz, Laude whispered, "Did you hear that?"

My pulse quickened. I tilted my head, straining for a growl of danger.

Nothing out of the ordinary. Frogs singing. An occasional rustle of leaves.

"Sorry, it must have been my imagination, Your Highness." She clapped the lid shut.

"Laude!"

"Sorry, Prin—" She stiffened. Her voice rose an octave. "I mean Miss *Cicadas*?"

The strange name hung on the night air. "Have you ever heard of anyone who goes by that name?" I turned toward Laude. Even in the dim lighting, I could see her hesitant grin.

"It's the first word that came to mind."

"Call me ehh … Cypress."

"Cypress?" Laude cleared her throat. "Miss Cypress."

"Just Cypress."

"I can't do that. It feels too strange." She settled on the trunk. "You know that Cypress is a plant? Isn't that kind of the same thing as an insect?"

I shook my head. I breathed in the cool night air and rested on my back. Pressing my eyelids shut, I pictured Lux next to me. How I wished I could be traveling with him. Really, anyone would have been a better companion than Laude. Even Duke Marden would have sufficed. Mamá said that I needed to be more kind to Laude. *Mamá must be blind when it comes to her.*

"Miss Cypress does have a nice ring to it."

Her words softened my frustration. Laude lay atop the hard trunk and brought her knees high to her chest to fit on top of it.

I turned toward the empty space beside me, guilt gnawing my insides. "You may sleep next to me."

"Excellent idea, Miss Cypress." She bounced over and nestled on the blanket.

Thousands of insects and snakes lurked nearby, but what choice did we have? At least it wasn't too cold. I shut my eyes. "Laude?"

"Yes, miss?"

I snuck a peek at her shadowed profile, and a lump formed in my throat. "You could head back home instead of joining me. We have no guide, and we're in more danger now than when we left. I must continue, but you don't need to go on with me." I hugged myself, feeling small and insignificant compared to the star-powdered sky. My hopes and dreams shrank to dust.

Laude gave my hand a gentle squeeze, just like Mamá would have. "I think *we* should continue your quest."

"Laude, you don't need to say that. The chances of us coming out of the valley alive are slim."

Our breaths came out in heavy sighs with only crickets trilling in the background.

"No," Laude raised her voice, "we need to finish this. You, because you're miserable knowing your gift is out there somewhere. Me, because I finally don't feel trapped. Sometimes, I wonder if the palace will suffocate me in my sleep."

I laughed. This wasn't what I expected her to say. In fact, I never considered what she felt—ever.

"I'm serious. I even have nightmares that the walls cave in over my bed. You call and call for me to help you, but the stones press in around me so tight I can barely breathe. And then I wake up."

The buzzing of the night surrounded me with the eerie sensation of awakening gripped by fear. A pinch of pity lodged itself within my ribs. "That's quite the nightmare. Let's not talk of such things. We have a long walk ahead of us, wherever we go."

"'Night, miss."

"Goodnight."

My marks itched, but my sleeves encased my upper arm too tightly to reach with my fingernails. I rubbed the silky fabric, but that didn't help. A lump in the grass jutted into my back, and I shifted. Another mound stuck out in such a way I couldn't get comfortable, so I returned to my original position. Laude's breaths slowed to a deep rhythmic sound.

Judging by my burning skin, I have very little time. The moon nudged across the night sky until my eyelids closed and I slipped out of consciousness.

When my eyes snapped open again, a gray-bearded man hovered above my head. Twilight shone around him, and a wicked smirk twisted his lips.

CHAPTER 10

Laude screamed. Several men laughed, their sinister rasps raising the hairs on my arms. I scrambled to sit up and take in my surroundings. Fog loomed in the air, blocking the view of the trees we'd seen yesterday, leaving us only able to see a circle of scruffy men dressed in shabby pants and dirty tunics.

"Good morning, sweet ladies. We hope we didn't disturb your sleep." The bearded man cackled as he stepped toward our trunk. He tossed the lid open. "We heard there might be something to fill our coin bags in these parts." He pulled out one of our pears and chomped into it.

Laude leaned into my shoulder, holding my arm while I counted ten men. Our chances of escaping were not good. *I've got to try something.* I shot to my feet and pulled Laude up. "Yes, sir. I am certain my papá will reward you greatly for bringing us back to Giddel."

The man cackled some more, slapping his thigh as if I'd told a joke. He was likely the leader. Strong hands seized me from behind. I kicked my captor's shins, but he merely cursed and tightened his grip.

Laude fought wildly as a burly man wrestled with her wrists to get her to stop punching. Another man pinned down her legs. She rolled her body, slipping out of their grasp. Might she break free?

The leader of the scoundrels tossed an exasperated gaze to the sky and descended upon Laude with a dagger to her nose. "You will learn to obey."

Laude stopped flopping. Her chest rose and fell in quick breaths.

The leader dragged his heavy-lidded gaze toward me, a malevolent curl playing at his lips. His boots padded the grass as he drew near. The first rays of morning light glimmered off his blade and sparked waves of goosebumps on my flesh.

He yanked my braid back, exposing my neck, and his hot breath lingered against my skin. It reeked of booze and rotting teeth. My stomach churned. "You are beautiful. I might have you for myself." He ran a hand against my thigh, lifting my skirt.

"Get away from me!" I tried to jerk free, but the man behind me tightened his grip.

The leader pressed the tip of the dagger to my jaw. "It would be a shame if I had to mar your perfect face."

I bit the inside of my cheek, and a quiver rattled down my back. My feet were still free.

"Tie them up." The leader unbuckled his belt and tossed it on the trunk.

My breath quickened. Panic flapped in my chest. A young man with dark hair approached with rope in his hands. He met my gaze and hesitated for a second, but that's all I needed.

I kneed his groin and threw my head back, smacking my captor's chin. He loosened his grip. Adrenaline pulsed through my blood as I ripped away and broke into a sprint toward the road.

My foot caught the ground, and I tripped. A body crashed on top of me, knocking the wind from my lungs. I gasped for air. Rough hands jerked my shoulder around.

My captor's dark brows knit into a fury. I screamed my throat raw. He clasped his hand over my mouth, and I bit hard. He jerked the hand back, and I reached for anything to help me pull away. There was only grass.

Desperation stormed through my blood as I twisted and pushed. I popped up to my feet. Intense warmth radiated inside my body. A black tunnel formed around the edges of my vision and narrowed.

I can't breathe.

Men shouted in the distance. Tree trunks blurred.

Need air.

Short, quick breaths.

More scuffling sounds that faded quickly.

Everything went black and then—nothing.

A breeze tickled my nose.

I blinked open my eyes and peered at blue skies through a ring of clouds. A thick layer of tall grass poked my arms. I sat up, and pain erupted from my ribs. *Where is the man who pummeled me to the ground?* I tried to call for Laude, but shards stabbed in my throat.

A man appeared above me. I clenched my fists, ready to fight.

"Miss. Miss, are you all right?" His brown eyes scrunched in concern. "You fainted."

I released air pent-up in my lungs. This fellow had a melodic accent, unlike the ruffians.

"Who are you?" My voice sounded hoarse.

He offered a hand, but instead, I shrank away and studied him. His dark wavy hair flopped past his ears. His face, clean-shaven and tan, reminded me of Duke Marden, but beautiful.

"Where's Laude?"

"There is another girl over there. We chased away those miscreants. My name is Zichri the Merchant."

That accent... and that name? I'd never heard them before. Though many kingdoms lined the Agata Sea, dozens of other provinces existed beyond the sea I knew little about.

Laude giggled somewhere nearby. *That's a good sign.* I sat up and scanned the hill. She stood among four men and threw herself toward one of them, hugging his torso. "Thank you, good sir. Thank you. I thought we were lost ... that we'd never see another kind person again." She threw her arms around another man, babbling the same words.

I struggled to my feet, and a wave of dizziness crashed around in my head.

Zichri blocked my view of Laude. "Are you all right? You laid there for a minute without moving. I thought you were injured. Or worse."

I rubbed my forehead and patted my wavy tresses. Hair dangled on the edge of my vision. Had I actually fainted?

"Do you need help walking?" He offered his arm. Unlike the men who attacked us, his white tunic was clean, for the most part. It had no embellishments or plush doublets like the courtiers.

"No. I can walk." I stepped toward the group by the well. "What happened?"

Zichri ambled next to me. "We were traveling along the road when we heard screaming. We rushed to help and chased those thieves away."

We could have been captured. I didn't want to consider what those men planned to do with us. I stifled a cry. My papá, mamá, and brother may never have seen me again.

"You don't look well. You should sit." Zichri touched my shoulder.

I flinched. Tears threatened to spill from my eyes. I pressed my hand to my mouth, unable to contain emotions welling up within.

Zichri's gaze shifted between the group and me. He bit down on his lip and reached to touch my arm but pulled his hand back. I filled my lungs until they might burst, but it didn't stop my ugly sobs from escaping.

"Miss." His voice turned weak. "What may I do to help?"

"Nothing." I sniveled and swiped my nose. Tears and snot smeared across my sleeve. Had anyone seen it? Zichri looked away when I glanced at him.

Heat rushed to my face. "I'm sorry for my lack of propriety."

Zichri chuckled. "There's no need to apologize. You've just been through an ordeal. We should move on, though. Where were you heading?"

I gulped. Should I tell him Valle de los Fantasmas or Giddel? "Where are *you* heading?"

He worked his jaw, seeming to consider the question for a second, then said, "Himzo."

I flinched. "Why would you want to go there?"

"Because it's my homeland." Zichri's careful tone etched a path toward scornful words about a cursed kingdom. A kingdom that snatched lands from its people and encroached on our treaties.

Mamá's words played in my mind: *Nothing good comes from Himzo.*

CHAPTER 11

Our new Himzo companions turned the crank at the well and filled their waterskins. They appeared like friendly travelers among the tangle of trees around us, but I knew better. Laude stood near them, oblivious and laughing at their banter while I ambled up the grassy hill. I couldn't decipher my thoughts. These men shouldn't have made it past the wards.

Clearly, the wards had failed; the five of them stood on Giddelian soil. How many more Himzos had infiltrated our lands? Did I need to abandon my quest to warn Papá? I let out a frustrated sigh.

Stick to the plan.

Marching back up to Laude, I filled with determination. Laude and I would get into the valley, but there was no way we'd travel alongside people of the very kingdom causing so much tension at home. *But what if they could help me?* The idea soured in my stomach upon wrapping my arms around Laude's skinny torso.

She flinched but patted my back in a hesitant embrace. Red frizz poked my nose as I leaned in close enough to graze my lips against her ear. "We need to get away from them. Say nothing. It might give us away. They are Himzos."

Laude stiffened. When I pulled away, her wide eyes glanced between the men and me. I nodded. She pressed her lips together, a slight tremble visible on her chin.

"We need to head out immediately." Zichri's voice rang with authority.

Laude and I locked stares while the five men stepped through the grass. Zichri waved us over to the road, but we hesitated.

"Prin—Miss Cypress, I will go wherever you lead. I meant what I said last night."

I glanced at the metallic lines that now had kissed my elbow. *I am running out of time.* My chest tightened. "To the valley."

Laude clapped her hands and bounced on her toes. "A quest for magic. I could scream for joy."

"Lower your voice," I hissed.

"Sorry, miss. I'm ever so excited. We'll also need some provisions." Laude flipped open the trunk and stuffed pears, bread smothered with refried beans, and waterskins into a woven bag.

"We'll also need to get directions." I stared out at Zichri and a lanky man waiting in our line of sight. Where had the others gone?

The three men came back into view, walking a black steed laden with supplies from wherever they left it during the altercation. I started toward them and called to Laude, "Follow my lead."

Laude carried the overstuffed bag, chattering the whole way down the hill. Did she truly understand how dangerous continuing the journey would be? Her smile swallowed her ears as she gazed down the lane. The road ahead curved downward out of sight, and another section of the path appeared on the mountainside across from us. The blisters along my heels and the side of my pinky toe suddenly throbbed, having not fully healed from my ball.

"So, what's it like out in Himzo?" Laude asked Zichri, shoulder cocked to one side under the weight of our sack. "I've heard only that there is no sea. I couldn't imagine not living near water and ships. They say the sea is good for your health."

An image of me covering Laude's flapping mouth flashed through my mind, but Zichri's offer to let us ride on their only horse silenced her more effectively. I could sing for joy at how thankful I was to ride the mountainous path, though we still needed to find a way to split from the Himzos without drawing unnecessary suspicions about my identity.

The horse shifted beneath our bottoms as we hit a steep decline. Laude clutched my waist, her head pressed against my back. Why did Zichri insist on Laude riding with me instead of taking turns? *I've worn girdles that were less suffocating than this.*

Zichri walked alongside the horse and held the reins. On the other side of us, the lanky man declared, "I could have taken those ruffians myself." He flashed a cocky grin in my direction.

A stout man clapped a hand on the lanky one's shoulder. "You couldn't even have taken one yourself."

The lanky man shook his head. "You, Gonzalo, forget what a little motivation can do. With such vile villains on the loose, my muscles growl with anticipation." The lanky fellow turned his turquoise eyes to meet my gaze. "Damsels, you are in safe hands."

I mumbled under my breath, "You Himzos aren't that much better."

The horse rounded a curve, clomping a steady rhythm.

"You never said where you were headed." Zichri patted the horse's black mane. "We'll take you wherever you need to go. It's not safe for young ladies in these parts. No one patrols the mountain roads."

"Yes, I understand. I'm certain no one will follow us where we go." I swayed with the horse's gait.

Laude's heat soaked into my back. What a most undignified way to ride, but what excuse could I give to kick Laude off?

Zichri combed a hand through his hair. "Where will you be going?"

"We'll pass it on the way to Himzo."

The stout man—called Gonzalo—growled, "For the love of all that is good, where are you going? We don't have all day. Besides, we're not even heading to—"

The lanky man jabbed an elbow into Gonzalo's gut. On closer inspection, something about the thin man looked familiar, but I had never met a Himzo before. I brushed the notion aside.

"What? I wasn't going to draw a map for her." Gonzalo rubbed his potbelly.

Perhaps we should slip away sooner than later. I felt my features contort with my anxious thoughts.

Zichri cleared his throat. "Maybe you'd feel more comfortable getting to know the men. Meet Gonzalo." He pointed to the stout man and moved his finger to the lanky fellow. "This is Blas." Blas did a two-finger salute and clicked his tongue. Zichri called up the two others at the rear. "That's Milo and Jaime."

I dipped my head. "It's nice to meet you all. I'm thankful for your help. But I'm confused at why a fine group of Himzos would be in the unpatrolled territories of Giddel."

Zichri eyed Gonzalo, who bowed his shiny head. Bright-eyed Blas turned his slender face away while Milo and Jaime slowed their gait. Should I press for answers? That's what my brother would do, but I was no spy.

"This path is lovely," Laude piped in. "All the trees for shade and the mountains ahead."

"Yes, I couldn't agree more." Zichri smiled back at Laude.

"Is Valle de los Fantasmas on the other side of that mountain?" Laude pointed to the tallest peak looming in the distance. Her other hand dug into my dress.

The Himzos gasped, and the horse even seemed to trip a bit.

"Yes, but the path is longer than it appears." Zichri clicked his tongue, patting the horse's side. "Why do you ask?"

"Because that's where we're headed." Laude straightened up, now clutching me again with both hands.

I pressed my palms into the horn of the saddle. She was supposed to follow my lead.

Zichri's brows furrowed. "Is that so?"

Back straight, I maintained my austere expression. Mamá would not approve of me socializing with Himzos. *Or anything about this trip. So, why am I worrying?* "Yes, we were invited into Valle de los Fantasmas."

Gonzalo spat in the dirt. "By whom? The ghosts?"

Blas jabbed him, laughing.

"For the love of the Ancient One, keep your sharp elbow out of my gut." Gonzalo threw up his fists.

Zichri laughed. "Stand down. Blas, keep those bones out of Gonzalo's gut. We won't hear the end of it if you bruise his sensitive skin."

The men roared with laughter while Gonzalo shook his head. Zichri tugged on the reins and led the horses to the side of the road. He lifted Laude down by the waist and slipped his fingers around my waist too. I started, caught off guard by a tingling heat where he touched me. Why did he inspire such a sensation? I fanned myself, averting my gaze toward the luscious green canopy, to the tree roots jutting out of the ground—anyone but Zichri.

Gonzalo passed Laude a skin of water. Laude's flirty wink caused an inward cringe to shiver down my spine. *Best to look away.* But I caught Zichri staring at me.

"Were you serious about being invited to Valle de los Fantasmas?" Zichri's blank face was unsettling.

I held my breath and pulled my shoulders back. "Yes. Does this road lead to the valley?"

"It does get very near it. Most people avoid that portion of the path." Zichri stepped close, forcing me to tip my head back to maintain eye contact. How would I pry details from him? Should I even try?

"Your assistance is no longer needed." I raised my chin at his lifted brow. "You needn't worry about us. We have no plans on turning you in to the authority. We also would prefer if you not mention this encounter to anyone."

Zichri maintained a stern set to his jaw. "We can't leave you two alone on this path."

"But you will. Leave us." I glanced at Laude, who giggled and patted Blas's elbow. My instinct was to reprimand her for such behavior, but that might give us away. "Zichri. I'm not sure you understand. We don't want you near."

His lips twisted into a smile while watching Laude jest with Gonzalo. "Have you talked to your companion about that? It appears you're the only one who finds our presence unwelcome."

I inhaled, trying to keep my poise. What would Mamá do in a moment like this? Of course, she wouldn't get in a mess like this. If

Papá found out about us running into Himzo merchants who wouldn't let us be, he might start a war over these nobodies. "Do as you please. Laude and I are not with you."

Zichri smirked, which dimpled his cheeks. "Fair enough. We can give you space if you like."

"Could we get our pack with our food?"

"Gonzalo, could you pass Miss ..." Zichri drawled.

What name had Laude and I agreed on last night? Not Cicadas. Cleo? Cy—That's it. "Cypress!"

"Miss Cypress's pack?"

Gonzalo held the overstuffed pack out to Zichri.

I snatched the brown satchel and swung it over my achy shoulder for appearance's sake. I'd pass this to Laude once we were away. No one had ever let me carry more than a basket of flowers at home. And why would Laude mind the extra weight? I linked arms with Laude and dragged her away. "It's time for us to head to the valley. We needn't worry about these men."

"But miss."

"Say your goodbyes." I waved a hand, tugging Laude along at my side.

The Himzos stood tall at the edge of the path, looking rather drab in their simple white tunics—perhaps Zichri held a splash of rogue appeal. I scolded myself for the silly thought. Zichri was a Himzo. Gonzalo stepped forward with saucers for eyes. Zichri flung his arm in front of Gonzalo's chest. No one else took a step to follow us.

"Why can't we let them walk us to the valley?" Laude's whine grated against my ears.

"They're Himzo. Do you want them capturing your princess for political gain?" I hiked faster, but the sack bumped against my hip, slowing my gait. When we reached the next bend, I'd ask Laude to carry the satchel.

One glance over my shoulder and my stomach dropped. So far, we only traveled a small curve of the mountain path.

"But they were mere merchants. And so funny." Laude dragged

her feet. "It sure is hot in the sun. Those nice men had a lot of extra water. I'm certain we can walk back up."

I clenched my teeth and maintained my pace. Was she daft?

"Miss, they said there are more bad men like the ones who overtook us." She jogged to catch up and looped her arm through mine. "I've never seen so many handsome, well-built, and jolly men in one place in my life. That Zichri sure had an eye for you."

"Laude! Is that all you think about?"

She let go of my arm and kicked at pebbles over the dirt path. "Miss, only bony boys and the old cooks ever make it back to the kitchen and mending rooms. All the male servants have their own rooms, and the soldiers pay me no mind."

"What would be the purpose? Your position doesn't allow for marriage."

"You're right, miss. But oh, how I dream." Laude clasped her hands together over her chest, letting her gaze drift out in the distance. "It would be so nice to at least have a suitor chasing after my hand. Your mother would say 'No!' while giving him a severe look, just like the ones you give. He'd sneak in the palace, leaving notes about his undying love for me, even after I tell him there's no possible way."

"Does this dream man have a face?" I skirted around a giant hole in the dirt.

Laude looked up, smiling brightly. "Oh miss! He's tall and portly, but it's all strength he carries over his torso. His crooked smile melted my heart, even if he's clean-shaven on the top of his head."

"Gonzalo? Really?" I couldn't help but scrunch my face at the idea of Laude and Gonzalo.

She paused mid-step. "Truth be told. Blas also has a very nice laugh. He's on the thin side, which means I'd have to give him an extra portion of food. His eyes make up for any of his other flaws. They're almost as bright as Lux's."

I snickered against my own sensibilities. The idea of Blas being compared to Lux? Nonsense. But the joy in her voice peeled away my irritation. "And what of the other two men?"

"You mean Milo and Jaime?" Laude released a sigh. "They were even more lovely. If they had talked, Gonzalo would be in danger of losing my affection."

Oh my! Now, I knew we must lose these men, for Laude's sake. It's unhealthy to have unrealistic dreams waved in front of a person. My misery should be enough to warn Laude about such things.

I stopped listening to Laude and let my mind drift. Each step forward meant my dreams could come true. And Lux would break off his engagement when he saw I had the gift.

A horse's hooves clomped somewhere behind us. I straightened my back and pursed my lips. Was it the Himzos' or another band of thugs? Apprehension pinched my stomach.

Laude squinted to make out who approached us. She giggled and clapped her hands in delight. "Miss, they're coming. Do you think they'll follow us?"

"No worries, Laude. We'll outsmart them."

"Oh." She hung her head, slowing her pace to the speed of an injured turtle.

CHAPTER 12

Of course, with Laude walking so slow, the Himzo merchants caught up to us easily. A steady clomp of their horse's hooves banged in my ears. The shaded portions of the path weren't long enough. How many inclines could there be on a downward slope? I tilted my waterskin, but only a drop fell onto my tongue. Zichri walked by my side. I sensed his perusal, but he looked away each time I glared daggers in his direction.

Gonzalo passed Laude a skin of water. She mouthed, "Thank you," and quickly glanced in my direction.

All my etiquette lessons had taught me to keep a rein on my tongue. How my tutors failed. I opened my mouth, ready to whip out words at Laude. "You have to be—"

Zichri pulled my arm, bringing me toward him.

"Excuse me!" I yanked myself free.

He gestured toward the road, and a pothole gaped right where I had been walking. I'm sure he expected a thank you. However, if the Himzos hadn't been there, I would have been focused on the road and not on them. I peeked at Laude, who turned her back toward me, trying to hide her mischief. She gulped from the Himzos' waterskin so loud everyone must have heard it.

My muscles begged for a rest. Even my tongue had gone limp. It was too much effort to reprimand her the way she deserved. We turned a curve, and another steep descent welcomed us. Our feet plodded on the packed dirt.

Beads of sweat dripped down my forehead. The strap of the sack dug into my shoulder. Why didn't I give Laude the bag earlier? My shoulders hunched to the side, sending forth a shooting pain. "Laude, could you take a turn with the bag?"

"Yes, Miss Cypress." Laude unhooked the bag from around my head and looped it over her own. "Whoa, miss! I think we need to take a break and eat some food."

"That's not a bad idea. We'll stop at that tall tree ahead." I limped down the last portion of the decline, straining toward the promise of relief. It took everything in me not to collapse on the ground. Instead, I sat against a tree, catching my breath. Laude plucked two pears from the bag.

"Would you like a snack?" Laude tossed Gonzalo a pear and dug for another one. The other men stopped along with us and adjusted their packs.

"What are you doing? They are not invited to our break and our food." I pushed off the ground to stand. The edges of my vision were spotty. Pain rippled through my skull. Seething, I wiped away more sweat than any girl should ever show in public.

Zichri held out a skin of water. "Please, drink." He dipped his head like a servant.

"I want nothing from you. I will not drink from your supply."

"Need you be so stubborn?" He raised his narrowed stare to mine. "You're going to pass out while giving me a tongue-lashing. Look at how you sway." He drew near, blocking my view of the others. A muscle twitched in his jaw. "Please, don't put yourself in danger because you find us disagreeable."

I yanked the skin from his hand and drank deeply. The water refreshed more than I wanted to admit. I stopped to breathe and drank again. Water trickled down my chin, and I swiped at it.

Zichri pretended to look away, though he snuck glimpses of me while feigning interest in the leaves above. "We'll refill at the river below. You can ride on Carmel."

"I will—"

Zichri lifted me by the waist and placed me onto the horse. Anger circulated through my weak body while objections lingered in my throat. Is this another form of capture? Laude trotted along next to Gonzalo, happy to join the men. Gonzalo carried the not-so-full satchel, and we all continued on our trek. So much for getting away. Ashamed of my relief for the walking break, I lowered my head.

The moment I regain a semblance of strength, they'll see what I can do. I swayed on the horse's back, too tired to think anymore.

At the end of the curvy descending trail, an emerald river welcomed us. A rocky ledge extended from each side of the river, followed by a green pasture. The pasture gave us space between the water and the forest. Old campfires sprinkled the riverside. Could those ashes be from the foul servants who left us? I shook my head. It was best not to wonder.

Zichri stopped Carmel in the pasture, and I jumped off. Gonzalo collected branches and piled them together, and Laude watched him scrape his steel knife against flint. She could have offered to start the fire with the touch of her finger, but that would end her time flirting much too soon. Poor Laude didn't understand his grumbling meant he preferred to be alone.

Behind them, Carmel gobbled greenery in a field. Jaime emerged from the forest with an armful of dried branches. I breathed in the faint scent of grass, wood, and flowers while swatting at some gnats buzzing in my face. Trees stretched around us, linking arms, while the waning sunlight glistened off the river.

The river water slurped as it moved around Zichri's, Milo's, and Blas's legs. They sharpened branches with which to spear fish. Zichri peeled off his tunic and threw it at my feet. Sculpted muscles covered his torso and rippled down his stomach. I averted my eyes to Milo and Blas, who fished alongside him. Though Blas's shirt was off, his skinny form was no distraction. Zichri thrust his spear into the water and pulled up a fish. A proud smile illuminated his face. My breath caught, and my knees weakened as he waded out of the water toward me.

"Are you ready to eat?" Zichri drew closer. Sweat trickled along his chest, so I focused my attention on his bare feet and rolled-up pants.

"I've never seen anyone catch fish like that." I gulped, unsure what to say next. Smoke drifted toward us. Either Laude helped or Gonzalo finally got the fire to start.

"I can teach you how to catch your own fish." Zichri pointed behind him and squinted, sunlight gleaming off his bronze skin.

"My other dresses were taken with the wagon. It might be more prudent to be a spectator."

"Nonsense. Blas has extra clothes you can borrow."

Blas shouted from his spot in the river, "I heard that! Why don't you lend her some of your extra clothes? You packed enough for three trips."

"She'd be swimming in mine. Your tunic and pants are closer to her size."

Blas kissed his biceps. "Don't underestimate the power of these weapons."

I shook my head. "It wouldn't be appropriate. I'll help Laude at the campfire."

Zichri chuckled. "Are you sure you want to intervene?" His dark eyes shifted toward the campfire then back to me.

Laude and Gonzalo sat together on a log. She'd edged up to Gonzalo, pressing her shoulder to his. Gonzalo dug in his pack with his lips pressed in a firm line. She talked on and on, waving her hands in the air, caught up in whatever she was saying. Pity swelled in my chest for her. It was one thing for me to get annoyed at her jabbering, but another thing for a man she found attractive to let her know she talked too much.

"Laude and I can help Jaime get more wood for the fire." I stomped toward Laude and grabbed her elbow. "Come with me. Jaime needs our help."

She fluttered her eyelashes at Gonzalo. "I hope you don't mind."

"Not at all. We're going to need lots of dry branches." Gonzalo motioned with his hands to show a pile large enough to fill two firepits.

Under the forest canopy, Laude snatched a few sticks. "So, we're letting them escort us to the valley?" She slowed her pace and leaned an ear in my direction.

My feet ached from the day's walk. A raw blister rubbed against my boot. The smart thing to do would be to stay with the Himzo merchants tonight. Laude didn't want to tell me what to do out of habit, and she wouldn't argue with me if I said no, so I thought. I patted down my skirt and folded my hands. "Yes, we'll stay with them until morning."

She lifted the end of her skirt and thrust her sticks into it. She humphed and grunted, which confused me. Isn't that what she wanted to hear? Bending over to collect more sticks, she peered up with narrowed eyes. I stepped back, the tension thickening between us. I'd never seen her like this before—wordless with an air of defiance.

I crossed my arms. "We don't even know who these men are. Doesn't it seem odd to you that Himzo men travel in Giddel's outer provinces?"

She barked, "They're merchants. And that's not your main concern." She squared up to me, still holding the edges of her overskirt, now full of dried branches. "They saved our lives. That is all I need to know."

"We might live to regret not prodding further. For all we know, they're leading us straight into harm's way."

"Isn't that where *you're* leading us?" She shook the sticks in her skirt as if trying to emphasize her words.

"It's different."

She scrunched her nose. "Valle de los Fantasmas isn't known for its kind welcomes." She released a slow breath. "I'm sorry, miss. It is not my place to speak to you so. Do you forgive me?" Laude dropped her head to her chest in her normal submissive posture.

"Let's get back to the others. I'm sure we've gathered enough wood to keep the campfire going all night."

We walked in silence out of the forest and through the field. Though Laude scolded me, there was something refreshing about seeing her less than perky. I wanted to tell her my thoughts, but my throat felt raspy. Instead, the only conversation between us was brushing grass and padding feet.

Laude stopped before reaching the riverbanks. Her freckles looked darker than they had this morning. "Miss, I'm glad to be here to witness you receiving your gift." Her twinkling eyes assured me of her sincerity. She had had this same spark as a child every time she found a conch to place atop the sandcastles we'd create. I followed a step behind, feeling a sweet release of something that had weighed me down.

The joy floating in my heart popped once I looked back at the seating arrangement around the bonfire. I breathed deep. *I'm stuck with them all night.* Laude had taken the spot next to Gonzalo. Blas, Jaime, and Milo shared a fallen trunk. I could sit on the rocky ground or sit next to Zichri on another smaller trunk. The ground suited me best, but it might be odd to sit so low with all the others perched up higher. Dread flooded within me. Nothing good would come out of his clear interest in me or … his dashing looks.

"I promise not to bite," Zichri said.

"That is yet to be tested." I settled on the end of the trunk as far away from him as possible. I stared at Laude, willing her to suggest switching seats with me, but she was too busy batting her lashes at Gonzalo. *Tonight will be torture.*

CHAPTER 13

GONZALO WATCHED WITH PRIDE as everyone around the campfire groaned with delight eating the fish he had prepared. He stowed the salts and spices meticulously into his sack. I had not expected this from him. The fish was better than I anticipated too. I licked my fingers in secret. Mamá would not approve. Lux would feign insult but chuckle when only I was watching. *I wish he were here.* Truth be told, I didn't want to admit I enjoyed the bonfire in the woods with these strangers.

Jaime pulled out a *güiro,* a hollowed-out gourd with stripes on the surface and a stick, tapping a rhythmic beat. *Bum-biri-bum-biri-bum.* The black sky spanned above us with a dusting of stars. Orange light glowed on our faces from the campfire. Blas rose to his feet and sang a rather pitchy ballad. The music rattled in my ears and danced through my shoulders.

Milo shot to his feet. "You're singing it all wrong." And he joined Blas in a baritone voice.

Laude giggled louder than a bugle leading soldiers into battle. I blew out my cheeks, unable to do anything to tame her. The men noticed her squeals as well and invited her to join them.

"But I don't know this song." Laude held out her hands, grinning.

Blas marched in place with a little swing to his hips. "We'll teach you. Just follow along."

Laude marched next to him and copied Blas with exaggerated movements.

A burst of hardy laughter erupted among the men. I tried to maintain my poise, but Laude's ridiculous version of Blas's song wheedled a smile out of me. Blas impersonated Laude, and my hands flew over my mouth to hold in a rush of laughter. Blas and Milo continued singing while Laude pantomimed them, waving her hands in a circular motion. I couldn't hold back any longer. My whole body surrendered to the giggles, and I gasped for air in between bouts of laughter.

Zichri scooted closer. "Your servant has a great sense of humor."

"That she does."

"Hmmm." He tapped his chin. A roguish smile tipped the corners of his lips. "Your father is wealthy, I take it."

I realized my mistake. He had gathered information about me. I pressed a palm on each cheek so they wouldn't tighten up again from laughter. "You're a very curious sort. What does it matter to you?"

Zichri raked a hand through his floppy hair. "I was just wondering. You called Laude your friend, but I can't help noticing that she always calls you Miss Cypress."

"Well, I don't think it's any of your business who we are. You aren't even supposed to be on this land." I pouted, turning up my chin.

"You make that expression often. Why do you do it?" There was no insult in the way Zichri asked.

But I took offense anyway. "Those of us from Giddel know better than to ask imprudent questions about the way a person looks." I turned my head away, attempting to focus on the dancing trio. Zichri's gaze bored into my skin. I kept my eyes on Laude. She belted a tune from Giddel, and Blas joined in. *How he butchers a good song.*

Zichri released an airy laugh. "You're doing it again."

"How dare you?" I turned toward Zichri, whose eyebrows were drawn together in question. "First, you pry into our personal matters. Then, you take license to mock me. Do you require a payoff to treat ladies with respect?"

"You were being assaulted. I did what any person should do." He held up his hand, quieting a quip ready on my tongue. "No, a payoff is not possible. I only ask that you let us escort you to your destination."

The pops and fizzles of the fire filled the silence between us. I hadn't noticed the music stopped until that moment. His giant brown eyes reflected our little circle. I searched his face for any hidden motives and found none. It was easy to follow his defined jaw and curve of his lips. He kept a serious look, reached his hand up, and placed the other hand over his heart. It took a moment for me to realize that he wanted me to press my hand to his. I'd heard about this Himzo practice for making pacts, but I'd never seen a Himzo before. I assumed they were vulgar and not so handsome. Well, only Zichri was the handsome one in this bunch. But he was also stubborn. Not a good quality.

"Promise to let us escort you? You can put your hand to mine. It usually helps to make pacts with both parties in agreement." Zichri shook the hand he held up between us.

I bit the inside of my cheek, uncertain if this was the right move. Papá always said that words matter. *Words could speak life into what once was invisible.* If I agreed, then I was bound to let these men walk us to our destination. My stomach clenched.

Laude knelt before me and grasped my hand. "Miss, please. For my sake, will you put aside your ill feelings about"—she pitched her voice low—"Himzos, and allow someone to help us in our time of need?" She dipped her head most humbly.

I peered up; the others fixed their stares in my direction.

Laude squeezed my hand. "Consider it a gift from the Ancient One."

"I've neither prayed for help on this trip nor given him any reason to intervene in such a way." I hadn't even thought about him since the morning of my ceremonia. My mamá is the one who walked through the garden singing songs to him. She was the one who felt his presence like a tangible breeze that spoke to her inner soul, as she claimed. I was my papá's child, lacking perhaps both the inclination and ability to cultivate such a relationship, though I had summoned the oath. Pain shot from my fingers to my elbows. Was this a sign? A nudge from the Ancient One?

Laude continued, "Either way, take this as a gift."

That word *gift*... it dangled before me and stung. That's what this whole trip was about, a gift. My gift. These men weren't meant to be here, but I could not admonish Laude in front of them.

I held up my hand. "Fine. We will neither verbally insist on parting ways nor escape in the night until we've reached our destination. You have my word." I waited for Zichri's nod of agreement before pressing our hands together.

The men applauded. Laude hopped up, pulling me in a tight, bouncy hug.

"That's great. Yes, we have enemies for guards. Yes, yes." I patted her back in dismissal and released her.

She squealed with delight while she skipped to Blas. He cleared his throat and puffed out his chest. Just when I thought he was about to sing, he winked at Laude. Hearty laughter burst from our circle.

Zichri stood. A hush fell over the campfire, and everyone around the fire leaned in. Anticipation built with each crackle while we waited. I expected him to give a toast or something to indicate his pleasure in our agreement. But instead, in a low, melodic voice, he sang:

"The heavens roared,
a fire to the ground
Escape to a place
A hope for better days
It would be so, if only ..."

The way he sang reminded me of the calm surf of the sea at night. And the story, a beautiful rendition of the escape from the valley of old, now Valle de los Fantasmas. I'd always heard that the Ancient One expelled the people from the city, but the details remained a mystery. This version of the story still told of their hope.

The other men joined in for the chorus, serious—but with a twinkle of something heartfelt in their eyes. It reminded me of ... I gasped ... my new pocket watch, but that could not be possible.

Yet it had the same melancholy tune, and Myla had snatched the watch from me when she heard the song. And the mysterious woman at the garden party? Could she have been a Himzo spy? Those in Giddel did not trade with Himzos. Impossible. I tucked my trembling hands under my legs while the chorus mingled in the balmy breeze.

Zichri finished the last note, and I took a deep breath. The fire hissed. Laude tossed in another stick. We had enough fodder for the flames to continue all night.

How I wished Lux were here to point out the stories hidden in the starry sky. Only then would this be perfect.

Zichri's gaze lingered in my direction.

I cast a sideways glance at him. "You should not stare. It's improper." I flicked my braid over a shoulder.

"You seem deep in thought." Zichri drew near.

My pulse quickened under his scrutiny, tightening a ball of doubt in my stomach. Doubt about Himzo affairs in Giddel, and doubt about my disdain for Zichri. I didn't want to stay among the Himzos. Tomorrow, Laude and I might happen to wander. Nothing was promised against doing that. I smiled so as not to reveal my plan. "Laude and I should go to sleep soon."

"You can take two of our hammocks." Zichri dug through a satchel at his feet until he pulled out a wad of rope and netting. "Here you go."

I took his hammocks, and Laude sided up next to me as I stood. She bounced on her toes, eyebrows arching high with glee. The Himzos said their goodnights.

"Don't go too far into the forest!" Blas shouted across the growing space between us. "No ruffians will take you on our watch."

Laude trudged behind me, looking over her shoulder, even as we crossed into the tree line.

"Come now, Laude. We haven't all night." I reached a finger in my opposite sleeve, scratching. "That's enough fawning after those Himzos. We'll figure out a means to part ways with them tomorrow."

"But you promised them—"

"Enough of your silly notions. Those men will not be so kind if they discover who I am."

CHAPTER 14

"SOMETHING IS AMISS WITH you," I said to Laude. Though the air was cool this morning, the red sunset last night forecasted a sunny day today. I cupped river water in my hands and splashed it on my cheeks. Cool liquid dripped down my neck and onto my chemise.

"Hmm? I don't know what you mean." Laude's words came out mumbled. She held pins between her teeth as she raced wet fingers through her red tendrils. Then she twisted locks at the top of her head and stabbed the pins into her hair. Her upper lip stiffened with concentrated effort.

Laude stood on a large rock and stretched her boot onto another boulder, and proceeded to shore in this manner.

I wiped my face with a sleeve and joined her. "You understand why we can't stay with them. I'm certain my markings make me distinguishable for even those who've merely heard about me."

Her eyes met mine for a moment. What was going on in that head of hers? She cast her gaze down. "We should join the others."

We continued along the rocky river shore when all five men came into view, loading the horse with our bags.

"It's going to be a long walk up Mount Giddel." Gonzalo smoothed his hand over Carmel's neck. "If you have any trouble, we can carry the satchels, and one of you can ride Carmel."

"I'm sure we can manage," I said.

Crunch. Whack.

I whipped around toward the sound.

Laude sat sprawled on the rocky shore. "Ai-yi-yi! I think I twisted my ankle."

Blas loaded Laude up onto Carmel, which inspired a twinkle in her sapphire eyes, and we were off on the rustic road up Mount Giddel, the rest of us walking alongside the horse. Why did she have to hurt herself? This ruined all my plans to run off.

Just when we turned the first bend, Laude and I locked stares, and a smirk slipped across her lips. Did she fake her injury? I stopped, craning my neck to get a better look at her ankle when Zichri smacked into me, and I stumbled forward.

After the awkward apologies, we continued for an hour or so on unforgiving stretches of road. When we finally stopped for a break under a mango tree, I took the opportunity to examine Laude's foot. But upon reaching for her ankle, a hairy spider crawled onto my sleeve, and I screeched, my muscles frozen in fear.

Zichri darted to my rescue and laughed when he saw what he described as a "kind little fellow." He gently shooed the creature from my person. Blas made no secret about his amusement either.

"Don't worry, Cypress." Zichri offered a hand to help me up. "We'll be out of the wild soon enough."

I pushed myself to my feet and pursed my lips. He chuckled. The deep sound of his laugh had an attractive quality. But I stuffed that sentiment away and arched my eyebrows in distaste. Why make him feel useful?

After the long day's walk, I longed for a bath, a new dress, to kick off my boots, and ointment to soothe the burning itch attacking my markings. When would this torturous walk ever end?

A home with stucco walls peeked through the forest. Sunrays illuminated the yellow color of its walls with a brilliant sheen. Relief flooded my body. Rest would come soon.

"Is this the place?" I asked as I turned to Zichri.

Zichri's eyes met mine, and my stomach did a strange flop. Perhaps I was simply grateful he hadn't left me when I fell behind the rest of the group? Or the heat had weakened my resolve?

"You suppose well. Wait until you see the accommodations. They might even impress you." His smile tugged up one cheek, inspiring a well-placed dimple.

I lifted a dubious brow. *Doubt it.*

Then more homes with flat roofs popped up along the road, offering a change from the sprawling jungle. Soon wagons lined the sides of the road, and the structures became larger. The roads were paved with cobblestone. A plaza with a large fountain in the center came into view.

"Cypress." Zichri touched my elbow, drawing my attention to him. "I meant it earlier when I said I want to get to know you."

Tearing my arm back, I inspected his drab white tunic and scuffed boots. Who was this Zichri? With tension between Himzo and Giddel so high, what type of merchant would risk his life for the purpose of trade? I tempered my suspicions with what I assumed was a graceful flutter of my lashes. "You are persistent. A lady can't be rushed when getting to know someone new."

The other four men and Laude chatted in front of an inviting arched doorway across the road. Laude bounced on her toes and clapped her hands, ankle not a concern. A flame of ire lit inside of me.

I strode ahead, ready to expose her lie, but got yanked back. A horse and carriage zipped past where I aimed to step. I gasped.

"Whoa there! You could get yourself killed like that." Zichri held my shoulders, examining my face.

My cheeks burned. Another blunder. This whole day, I had made a fool of myself. First colliding with him, overreacting to the spider, and then punctuated by my inability to keep up with the group. Laude and I needed help since we hadn't a clue where we were going, no weapons, and hardly any supplies. My chin fell with my thoughts: *You are useless and incapable of anything.*

Zichri tipped my chin up. "Cypress, you needn't be flustered. You remind me of my little sister when she thinks she made a mess of things."

Splendid, I remind him of his sister. I smashed my lips together.

Zichri continued, "You don't need to prove anything to me."

"Why would I? I barely know you."

His mouth cocked into a crooked smile. "We can change that."

My heart flapped like a trapped bird caged within my chest. The combination of his large round eyes, the curve of his nose, and his full lips could unsettle even the most detailed woman on a hunt for faults. In that instance, my mind settled on allowing this merchant to assist Laude and me.

We looked both ways before crossing the road, and I followed him into an inn decorated with painted tiles depicting a valley with a river running through it. Laude and the others talked amongst themselves while waiting in the narrow entrance.

"Good fellow, do you have our rooms?" Zichri tapped the tall wooden counter at the end of the foyer.

A portly clerk wiped his brow with a handkerchief and paged through his check-in book. "We nearly gave them away."

Zichri's eyes flashed, and three long breaths passed before the muscle in his jaw relaxed. "We always pay our dues and then some. You wouldn't want us to choose the inn across the way."

The clerk stuffed his flower-embroidered handkerchief in the front pocket of his vest. A scowl crossed his plump face while he shook his head. "Here are the keys. You know the rooms."

"An extra coin for your troubles." Zichri slid the metal across the wooden top. "Oh, and please send a maid with hot water and extra lamps to both rooms."

The clerk snatched his payment and rang a bell, a grimace deepening on his mouth lines.

I wiped my palms along my skirt. Laude gazed wide-eyed as she stepped from the foyer into the dining area, where dozens of other guests ate. I'd never seen an inn before, so I understood her curiosity.

She skimmed a fingertip over a parlor table. The polished surface shined like all the others in the room.

Men and women dined near the tall windows, conversing in low tones over a single candle. The evening light painted the white walls with a bright orange glow. A maid dashed from a back door, carrying a tray laden with food, enveloping us with a meaty aroma. My stomach growled.

"Miss, that sure looks tasty. I hadn't realized how hungry I was, but it sure makes sense since we only ate fruit and nuts all day. Well, besides the fish from breakfast. Do you think we could ask the Himz—the men if we'll be dining?" Laude's eager eyes became saucers when another platter of sizzling meat and fried plantain passed on a tray in front of us.

Looking over my shoulder, I strained to hear Zichri and the other merchants talking amongst themselves. Milo pinched the bridge of his nose. Blas tipped his head in our direction while Gonzalo pointed to the stairs and then toward us. Heat climbed the back of my neck. How dare they treat me like a child?

But before words flew out of my mouth, Blas and Gonzalo strode out the front door. Laude clasped her hands and beamed as Milo and Jaime walked past us. They continued up the stairs at the far end of the dining room. I nudged her side.

"I'm sorry, miss. They're just so lovely."

"Straighten up and have some decorum. We're in public."

Zichri appeared by my side, and I jumped. "Pardon me. I didn't mean to frighten you." He extended Laude a piece of wood etched with the number thirteen. A key dangled from it by a leather cord. "This is where you'll stay. Why don't you wash up? Miss Cypress and I will dine in the meantime."

Laude's cheeks bubbled with a conspiratorial smile. I glared at her, but she giggled, unaffected by my scowl. She strolled up the stairs. Should I demand that she stay by my side? The opportunity fled when her boots disappeared up the steps.

"Shall we?" Zichri jutted out his elbow.

I nodded and wrapped my hand around his forearm. Warmth radiated from his body. We found a table in the back corner and ordered two house specials. I drummed my fingers on the tabletop, unsure of what to say, so I feigned interest in my nails. But I could still see him watching me as if he studied my reactions.

A thousand butterflies fluttered in my stomach. By the time the server arrived with our meals, I was ready to thank her for giving me something to do, other than sitting under Zichri's keen perusal.

"What's your favorite color?" Zichri scooped a mouth full of sautéed vegetables in his mouth.

I finished swallowing my first bite and dabbed my lips with my napkin. "Sea blue. The type that has a hint of green, just like the shallow waters near the Agata Sea." I cut another morsel of meat and placed it in my mouth.

"That's fitting."

I gulped down the bite of food. "What do you mean?"

"You live near the sea. It makes sense you'd like that color. That's all I'm saying."

His assuming anything about me pricked like grazing a hand on a thorn when reaching for a flower. My lips pursed, cheek muscles tightening.

He snickered.

"What do you find so amusing?"

"You."

"I beg your pardon."

He took a long drink of water. "We don't know much about one another. I make conversation. You get angry about everything I say. Or pretend you didn't hear."

"I'm not angry." I hacked a portion of meat and shoved it in my mouth.

"No, not at all." He inflected his voice with a hint of sarcasm.

I shifted the half-chewed meat into my cheek, despite it breaking every rule in refined society, and said, "What is it that you want? You saved us from danger, and now you feel you own us."

A faint smirk crossed his face. "Not at all."

I chomped down on another morsel of meat, trying to eat as fast as possible. Taking my glass of water, I sipped. The chunk lodged in my throat. I gasped for air, but none came.

"I did what any human should do like I said last night. These paths are unsafe for even a lone man. Any good fellow passing by would have helped you. And after beholding such beauty, do you blame me for wanting further acquaintance with you?" A look of concern knit his eyebrows. "Are you all right?"

Gasping for air, I dropped my utensils, and they hit the table with a clank. I waved my hands and my torso tightened until I coughed.

Water and the chunk of meat shot from my mouth and straight at Zichri.

My mouth hung open in shock. I continued to cough, and something akin to a laugh or cry sputtered from my lips.

Zichri wiped his face with the back of his hand, eyes wide and lips pinched together.

I couldn't hold back any longer. Laughter quivered out my burning throat until I slapped my hands over my mouth.

He placed his napkin on the table. "How about a walk? That might prove less dangerous."

While wandering the boardwalk overlooking the shadowy mountainside, I let go of the tension building up in my mind as I ambled by Zichri's side. I may not be able to share everything about me, but something in his demeanor allowed me to put off regality. Well, it also could have been that I launched a chunk of chewed meat at his face, and he hadn't run away—yet.

He glanced in my direction. "What's something you hope for?"

I crossed my arms. My real answers could not be shared. Would he even understand the need for my gift? I doubted the weight of being useful to an entire kingdom would be fathomable for him. Instead,

I said, "I hope to travel the forest like a bird, seeing all from above without a care in the world."

"Hmm … birds do have cares." He stepped closer to me, and then a man shoved past him.

A peasant with scruffy hair caught my attention. Could he be one of the wicked servants? My foot caught on a wooden slab, and I began to tip forward.

Zichri grabbed my arm and braced my waist. "That was a close one."

Three other peasants, a male and two females, knocked into us, and Zichri pulled me into his body.

My heart lurched. "I'm not quite myself today." I fanned my face, heat rising up my neck. The men who careened into us dressed better than the drivers, and these women covered their hair with kerchiefs. Goosebumps prickled on my arms.

Zichri followed my gaze. "I've never seen them here before, but many visitors pass through all the time. Should we continue our walk or head back?" Torch lights danced in his eyes.

More people gallivanted out a saloon, singing. They bumped my back, pushing us closer together. I could hear his heartbeat quicken in his chest. A delightful sensation danced along my spine. I lifted my gaze and met a look that turned my knees to water.

What's wrong with me? Hold yourself together, Beatriz.

I cleared my throat. "Is it always a ruckus here at night?"

"Not always." There was a lightness in his voice.

"Maybe we should head back. I'm sure Laude is done cleaning up, and I'm in desperate need of a wash." I stretched my neck to see around Zichri, to ease my apprehension about the four peasants. They had either woven in with the crowd or entered another establishment.

He gently squeezed my hand. "It's getting late. We should get as much rest as possible before our journey tomorrow."

His warmth comforted me more than I wanted to admit. I let him hold my hand as we strolled down the rest of the boardwalk, curving around a set of establishments. We crossed the street and entered the inn. The clerk peered at us with a suspicious look. I pulled my hand away so as not to give the clerk reason for unwholesome thoughts.

Zichri continued up the stairs to the rooms, stealing side glances at me as I followed close behind. Something about him sent tingling currents through my blood. I knocked on door thirteen, and the bolt clicked to unlock. Laude peeked through a crack and beamed.

"Good night, Zichri." I tried to slip in quickly, but Laude stayed at the door, making it difficult to sneak past her.

He dipped his head. "Good night."

I shut the door and leaned against it—potpourri perfume mixed with a lingering milk and cinnamon scent. Laude must have had her dinner up here. A dim lamp glowed in between two small beds. The gentleness of it all contrasted my pounding heart. I pressed my palms over my chest to steady the beat.

"What happened? I must know. You're in love," Laude squealed. "I can see it all over your face."

"Enough, Laude. I'm not sure how much more of him I can take." It was the truth.

Laude's smile fell. She passed me a nightgown and stacked dishes onto an empty tray on a desk. "The maids brought us extra clothes."

Focusing on breathing, I told this strange sensation to disappear. But it flowed like a river through my mind, bringing each of Zichri's touches, stray glances, and words through my thoughts.

I changed into my nightgown and slid under a quilt cover. *Having such ridiculous feelings for a merchant ...*

A tiny whisper stirred in my mind: *But no one would know about flirting with a Himzo nobody.* What harm could it do to enjoy Zichri's attention?

CHAPTER 15

"MISS, WHAT ARE YOU looking at?" The playful melody in Laude's voice chafed even after a good night's rest. "Zichri perhaps?" She waggled her eyebrows and perched on the edge of the small bed across from mine.

"No, Laude, I have other things on my mind besides a handsome face." I held the floral print curtains to the side, letting in the morning light.

"So, you admit it. You favor Zichri! The way he stayed back with you to dine. He only had eyes for you when he said good night. Oh, it's too good to be true!" Staring at nothing in particular, Laude clapped daintily while she most likely planned my wedding.

Shaking my head, I rolled my eyes. Zichri could be considered cute and perfect for a lowborn like Laude. I, on the other hand, could never dream of such a match. "It's not that. Take a look at the horses and wagon across the way." I pointed out the small window.

She hopped off the bed and pressed against the glass. "There's Milo! He must be buying supplies at that shop." She waved, almost smacking my face in the process.

"Please don't tell me you favor Milo now?" I pushed her hands to the side.

Milo trudged from the wagon into the store without glancing up at us.

"You should have heard the clever stories he told. I think he said them to make me laugh."

"Oh, Laude." I had a mind to rebuke her. "At least you don't like Jaime too."

"I think Jaime is the most handsome of the bunch."

I pressed a palm to my forehead. Even if I tried to point out the silliness of liking each of the Himzo merchants, she wouldn't care.

My eyes wandered back to the horses and wagon in question when a raggedy man carrying a basket approached the horse. Anger rose in my throat. "Look! The one feeding the horse." I pointed, jabbing my finger into the glass. When Laude gasped, I knew I hadn't imagined it. One of the vile servants who left us stranded was here.

Laude backed away from the window. She clasped the ruffles on the neckline of her dress. "What do you think they will do if they see us?"

I didn't know. It might suit them best to disappear. Perhaps they'd give away my identity, and our new guides would take us to the Himzo king and queen. But could the Himzos abduct us in a populated place and with a single horse? In some ways, I sensed they would never hurt us. Nevertheless, one in my position could never be too cautious. But I did need another dress besides the one on my back. "We should tell Zichri and his companions. They said they'd be in the room across the hall or downstairs dining."

Laude stormed across our room, whipped our door open, and crossed the hall to the men's room. "What are you waiting for?" She waved for me to hurry with a blaze of determination in her eyes. The moment I stepped beside her, she pounded on the door.

The door creaked open. Zichri appeared in a clean tunic, running his fingers through his wet hair. A fresh lavender scent rolled off his body, and instinctively, I inclined toward the aroma and inhaled.

"Whoa there." He patted my shoulder. "They only have this scent of soap. It's going to take some time before my usual forest smell comes back. What brings you two here? Is something amiss?"

I folded my arms, swallowing my bruised pride from having been caught smelling him. "We saw one of the men who abandoned us."

Laude added, "He might have our trunks and supplies."

A muscle in Zichri's jaw flexed. "Where did you see him?"

"Across the way." Laude pointed, furrowing her brows in a way that did not befit her jovial face. I suppressed a smile.

Zichri bolted between us, taking the stairs two at a time. Laude hurried behind him, allowing me a minute alone to gather my thoughts. *Will we be found out?*

I locked my door, closed Zichri's, and trod down the creaky steps.

"Ai-yi-yi! Miss Cypress! Zichri and all the merchants went to confront the man. I'm scared they'll get in a scuffle, and someone will get hurt. They said we should be safe here." Laude pulled on my arm. "Do you think they'll get your beautiful dresses back? I hope they show them a thing or two about double-crossing"—she leaned in—"the Princess of Giddel."

"That's enough," I hissed. But a puff of pride remained in my chest after hearing the way she said my title. "Someone could hear you." I glanced around the dining room. Empty tables covered the front of the sunlit space, and other guests at the far table near the foyer eyed us with curiosity. A long counter where servers picked up food and beverages lined the back of the room.

I tipped my head to the side. "Let's take a seat so as not to make more of a scene."

I kept my chin high, and my pace measured. Laude followed. We slid into the seats near the window, staring at the Himzos. The inn across the road sat between a store and a bakery, and many people either stood in windows or off to the side with shocked expressions. Zichri held a gruff man by the collar while Gonzalo, Blas, and Jaime stood behind like soldiers waiting to attack. Another man launched a punch at Blas, but Blas ducked in time.

I turned my gaze to the clerk behind the front counter just outside the dining area. A frown drooped on his face as he looked out the front door. He met my stare, not a hint of kindness touched his features, and he returned to observing the scene outside.

A fresh heatwave simmered on my skin, and I fanned my face.

Milo exited the store with his arms full of supplies when he noticed the others. Blas approached Milo and patted his shoulder. They spoke for some time. Blas's hands flew in every direction, and his face contorted with wide-eyed outrage to pinched anger. With a cock of his head and pursed lips pointing toward our inn, Blas seemed to send Milo toward us. Milo shoved the supplies into Blas's arms, walked across the road, through the front door of the inn, and past the clerk. He stopped for a second, scanning the dining room before he stalked toward us. "Are you ladies all right?"

"What's going on over there?" Laude blurted.

"Zichri confronted the man to get information about the trunks, but that man insists he and his associates don't know what Zichri speaks of." Milo set his bag in a seat and sat across from me. He tugged the curls at the top of his head, more frustrated than I would have expected.

Did the fight cause more problems for the Himzos than they let on? I leaned in toward Milo. "Is something the matter?"

Milo lifted his dark eyes. "The mountain people don't take to strangers causing trouble."

Laude smacked the table and pushed her chair back. "That's it!" She marched out of the dining area, stomped through the foyer, flung the front doors open, and headed across the street to the other inn. Moments later, she pulled Cata, one of the thieving servants, out of the doorway by the ear.

How did Laude see her from here? I smoothed out my skirt with my clammy palms, noticing the tiny pink flower pattern that reminded me of the gardens at home. Why couldn't Papá and Mamá have sanctioned this trip? We would have had guards and reliable servants.

This is no time for what could have been.

But I couldn't stop the surge of apprehension sinking in my belly. Cata had always unsettled me, and those other servants were unscrupulous. What if this fight turned for the worse? Part of me expected one of those villainous men to pull out a dagger.

A loud pounding noise resonated through the dining room, bringing me back from my thoughts. Our clerk slammed his fist on the front counter again, shaking his head. His face reddened the more he continued to watch the events outside.

I stared out the window. Laude pushed Blas away while she wagged a finger at Cata. Her mouth opened wide, and we heard a squeaky scream—from this distance, her words were difficult to decipher.

Zichri surely knows who we are. Would the king demand riches, unfair treaties, or even worse ... Papá to abdicate his throne? I drew a slow breath. *Settle your thoughts. After all Zichri's chivalrous talk, he might not hand us over.*

A creak from the floor startled me, and I whipped my gaze back into the room. The clerk's girth bumped our table. He wiped his brow and bald head with a handkerchief. "Soldier," he addressed Milo. "We don't take to Himzo enforcement in these parts. We allow you passage, but that's all."

My eyes snapped wide. *Soldier? The Himzos are soldiers?* That could not be a good sign for Giddel or for us. And Zichri with all his kindness and attentions. Him, a soldier? A plummeting sensation sank to my toes. I didn't want Zichri or Milo or any of the men to be my enemies.

Oh, Ancient One, help! How did Zichri and all the men get past the wards? The wards should have held soldiers back unless ... another ward disappeared. Maybe, a ward would not prevent men dressed like merchants from passing into our city even if they were Himzo soldiers. I should have paid more attention to my brother's friend at the ball. All I had thought about was how Cosme pulled me away from Lux.

Milo got to his feet, and I saw the warrior in him. The stern expression, his muscular form, the way he carried himself. All of it screamed soldier. How daft of me for not noticing before. The clerk trembled under Milo's cold stare. I might shake too if I was the recipient.

Standing to break the tension, I said in my daintiest voice, "Good sir! The men only mean to retrieve what was stolen from us ladies."

The clerk didn't break eye contact with Milo. "Miss, we're an independent village. We take care of our own and allow visitors to pass through as long as they stick to themselves."

"What of justice for someone like me?" I lifted my chin.

"Justice is a funny thing. Everyone seeks it for themselves and twists it for their cause. We are no different here." The clerk dared to look away from Milo and met my gaze. "You have a pretty face. I can see why the Himzos took to you and your friend, but I wouldn't trust them. They travel outside their borders, and I 'spect they're looking to stir trouble abroad."

"That's enough, old man." Milo grimaced. "You presume much."

Milo insisted I gather our things upstairs. I hesitated but obeyed him even though my heart pounded as I scampered to our rooms. I collected the little Zichri left behind and my small satchel while begging the Ancient One for the clerk to be wrong. The weight of the old clerk's words stiffened my shoulders. I raced down the stairs and halted before reaching the last step.

The clerk laid on the floor, cheek swollen and shouting at Milo, leaving me no doubt about what had transpired.

Blas plowed into the dining room. Upon seeing the clerk, his face enlivened with a smirk. I didn't blame him for it either. The clerk reminded me of a beetle stuck on his back, trying to get to his feet. He spat foul words in Blas's direction while flipping over to his knees.

"We didn't want to stay in your dirty old inn anyway," Blas said.

"I mean it!" The clerk pushed up and stuck his rear in the air, attempting to stand. "You can never come back to this village." The foul edge to his words lost their bite as he was still bent over.

We exited the inn and were met by Gonzalo, who was readying the horses and wagon. Zichri held a dagger to one of the men's throats. Behind them, Jaime carried our stolen trunk. Laude barked orders at Cata and Mattha, who had been hiding by the doorway. They carried the other trunk and heaved it onto the wagon bed.

Laude, smiling from ear to ear, hopped on the wagon, impervious to the anger seething from the other servants. She waved me over to join her. My throat tightened, and I stepped onto the road and back onto the sidewalk. What if the clerk was right?

Zichri threw the vile man to the ground, kicking dirt at him. Cata tugged the man by his elbow while Mattha scrambled to Cata's side. The other despicable man rubbed his swollen jaw and backed into

Mattha. The sight of the wicked servants getting what they deserved spurred confidence into my step, and I crossed the road.

I lifted my chin and strode near our four previous guides, cocking a satisfied grin on my lips.

Zichri, Milo, and Jaime climbed on the wagon bed behind me, whooping in victory. Gonzalo clicked his tongue while tugging on the reins. The wagon jerked and rolled out of the town. Blas rode the Himzo horse behind us. Pride for Laude's loyalty overtook any other emotions welling up inside of me. She leaned over the side of the wagon, the breeze tousling her curly hair from her pins. I joined her.

The men and Laude sang the whole ride until there was almost no sunlight left. Laude improved in her ability to follow the lyrics. The words began sounding familiar since the men broke into song rather often. Gonzalo pulled over to a grassy area. Without an order, the Himzos jumped out the wagon, working together like a well-trained team.

Though everyone still exuded the joy of victory, the word "soldier" bounced through my skull, pumping fury in my blood. It stole my relief at getting our things back.

The men continued their songs while kindling a fire and readying a campsite. Laude opened a trunk and gasped at the sight. Complaining about grimy hands undoing her hard work, she plucked out dresses and refolded them.

Zichri, finally, sauntered over while the other men gathered wood. His self-satisfied manner struck a nerve. He might have saved us and our things, but he also lied to me.

I crossed my arms and held my chin high, relishing in my rather high position on the wagon. "When were you going to tell us you all are soldiers?"

His smiling eyes rounded into moons at my question. I assumed he had hoped for a thank you. He should know the adage: when one discovers a lie, etiquette ceases to be an obligation.

CHAPTER 16

ZICHRI'S MOUTH HUNG OPEN. He stuttered for the first time since I had met him. Instinctively, I pursed my lips and raised a brow, but I remembered him asking me why I pouted. I relaxed my facial muscles. Laude still fussed over the trunks.

I crossed my arms, blood pulsing in my temples. "Well? Are you going to weave more lies and say it's all right since you saved us poor, helpless girls?"

"No, it's not that." He raked a hand through his hair. "Please sit so we can talk."

"No, I demand an explanation." I stomped my foot. The sound vibrated across the wagon bed. Uncle Uly's gift for sensing truth would have been a nice thing to have at that moment. Even Cosme's ability to levitate people would have given Zichri a good scare. Instead, I needed to use old-fashioned lady powers, so I maintained a hard edge.

He looked behind me. "Laude."

"They should have throttled those—those scoundrels. Who does this to lace?" She got to her feet. "I'll be pulling apart those threads for hours." She turned around, still rambling to herself before she saw Zichri, and snapped her mouth shut.

"Could you please give us a moment alone?" He cocked his head just the right way to elicit sympathy from her.

She chortled. "Of course. The men look like they could use some help maintaining the fire. You and Miss Cypress can take all the time you need. Those dresses can wait." She spread a rainbow of fabrics to one side of the wagon and slammed the trunks shut. Wagging her brows, she nudged my side and hopped to the ground.

I ought to scold her for the insinuation. Her giggles carried off in the cool breeze as she skipped to Jaime, who was standing near the fire. Zichri waved a hand in front of my face, startling me. I hadn't seen or heard him climb up, but there he was.

My pulse kicked up to a gallop. Lifting my chin higher, I looked him square in the eye. "Why did you send Laude away?"

He touched my elbow. I yanked it back but swallowed hard, feeling his warmth lingering on my skin. It distracted me more than I cared to admit. I was sure he could sense my thoughts—not in the magical sort of way.

He slid his fingers along my wrist. "You're riled up. Let's sit so we can have a real conversation."

"Fine." I sat on a trunk, folding my hands on my lap. "Speak."

"Our king sent us to make a secret transaction. He ordered us to say we were merchants. So, you see, I told you the information I was at liberty to share. I meant no harm. Truth be told, my superiors instructed us to go directly there and back."

"I see. Laude and I ruined your secret mission."

The fading, golden light cast shadows over half his face, revealing a scar under his eyebrow and another small one on his cheek. He leaned in. "No, that's not what I'm trying to say."

"Why would Himzo soldiers enter our territory to trade? It sounds suspicious, don't you think?" Judging by the way he stilled, there was more to the story. "Never mind. I prefer you not to answer. It might tempt you to spin another tall tale." That was a lie. I wanted to know everything, but I didn't think he'd tell the truth. Why not let him relax and think I was not so desperate for information? He might slip up.

"I followed orders. The rest of what I've said is true. Why don't we start over again? My name is Zichri. I'm a Himzo soldier. I'm completely sidetracked because I stopped to save the most beautiful woman I've ever met." His face was now too close for comfort.

I exhaled a slow, measured breath. No man had ever told me I was beautiful. I had imagined Lux saying those words countless times, and part of me still wished he'd say it. Heat bloomed on my cheeks. A fog covered any previous thoughts, feelings, and conversation.

Zichri tipped my chin. "Cypress, will you let me accompany you to your destination?"

The name jolted me back to reality. I was Princess Beatriz, not Cypress, and I sought my whyzer to bestow a magical gift. My life is worth nothing without this gift. I thought: *He'll serve my purpose.*

I swallowed hard and said, "Yes."

"Can I ask a question?" He held my hand and gave it a gentle squeeze. "Why are you headed to Valle de los Fantasmas?"

My body tensed. His rough fingers interlaced with mine, distracting me from thinking clearly. A tingling radiated up my arm and through my chest. I cleared my throat and attempted to focus again on his question.

All explanations would give away my identity unless he knew nothing of Giddel. That could be a real possibility. Noblemen and commoners alike received gifts from whyzers. "The whyzer of the valley invited me to the ruins so I may receive my gifting."

Zichri nodded. "Then it's settled. We will guide you into the valley. If you were promised a gift, the whyzer will surely allow all of us to enter and exit safely. Giftings, like the ones you receive in Giddel, are worth the risk."

His words sent a spring of hope surging through my body, comforting my soul. I didn't realize bits of doubt poisoned my joy. Papá never thought this trip would be worth risking my life, and Mamá would never speak negatively against Papá. Cosme teased me about making the trip—nothing more could be expected from him. Laude always agreed with any plans I made, so her approval never meant much.

Tiny dancing flames reflected off of Zichri's eyes, much like the one being kindled inside me. His nearness would never be allowed back home, but I wasn't home. In the dark forest, while the soldiers and Laude sang around a fire, I allowed myself to cuddle closer to the man who saved me.

I leaned my head on his shoulder and said, "Thank you for everything."

He released my hand and wrapped an arm around my shoulders. "I wish the trip was longer."

I melted even more into his embrace, choosing to trust him despite logic.

CHAPTER 17

Shades of green leaves swayed above the wagon as the horses pulled us down the mountainside. I sat next to Zichri, leaning against a trunk. His hand grazed mine as if he were trying to hold it. At home, this sort of thing never happened. It awakened a tantalizing feeling that swarmed inside of me like bees in a hive brimming with honey, and I liked it. I wove my fingers through his, and his cheeks dimpled.

I told myself, *What better way to gain Zichri's trust?*

We hit a bump on the road with a thud and knocked into each other.

Gonzalo peeked over his shoulder, holding the reins. "Sorry, Blas distracted me."

Blas shouted from next to Gonzalo, "Don't believe a word he says. The old man is going blind."

Zichri leaned over my shoulder, his breath brushing against my neck. "Gonzalo can't see well, but he'll never admit it."

"Why do we allow him to drive?" I pursed my lips.

"No one wants to fight him for the driver's seat." He rubbed his thumb into my palm, keeping our fingers intertwined. A thick campfire smell lingered on his clothes, drawing me in closer. "We've driven down this road many times before, and we're still alive."

I forced a smile to my face. The thought of being driven by a blind driver didn't seem to bother any of the men.

Zichri shook his head at Blas's laughter. Blas smacked Gonzalo's back, and Gonzalo grunted. Milo sat across from us, glaring at the scene on the driving bench, not a touch of amusement gracing his face. I hoped he'd take the reins.

Jaime rode on Carmel behind us, gazing at the forest and studying the mountainside. I agreed with Laude—Jaime was the most handsome of the bunch, besides Zichri, of course. Jaime's eyes reminded me of my papá's with a mix of green, gray, and brown flecks. Just like the other men, he was tall and strong. But something about his presence calmed the soul. Perhaps, it was that he chose his words carefully or that he remained steady under pressure.

I'd approve of him for Laude, though I'm not sure she wanted my approval anymore. Slumped at the back of the wagon, she screwed up her lips, scrunching her nose. All morning, she had acted out of sorts. She didn't offer to fix my hair and she knocked over a pail and left it there. I had thought that maybe she didn't sleep well. She glared at Blas, who glanced over his shoulder, flashing a toothy grin.

The wagon jerked again. My heart leaped. Zichri steadied me by wrapping an arm around my shoulders as he gripped the side of the wagon with his other arm. I breathed in a remnant of the lavender soap from the inn and relaxed against his chest.

"Old man!" Milo pulled himself up to his feet. "If you need me to drive, I'll take the reins."

Gonzalo snickered. "You'll need to wrestle me first, and we both know how that ended last time."

Zichri leaned close to my ear. "Last time, Milo laid on the floor all afternoon catching his breath. Gonzalo didn't break a sweat." The jovial way Zichri nodded inspired a faint chuckle. Back home, my brother and Lux sparred rather than wrestled. Lux said that barbaric people do that sort of thing. And here I was spending time with—and enjoying—the barbaric sort. Never could I have imagined this.

Laude's expression dripped with disdain. Her stare could have sent fiery darts in Blas's direction if she had that power. It was so unlike her to hold a grudge. Yesterday, she had belted tunes and laughed much of the night. I'd fallen asleep before she came to lie on the wagon next to me. What could have changed in that short time?

I patted Zichri's arm and tilted my head toward Laude. He let go of my hand, and I pulled myself to the back of the wagon bed, next to Laude.

I nudged her side. "You've been sour all morning. What's wrong?"

"Nothing." She curled the corners of her mouth up and squinted her eyes.

"That's the most ridiculous smile I've ever seen."

"Go back with Mister Handsome and enjoy his muscular arms." Her pitch rose as her mouth fell back into a frown. "When we run off, there won't be any more of that to go around."

"I agreed to let them take us to the ruins."

Laude's jaw dropped. "You didn't even want them to walk us five paces. Now they're going with us all the way into the valley? This is the worst day of my life." She grunted.

I leaned in near her shoulder. "Be civil. We don't want any stray word giving away our identities." I pulled away. "Besides, I thought you liked all our companions."

"I did. Then Blas made a crude joke at my expense. They all laughed at me. Can you believe that? I will never like a Himzo ever again."

"What of Zichri?"

"He would have laughed too."

I cringed at the whine in her voice. "Well, what did Blas say that hurt you so?"

Laude turned her face away, crinkling her nose.

Wasn't she the one so determined to stay with these men that she faked an injury? I gave a mirthless chuckle.

"You laugh at me," she said in her squeaky voice.

"It's not—"

"Go enjoy your Himzo and all the hand-holding and hugs and sweet words. He'll soon be gone when you get your gift."

Why is she shouting? I flicked my eyes toward Zichri and Jaime, wanting to shake the insolence out of Laude. "Have it your way."

Jaime feigning interest in the sky. He had to have heard her. In the time I had spoken with Laude, Milo had—somehow—squeezed between Blas and Gonzalo. Blas had part of his bottom on the bench, appearing to hang off the edge. Was this any safer? I clutched the side panel and made my way back to Zichri.

He took me in his arms. "We're almost there. I'm sure she'll forget Blas's joke once she sees the waterfalls. They're said to have magical properties since the water flows from Valle de los Fantasmas." He lifted his brows. "We are going to climb the falls to enter the valley."

I held tight to his arm while the wagon pitched and settled again. The idea of finally reaching our destination mixed my emotions into a ball knotted up against my heart. *Will we survive? Is this a death sentence for Laude, Zichri, and the others?* I tucked wayward hairs behind my ears, brushing away my concern.

Soon I'd possess the one thing I had always wanted ... and Lux. He promised to marry me. Would it be everything I had hoped? I sat up straight, causing Zichri's hand to slip down my itching arm.

Though my skin hadn't stopped burning, I hadn't been as bothered by it. My fingers slipped under my collar, and I tugged the fabric over to glimpse the designs on my shoulder. The curve of a faint marking peeked out, unchanged. I released a pent-up breath.

We still had time.

CHAPTER 18

WATER CASCADED DOWN PROTRUDING rocks and splashed into a teal pool. A lazy flow slithered away into a cave and continued downstream. Blas took off his tunic, threw it to the side, and dove in. Gonzalo and Milo raced behind him. The water seemed to welcome them after a morning of the sun beating on our foreheads. I wanted to join in, but I had not thought to bring my swimwear.

Blas popped his head out of the water. He pointed twelve feet high, up a ledge with a giant boulder on it. "I doubt Giddelian ladies would dare to jump from such heights."

My hands balled into fists.

"Do you know how to swim?" Zichri took off his boots and tunic, tossing them on the back of the wagon.

"I'm from Giddel. We're creatures of the sea." I averted my eyes from Zichri so I wouldn't stare at his sculpted chest. A flush crept up my neck. Should I sit out with Laude and skip out on the chance to show these Himzos a thing or two about the strength of Giddelian ladies? I removed my overdress, untied my boots, and placed them over the side of the wagon. Did my clothes cover my body properly? I glanced down. My white underclothes covered my skin from my neck to my wrists, and the loose skirt flowed all the way to my shins.

Jaime stayed back, patting his horse's mane and speaking tenderly to it. Laude neared the water but plopped on the dirt with her arms crossed. The contrast between the whooping men and Laude stirred a need for me to breach the gap.

Zichri extended his hand, drawing my attention away from Laude. "One can never be too certain. I was looking forward to teaching you how to swim."

A nervous laugh escaped my mouth. The idea of him being so close twisted in my stomach. To ease my jitters, I walked over to Laude and tugged on her arm. "Come in with us. When will we get another chance to do something like this again?"

She glared up at me. "If you would have heard what they said about you, then you wouldn't be so willing to jump in after them."

I groaned and sat on the ground. "Just say what you mean to say."

"They said that every single lady in Giddel is silly. Then Blas mocked me. All of them laughed. They even made a strange gesture in your direction, laughing about how Zichri was making his move. So, you see, I'm not overreacting. These men are vile and don't deserve our attention. We don't need them anymore since we're at the valley entrance." She turned toward me, bracing my shoulders. "Why can't we just do what we originally planned?"

"Shh!" I put my index finger to my mouth, certain Zichri overheard her rant. Unclasping her hands from my shoulders, I tipped my head back, considering her words. It stung to think Zichri used me. "Laude, you can either make the best of this moment or wallow in self-pity. We don't think much better of Himzos either."

She mumbled to herself.

"What did you say? Speak clearly. You know how I hate when you mumble."

"Make the best of this moment, Your Highness." She turned her body away and hugged her knees.

Laude was not going to be reasonable. That had never been her forte, so I shouldn't have expected it. Zichri waited at the edge of the water. I strode toward him, packed dirt and pebbles poking my feet, and I took his hand. My frustration melted as his warmth seeped into my skin. The blue-green water lured us to dive into its depths, though the gap between the ground and the surface of the water appeared wider than I had thought from afar.

"Are you scared?" Zichri tugged on my hand.

"What makes you think that?" I tried to shift my face into a neutral position, but there was no hiding from Zichri.

"You do this thing with your eyes." He set his mouth in a crooked grin.

I lifted my chin. My need to prove him wrong held me in place, even though everything in me wanted to run back to the wagon in defeat. "Don't worry about me."

"If you're sure, then. On the count of three, we jump in. Ready. One. Two—"

I jumped in the air, pulling Zichri with me. Cool water smacked my feet and swallowed my whole body. I swam toward daylight. The blue sky and tall tree branches hovered around the edges of my water-distorted eyesight. I broke through the surface and gasped. A chilly, humid air met my cheeks.

Zichri popped out of the water, coughing. "Why didn't you wait for three? My mouth was open when I hit the water."

I laughed. "I didn't think I would have jumped if I waited any longer."

He gave a low chortle in return and stroked toward the men who climbed up to the ledge and onto the boulder. "Come, let's see how fearless you really are."

Blas hung off the vines creeping up the side of the boulder. Milo dove from the top, breaking the water's surface with a splash. Ease passed between the men like they had done this before.

Zichri climbed up the ledge to join them. Waves of tension rolled through my body. Running from home took every ounce of courage I could muster. Didn't that prove my grit? Why did I now need to prove my fearlessness?

I looked over at Laude for an excuse to get out of this challenge. Instead, Jaime sat next to her, and she smiled. *Nothing keeps Laude down for long.* What could he have said to make her forget her anger?

Zichri waved me over. I told myself that I was unafraid as I stroked closer to him. I set my palms on the slippery rocks on the ledge and hoisted myself out of the water to the base of the giant rock. My fingers met slick roots and crevices, but I set my foot to climb, determined to cling for dear life. Zichri offered me his hand, and I smacked it away. Blas teased Zichri with a strange twiddling finger gesture. *They will not think me weak.* I lifted myself upward.

At the top, the jungle swayed, or maybe that was my vision. Blas jumped, and my arms and legs quivered. Seconds passed, then plop. Blas reemerged—all smiles. The men cheered and hooted.

"Cy-press, Cy-press, Cy-press," the men chanted.

That was me. I stepped closer to the ledge, regretting my quick decision.

Zichri said, "You don't need to—"

I flung my body as far from the boulder as possible. During the fall, a rush of exhilaration tingled through my body, and air flapped my clothes. My feet smacked the water. Bubbles and water streamed up my body as the river slowed my fall. I paddled to the surface, ready to do it again.

By the time we were done enjoying our downtime, Gonzalo had prepared a campfire and food. I hadn't seen him exit with all the jumping. All of us enjoyed fresh fish and zapotes—an orange-fleshed fruit found in the land around Giddel. Our plan to enter the valley developed while we ate, though they wouldn't look in my direction.

Gonzalo would stay behind to tend to the horses. I suspected he didn't want to do all the climbing and swimming required to make it into the valley. The men would carry packs with the hammocks and one set of clothes for each of us. We all would wear our boots because we'd need to hike when we got in. No one alive had seen the ruins, but the legends of old told of a city overlooking a waterfall.

Zichri, Blas, Jaime, and Milo dashed to gather all the supplies before I had a chance to agree or disagree with the plans.

"Are you nervous, miss?" Laude nibbled the last of a zapote.

Gonzalo sat across from us and bit into his pear, letting it dribble down his gruff chin and rough knuckles. He kept his gaze fixed to the ground as he made his way to the rest of the men beyond the wagon.

I shook my head. Why was he behaving so strangely? It must be a Himzo thing since the others acted awkward too. I turned my attention back to Laude. "Does it matter what I feel? We're going to climb up and hope the whyzer really invited us."

Laude flung the pit of the zapote into the forest and wiped her hands on her dress. "I remember that day the whyzer was supposed to give you your gift, and the boy came instead. Your uncle Uly said that the boy spoke the truth, so we should be all right. Right? You said he invited you in your head."

She passed me an earnest look and continued, "Still, I think I might faint from fright. I'm sorry for mistreating you this morning. If I die, I want you to know that you are a sister to me." She flung her arms around me, squeezing the air from my lungs, red curls tickling my face. For once, she wasn't overexaggerating.

I hugged her in return. Did I really mean that much to her? She had always been a presence in my life, and I in hers. When had we stopped being playmates? When had I become so ... I bit my lip. A day at the beach sifted to my memory when Lux pointed out how Laude stole Mamá's affection from me. His words had driven deep.

What if I lost her? My stomach clenched. "We are going in and coming out with the gift, both of us—alive."

Could I make that promise?

"Are you ready to leave?" Zichri's voice pulled Laude and me apart. He held out a stack of folded clothes to each of us. "Why don't you change into these? You might be more comfortable climbing in pants and tunics. And Laude, Jaime lent these to you."

Zichri kept his eyes trained on Laude. How odd. I wouldn't say I was jealous, but something inside of me bristled. I hesitated to reach for Zichri's spare clothes. This broke every rule I'd ever learned: using a man's clothes—a Himzo soldier's clothes for that matter. Laude ripped the garments from him, hugging them like a child's special toy, rather than a worn-out tunic and pants.

Eyes cast down and anywhere but at me, he said, "You

do understand that wearing a gown could mean your death, and those wet undergarments could be a … distraction." He smashed his lips into a line as if he was uncomfortable.

For the first time since jumping in the water, I peered down, catching how the thin fabric clung to my skin and revealed more than any person, besides my future husband, should ever see. Heat rushed up my face. I crossed an arm over the front of my chest. Why didn't anyone say anything? To think I'd climbed the boulder several times in these translucent garments. No wonder all the men wouldn't meet my gaze.

"Thank you." I swiped the clothes from Zichri's arms and pulled Laude by the elbow, not bothering to look over at Zichri. Rushing to the trunks, I leaned my chin over Laude's shoulder. "Why didn't you say anything about my shirt being transparent?"

"Ai-yi-yi! I didn't notice. My mind was elsewhere."

A growl vibrated low in my throat. "Now, what could Jaime have said that distracted you so?"

Laude tittered with glee. "Miss, I never supposed you'd care for such things."

"I don't. It was a passing thought." Now, why did I say that? Curiosity flooded over my frustration. I climbed up the back of the wagon.

She hopped up and opened a trunk. "Then, I'll keep it to myself."

"Don't be silly. You know you want to share." I set Zichri's garments on a trunk. As I was about to rip off my damp undergarments, I noticed the men in clear view, staring up at the rocks and vines we were about to climb.

Laude followed my gaze and shouted, "Don't you dare peek or else we'll—we'll …" She turned toward me, "What will we do to them?"

"I'll use my gift on you, Zichri of Himzo," I yelled with as much threat as a screeching kitten.

Zichri turned toward us, laughing with all his men. "That doesn't encourage us to help you."

"You will be gentlemen or …" I couldn't think of a sly comeback, but I knew I had to say something. "I will send my brother after you, and he will levitate you to the moons."

"You're lucky I find you irresistible and that we are men of our word. We will not look. Just get to changing already." Zichri turned his face to the falls again.

Though they said they were men of their word, Laude and I changed fast before the temptation to peek overtook them.

CHAPTER 19

WATER GUSHED OUT THE top of the cliff and splattered into the river beside us. A slick, brown wall of rock stood guard over the dangers in the jungles beyond, giving me just one more chance to reconsider my choices. I looked down, trying to adjust to the way Zichri's pants sagged over my legs. And no amount of rolling up my sleeves could make the borrowed tunic sit correctly. I pressed my shoulders back, determined to appear confident for Laude and the Himzos behind me despite the nerves clawing at my stomach. Were we insane for going into the valley?

Before I could scare myself further, I led the group. We ascended the rocky side of the waterfalls with ease, taking our time to place our hands and feet in each crevice. Milo and Blas made it to the top first.

Smack!

"Blas," Milo yelled. "What in all—"

Smack!

"My word," Milo said with a hint of shock in his voice.

"What is that?" Blas asked. "Jaime, come here. You've got to see this."

Upon reaching the crest, I perched on the edge, catching my breath. Between us and the next waterfall lay a teal pool the size of the palace grounds. Above the next fall, another taller waterfall cut through slabs of the mountain like a staircase made of rock and water. We hadn't been able to see any of this from below because of all the tree branches.

The men huddled near the falls, and Laude crawled up a second later. The steady roar of the water shooting off the cliff calmed my nerves. A gentle breeze kissed my heated cheeks. Zichri stepped beside me and eclipsed the sun, offering a helping hand.

"Should I be worried?" I slipped my hand in his and pulled myself to my feet.

"No," Zichri said. "Blas found a strange bug." He combed his fingers through his hair while staring straight down the fourteen-foot cliff.

"That wasn't so bad."

"Why had we been so hesitant to come?" Zichri teased.

"My uncle, for one, and the horror stories about bodies washing downriver can give a lady quite the scare."

"Oh, but you don't look like the fretful type." His smile lit up every other part of his face and melted my heart like butter on warm toast.

"I'm not." My chin cocked up.

"What happened to your uncle?" Zichri asked.

"I remember him from when I was a child. Tall, thin, looked like my papá, but he had a scraggly beard. He was plagued by nightmares and thought he needed to come here." The skin on my bicep burned under my sleeve, and I gripped it, hoping to stop the metallic lines from spreading further up my arm. "I don't know what happened to my uncle, but Papá was mad when he left." I glanced at the waterfalls we'd still need to climb. "Let's keep going."

Milo patted Zichri's shoulder. "I suggest we swim to save on time."

"Anything to save on time." I jumped in and swam, clothes clinging to my body.

We crossed the pool of water, climbed another waterfall, and hiked to the base of yet another, taller fall. Muscles aching like I'd swum the width of the Agata Sea, I sank my fingers between slick rocks. A grayish haze floated around us. Jagged boulders protruded from the mountainside, our cushion should we misstep. Would we ever make it in?

"Do you still want to go forward?" Zichri propped his foot on a rock and adjusted a sodden boot.

"Is this fear I'm detecting from a soldier?" I shook my head as I clicked my tongue.

"Forward and onward!" Zichri called to the rest of our companions.

Jaime assisted Laude by making suggestions on where to place her hands and feet. Blas and Milo raced to the top, crossing distances with ease. I picked a spot and climbed.

Left arm. Left foot. My right foot slipped, and I curled my fingers around the rocks, praying not to fall. I recovered and started up again. Right arm. Right foot. Push up. I continued until halfway to the top ledge. Something buzzed about my head, and I swatted it—more buzzing. The little critter knocked against my cheek.

I cringed and glanced at Zichri, who was about an arm's length away. "Do you see bugs swarming about?" My arms trembled under my weight.

He stopped moving. His expression contorted until his eyes grew a couple sizes bigger and his nostrils flared.

"What is it?" A pinch pricked my neck, and I yelped.

"Just keep going. Faster," he urged, continuing his ascent.

I reached for a nook, and something stabbed my palm. I screamed. A hornet, larger than any I'd ever seen before, remained stuck in my skin. I flicked my hand, throwing the yellow monster. Even with the pulsating sting, I increased the pace—more buzzing. I swatted. Another stab on my leg.

Keep going, Beatriz.

Mumbled voices filtered from above. I couldn't hear past the throbbing pain of my stings.

Dirt and pebbles trickled onto my forehead. But I didn't stop clawing and pushing skyward.

"I think the dirt's helping!" Laud's voice blared above the roar of the waters. "Almost here!"

Ragged breaths puffed between my lips. More dirt pricked my eyes and burning pain pulsed. Many hands yanked my body over the top of the ridge. I lay on a hard surface. Blue skies above.

"You climbed into a swarm of strange bees," Laude said. "Jaime has never seen such creatures before. The fellows believe it's one of the beasts of the valley."

Her statement brought no comfort. *Will we be the first to come out alive?*

My forearms and calves protested any further movement, but I got to my feet anyway. It seemed everyone else needed a break just as desperately as I did. Thank the Ancient One!

We stood on a rocky ledge, squinting at another large expanse of glistening water. The slow-flowing current cut through dark slabs of rock, making swimming our best way to officially enter the infamous valley.

Tucking stray hairs behind my ears, I peeked at Zichri. "You could still turn back."

"Why don't we stop here?" He squared up to me. "We'll decide tomorrow when we're not so tired." He walked around me and swiped a yellow-orange fruit from the ground. The floor was littered with mangoes.

Nothing had ever looked so sweet. By the time I ate my second mango, Laude, Milo, Jaime, and Blas had their hands coated in sweet juices from devouring the treat. No one argued about camping at the top of the cliff for the night.

Since the land on the cliff could fit my bedroom inside of it, and roots and brush took up more than half the space, the Himzos chose to sleep in the brush while Laude and I got a grassy spot in between the tree roots.

Laude curled up and slept before the sunlight disappeared from the sky. As clouds covered the moonlight, I sat, legs curled to the side and back straight. The stings on my hand and leg pulsed. The marks along my arms throbbed with an itch that would not be satisfied, reminding me of my oath. Was my time running out?

Footfalls approached. Zichri took a seat, with one leg extended and the other propped up. He leaned an elbow on his knee and turned toward me. "You should get some rest."

Now an inky black, the calm water lay as the boundary between being inside the sacred land and outside. I inhaled a hissing breath, subduing the urge to tear at my skin. "I can't sleep."

"Nerves getting the better of you?" His piercing eyes searched mine.

"If the whyzer, who hears from the Ancient One, told you to come, then he'll protect you." Zichri sounded so certain.

"Who has that sort of faith?"

"If you don't, why did you come?" Zichri fit his hand into my unscathed one and asked again. "Why did you leave your family?"

I closed my eyes, seeing the vines glowing on my skin the day I made the oath. Alexa whispering to her ladies in waiting: *She might as well be a useless Himzo.* Those words stung even this far removed from the court. But I could not explain that to Zichri. "Because I had no choice."

"We all have choices." He squeezed my hand. "If you want to go back, we can jump down each waterfall and pretend that this is what we came to do."

"I thought you said that this gift was worth the risk."

"Or … we can step forward and see what the Ancient One destined for you." He pressed his lips to my knuckles. His soft touch ignited waves of goosebumps.

"Zichri, why are you here? You've done what no one else was willing to do for me, and we've only known each other four days."

He pulled away and looked up to the sky. "I mean what I say about the Ancient One protecting us. But you're right. That's not why I'm here." Moonlight emerged from behind a cloud and kissed the slope of his nose. "Have you ever wondered if our efforts are worthless?"

I flinched. The question caught me off guard. My focus had always been on attaining my gift and working through my nightmares.

"When you get your ability, you might help me deal with my troubles." He let out a mirthless laugh. "I'm sure you understand being helpless to change your life."

A smile crept up my cheek. Why did I let him affect me this way? I was supposed to gather information. Instead, I had the urge to hug him. "Tell me something most people don't know about you."

He scrunched his brows, contemplating. "I would much rather read than dine in style." The corner of his lips tipped up. "Where did that question come from?"

"It occurred to me that we might die, and there's so much I don't know about you. Is reading your favorite thing to do?"

"No, but close." His eyebrows rose halfway up his forehead.

"What is it then?"

"Trespassing in forbidden lands, of course."

I laughed, unsure if he was telling the truth.

CHAPTER 20

I LAY NEXT TO the mango tree, somewhat aware that I was sleeping. Even so, my mind whirred with a vision of tall grass poking at my legs in a meadow with a cabin. Sunny skies stretched overhead, but I glanced into the jungles to my right. A sensation rushed into my mind like string connected me to another living being. The invisible cord throbbed. I followed the unseen string from the open meadow and into the deep shadows between the trees. A greedy urge pumped through my veins, but it wasn't my own feeling.

"We want you," a voice hissed, and a dark shadow shifted between the trees.

I whirled around, smacking into someone's chest.

My body jolted. I gasped for air and awakened to a dull blue sky overhead with branches reaching into my line of sight. My heartbeat galloped.

It was only a dream, Beatriz. But why do night visions have to feel so real?

A constant rush of water louder than the sea flowed somewhere nearby, calming my nerves. I lifted my head. Zichri, Blas, and Milo's backs faced me while they perched on the cliff edge several paces ahead. Following the curve of a narrow stretch of land between the pool of river water and the cliff's edge, I spotted Laude and Jaime sitting and eating mangoes nearer the waterfall.

Had I slept in that long? I flinched, imagining their judgment. *No wonder she hasn't a gift. She's quite the sluggard.* Tears stung my eyes, but I blinked them back.

We'd enter Valle de los Fantasmas today. What would we search for? The image of the meadow from my dream entered my mind's eye. I pushed myself into a sitting position. Every muscle ached from so much climbing and swimming from the day before.

I gripped the collar of my tunic. How much time did we have? I peeked beneath the rough linen, catching the swirl of faint lines. Not metallic ones. A sigh of relief poured out my mouth. We still had time to find my whyzer.

"Cypress!" Zichri called. He swiped a mango from the ground and approached me. "We'll head out when you're ready."

"Let's go now." I got to my feet and smoothed off my rumpled shirt and pants.

"It's quite the swim, and we had a long day yesterday." He shook the mango and lifted a questioning brow as if to ask if I wanted to eat.

"We need to get into the valley. Time is running short and—" I snapped my mouth shut. How did I let my words get away from me? No one else needed to know about my oath.

He gestured with a circular hand motion for me to continue. "And?"

"I'll eat first," I said, resigned.

Zichri tossed the mango, and I fumbled to catch it. He stood beside me while I dug my fingernails into the fruit, peeling the skin. I devoured my breakfast, juices dripping along my chin. It was so awkward, but these weren't normal circumstances. I mopped my face with my shirt sleeve. So undignified. He laughed, but I was in no mood for any talking or amusement. The skin along my biceps squeezed, and I winced.

Was it the dream that hurried me forward? Or the constant reminder of my impending death should I fail to complete my oath?

I threw the mango pit over my shoulder. "Now, can we go?"

Zichri scanned my face, and whatever he saw in it must have told him that I could not be swayed to idle any longer. He whistled to his companions, calling them nearer. Everyone ambled toward us and listened to Zichri lay out a plan of who'd be swimming near whom and what we'd do upon entering the valley. His melodic accent broke through in certain phrases, and he projected an air of confidence. I turned my gaze down to our boots, trying to focus on our current task.

"Lead the way," Zichri said in a gentle tone.

Dipping my boot in the turquoise water, I walked deeper. I would let the promise of more time with Zichri sustain me as I swam. He waded next to me, and I plunged ahead, thankful for all the swimming I did back home. A splash sounded beside me, Zichri. On my next stroke, Blas rushed to join us. I slowed my pace, catching a glimpse of Milo, Jaime, and Laude stepping into the water together.

The falls hummed in my ears, strangely calming despite doubt licking at my heels. I arced an arm over my head, breathed, and switched arms. My legs kicked in perfect rhythm.

A large bird glided over our heads and dove to the water, skimming the surface. It zipped away, a flopping fish in its talons. *Will we be hunted like that fish?*

My aching arm muscles tightened. Splashes sounded on each side of me. How much more to go?

The rocky shore grew closer, and I continued forward until smooth stones grazed my fingers. My limbs begged for a break. A few more strokes. Sucking in a deep breath, I lunged onto the shore, unconcerned about dirt or anything else.

Zichri followed behind me and staggered to his feet, looking into the jungles all about us. He paced, hands on hips, and panted.

Blas collapsed once he made it out of the water, breathing hard, and sat up. "Something's not right." He pointed a thin finger toward the others.

I lifted my head, propping it onto my elbows. Two brown-haired heads peeked above the water offshore. I stood to get a better view, but it was the same. My heart dropped. "Laude!"

Milo swam back a few strokes, and Jaime disappeared under the water's surface. My world spun. What could I possibly say to Mamá if they couldn't save Laude?

What am I thinking? She isn't dead yet.

I ran into the water, but a strong hand grabbed my shoulder.

"They have her," Zichri said. "Milo and Jaime will get her to shore as fast as they can."

The two men flipped a lifeless-looking Laude on her back and hauled her in tow while they sidestroked. Each precious second tarried as I waited for them to make it to shore. I wiggled free of Zichri's steel grip and plunged in until the water reached my waist.

Zichri barred my way again with an arm and scooped me close to his chest. "Wait until they pull her onto the shore. You'll only hold them back."

"Is she alive?" I called out to them. Jerking to get free of Zichri, I elbowed his side. "Let me go."

Milo and Jaime dragged Laude to the rock-laden shore. She erupted in coughs. Jaime turned her onto her side and she retched water. *Is that a good sign?* I ran to her and wedged myself between Jaime and Milo. She wouldn't like them seeing her in such a state. Still coughing and gasping for air, she propped herself onto an elbow.

"Let it all out." I patted her back. Hot tears streamed to my jawbone. "Never scare me like that again."

Her swollen eyes looked up at me, reflecting the murky waters rather than the usual skyblue. More tears gushed out of me like hot springs. I lifted her torso and wrapped my arms around her body, squeezing tight. She spewed again. Warm vomit soaked into my shoulder. I didn't care—well, not much. Laude was alive.

"Good thing she got all that out," Blas said.

I whipped my head, glaring.

He bit his nails, concern etched on his forehead. At least he looked worried. Though, any loose comments might have brought out a fresh batch of fury from me. He'd caused Laude enough grief with his insults.

"Miss, I thought I might die ... I'm sorry. My arms gave up." Laude still caught her breath. Curls clung to the side of her face. Her chest puffed out and shuddered as it fell.

"Don't be sorry." I should have known better. She never went for the long swims with Lux and me, and the thought poured guilt into my heart. She never went because I disinvited her years ago.

Blas paced, his boots crunching. "I'm guessing we will relax the rest of the day." He hesitated for a second, looking down and adjusting his soaked tunic. "Gonzalo isn't here, so I'm the new chef. I'll start the fire." He lumbered toward the small clearing in the shadowed forest behind us.

Sunlight painted the mountain peaks and cast dark silhouettes of the lush trees covering the valley side. On the opposite end of the river, grass and plants bunched together in a larger clearing. Next to it, trees bursting with zapotes and a plume of smoke smudged the lilac skies. My whyzer was the valley's only known resident.

Zichri crossed in front of my view. "We'll head out tomorrow. You both can relax near the fire while we fish and gather from the forest."

"As you wish." I reached for Laude's hand to help her up, but Zichri scooped Laude into his arms. Her legs dangled, and her head lolled against his chest. Gratitude swept over me for his kindness.

Could she still die because of injuries within her body?

Looking over the river, I lifted my voice, hoping the Ancient One could hear more clearly in this valley. "Please, I beg for Laude's life and for all the men too."

A cool breeze touched my skin, like a small gesture to affirm my words had been heard. Maybe it was wishful thinking, but in that moment, I needed any sign of hope. The wind shifted, restoring the humid air.

I walked straight to Laude, who watched Blas fiddle with flint and steel. She could light a branch with the touch of a finger, but did the Himzos know? Probably not.

"No luck with the fire yet?" I placed a hand on my hip.

He hunched over a pile of leaves, striking his tools together. Not bothering to make eye contact, he said, "Yet? Don't worry your pretty little toes. Not even Gonzalo could get a fire kindled so fast." The cocky undertone of his voice chafed my ears.

"I bet Laude could get a fire going before you light up those leaves."

Laude's swollen eyes flicked wide. "But Miss—"

"Laude." I turned toward her and winked, trying to push my thoughts at her. *Don't mention your gift.*

She sat back, mouth snapping closed.

"Blas, Laude's victory will be all the better, especially since," I tapped a finger to my cheek, watching Blas meet my gaze, "all ladies from Giddel are silly. Isn't that what you said?" I raised an eyebrow in challenge.

"We only have one set of steel and flint." Blas continued to strike the pieces together.

"I packed another set." Jaime's voice came from somewhere behind us. He carried an armful of colorful fruit and odd leaves. Then he plopped them next to me and shook off his pack.

"This is silly. She's upset over comments between men around a campfire. She shouldn't have taken it personally." Blas grunted in frustration when a spark hit a leaf, but it did not catch fire.

Jaime handed Laude the metal set and added, "I'll get you some dry leaves."

Laude and I fixed our gazes on each other. I smashed my lips tight and ran an index finger across them to try and tell her to stay silent. She giggled weakly.

Milo and Zichri ambled toward us from down the shore, carrying several fish skewered on long branches.

I waved them over to quicken their steps. "Come see, come see who can light a fire first. Blas or Laude?"

"You can't be serious." Blas remained seated on the grass. "Are we going to make this into a show?"

Zichri, Milo, Jaime, and I stood between the two competitors. Poor Laude managed a swollen-faced smile when she lit up a leaf with her finger, pretending to use the tools. I bit on my lower lip while Jaime scooted the leaves under our firewood. None of the wood seemed to kindle, so Laude snuck a peek over at the others. All of their gazes fixed on Blas, and she reached with a glowing finger to a branch near her leaf.

Blas finally got a flame going when Laude's wood ignited into a full campfire. I passed her a conspiratorial grin. She snatched her finger back, firelight illuminating a sly expression. Smoke wafted in the air before Blas could take credit for helping. He dropped his tiny leaf to the ground and stomped on his flame. His angular features pinched together in a way that added more delight to the victory.

Laude hugged her knees, and Jaime sat next to her, scratching his beard stubble. Flirtatious glances passed between them. It appeared more than firewood got kindled in the competition.

What would I have done if the worst had transpired? A well of emotion filled me with a strange new sensation that swarmed through my chest. I hadn't realized how much she meant to me.

I settled between Laude and Milo and curled my legs to the side, positioning myself to give Laude some privacy. Then again, why shouldn't I eavesdrop on them?

Wind howled through the leaves. For a moment, I almost thought I had heard my name in the rustling: *Beatriz.* I shivered despite my proximity to the fire, feeling the hairs on my body raise.

"Hey, beautiful!" Zichri cooked his skewered fish on the other side of Milo. "Come sit with me. Tonight, we'll feast and get some rest."

"I *am* sitting next to you."

"No. Milo is sitting next to me."

Milo partially rolled his eyes and migrated to the other side of the campfire. I scooted closer to Zichri and flipped my sore palm up. The sting stretched my skin into a tight red color.

"Let me see that." Zichri cradled my hand. "Jaime, did you find anything to help with the swelling?"

Blas stood. "Jaime knows about *all* sorts of plants. Did you find any to season the fish?" There might have been a hint of envy to his voice, but I couldn't say for sure.

Jaime blushed and pointed to the mix of leaves he had left next to me. "No. Those are for Cypress. Can you heat up some water to make a poultice?"

Blas snatched the leaves and grunted. "I didn't need your stinky herbs anyway."

Another warm gust of wind brought a louder howl. *Turn back.*

Had anyone else heard the eerie words? Zichri stilled, and Laude sank into Jaime's embrace. But no one mentioned the strange voice.

The fire crackled, casting light over our small group as the sun's glow disappeared.

"Let me sing you the best tune you've ever heard." Blas stood closer to the fire.

Milo slapped Blas's back. "It's all right, brother. You don't have to prove yourself now. I'll take this one. I think we've had enough of your … exhibitions."

Laude and I met gazes, and she curved her lips in conspicuous surprise. I snorted, nearly spitting the tea I just drank. My hand shot to my mouth. If only they would have known how Laude won so easily.

Laude dropped her chin to her chest while the others watched my outburst.

Zichri nudged my elbow and leaned closer. "What's so funny?"

"It's a secret."

"Now we have secrets?"

"Look who's talking, Mister Zichri of Himzo." I pinned him down with a long, narrowed stare.

"I'm bound to secrecy. My king could hang me."

I gulped, feeling the weight of his words. Papá executed treasonous soldiers, not that it happened often. A memory flashed through my mind of dangling feet. I sat with my family, overlooking the gallows on a perfect sunny day in the main square. No amount of sea breeze could blow away the stifling air or stop my lungs from becoming iron in my chest. Papá explained that this one man's mischief stole many fathers from their families. Even with the explanation, it didn't change the morose and sickening feeling of watching another person die.

"Laude has," I glanced to be sure Blas wasn't close enough to hear, "the gift of starting fires."

Zichri guffawed.

"But don't tell Blas. Promise?"

He lifted a hand in the air and another on his heart in the Himzo fashion. It took him a good while to subdue his laughter. "Promise. Though you should know, Blas will practice using the flint and steel every spare moment he gets."

I placed my hand on his. "Good."

One by one, we set up our hammocks in nearby trees. Laude, Jaime, Zichri, and I were the last to part ways. I wished to stretch this small thread of time as long as possible, but Laude needed her rest.

Laude and I climbed into the hammock Gonzalo lent us. Not exactly like my bed back home or even the beds at the inn. She jabbed my stomach with her elbow, and I turned to my side, facing Laude's profile. The netting wrapped tighter around us. Laude's wild curls tickled my nose.

I had to ask. "Are you going to tell me what Jaime said to change your mood?"

Laude sighed in awe. "Miss, he apologized and assured me I impressed him with my ability to stand up for myself at the inn."

"That's all?"

"Of course not. Like I said before, he's the most handsome of the bunch with the most tender heart. Even your Zichri does not match him anymore."

"*My* Zichri?"

"I assure you, he is *your* Zichri. Jaime even said that he's never seen him give such special attention to any lady before."

"Go to sleep."

Long after her breath became soft and even, I lay awake, cheeks tight from a smile I couldn't release. Laude's words hit me with such a force that even the howling wind couldn't steal the happy sensation of floating among the clouds until I, too, drifted to sleep.

CHAPTER 21

Turn back.
You aren't welcome here.

I AWOKE TO LEAVES rustling overhead. Had the wind whispered again, or had I been dreaming? A gray palette sky peeked between the tangle of branches, just like the uncertainty at the base of my thoughts. What if Zichri had ulterior motives for helping us? My heart throbbed with doubt more than the stings on my palm and calf. The hammock netting squeezed me on one side, and the other side felt heavy and lifeless. I shifted Laude off my shoulder, allowing blood to circulate.

Zichri had saved us. He seemed sincere. But he was a soldier, and he had sneaked into Giddel, probably on more than one occasion. Was it for trade, like he said? The kingdoms around the Agata Sea enjoyed many resources. However, Papá enforced strict policies preventing free trade with Himzos. These suspicions continued to work through my thoughts like wildflower seeds cast over a manicured lawn.

Someone whistled at the campsite, and another person whistled from upriver. All this thinking sat ill in my belly. Perhaps I should join the others? I shifted toward the side, trying my hardest not to wake Laude, but the hammock jostled. We hadn't considered this when we agreed on sleeping arrangements. She flipped to her shoulder and groaned. Her fiery mess of hair acted like a wooly face mask.

I stuck a leg out, rolled to the side, and hit the ground hard. Laude plopped next to me. At least her arm hit the dirt before her head.

"Miss," she squeaked. "Did you need something?"

"I tried to escape your hair."

"Do you think I should have brought your comb?" She pushed back the curls that sprang out like a halo around her face. "Well ... since you're out of the hammock, it's best I"—Yawning, she climbed back into the netting—"take five more minutes."

I shook my head but said nothing to stop Laude. She was still recovering from nearly drowning after all. A cool breeze fluttered my oversized tunic. Tucking it into my pants, I tightened the belt and hiked through the woods rather than by the river. My boots sank into the mossy ground, barely making a noise.

Blas squatted near the fire pit, striking steel to flint. I stayed under the tree canopy and laughed to myself. *Maybe I should go back for Laude so she can help him.*

Someone whistled upriver, and I continued strolling through the forest. Dragging my fingers along the smooth tree trunks, I remembered Zichri's hand grazing mine and how right it felt. Perhaps I just had a bad dream, and that's why doubt pinched within my gut.

Water gurgled loudly, and deep voices murmured just beyond the tree line. Milo and Zichri stood, backs facing me on the edge of the river, holding spears. I tiptoed forward but stopped when I heard the harsh tone in Milo's voice.

"We should have arrived yesterday. All this dawdling could cost us ..." Milo continued to speak too low for me to hear.

I crept behind a trunk, not even a body length behind them, waiting for Zichri's response. Might I get some answers to my questions?

Milo grunted in frustration. "We could still head down and make it tonight. You did everything you promised." Slow seconds passed with only a burble of water for an answer. "Consider your brothers. They were already apprehensive about sending us."

"I will make sure the young ladies get out of this valley." Zichri's measured words assured me he meant us no harm. "You may go back if you like."

"We may not be able to keep them safe, and you know it. What benefit is this to us?"

Holding my breath, I peeked around the trunk, hoping to see more than Zichri's back.

No such luck. Zichri speared the water and lifted his bare stick. "This was much easier yesterday."

Milo jabbed his spear between the rocks on the shore, gaze drifting from the river. I twisted back behind the trunk, hoping he didn't see me. Hands over my pounding heart, I counted to ten. My breath slowed, though my heart still thumped loud in my ears. I crept around to spy some more. Milo tugged on his dark curls like he had at the inn and paced.

"Stop that," Zichri said. "You are scaring away the fish. Trust me. I've never made rash decisions before."

"A pair of fine eyes can cloud one's judgment."

"You know where I stand." Zichri's voice was serious.

"Do I?"

Laude squealed in the distance. *No!* I sank onto my bottom and pressed my back against the hard bark, hoping they'd follow the shore to our campsite. What could Zichri have meant by *You know where I stand*? Would he use me for the powers I would wield? It would make sense since no one in Himzo received gifts, and the powers Giddelians wield have held back Himzo invasions for many generations.

Milo's gruff tone broke the silence. "Forget this. I'm going back to eat Jaime's food." Rocks crunched along the river and faded into the distance.

Water splashed. I kept still and waited, tipping my head to the side. Sounds of flowing water, birds tweeting, and insects buzzing rattled the forest.

Slosh.

I poked my head out from behind the trunk. Zichri raised his stick from the water, and a fish flopped at the end.

CHAPTER 22

I HID AGAIN BEHIND the tree, back to the bark. The shadows under the jungle canopy seemed to grow darker, enveloping me in its ominous blanket. Zichri sighed. Then water sloshed, and crunching pebbles followed. I held my breath. The sound of footsteps waned and disappeared in the distance. Zichri had gone in the direction of our camp.

"Miss Cypress!" Laude called. Strain marked her voice. "Miss Cypress!"

The men would suspect I heard their private conversation if they found me here. I needed to move somewhere else. Traveling deeper into the forest, I hiked with no direction in mind. A pitter-patter of droplets played music on the treetops. Sprinkles of water dripped onto my nose. Still, I plowed ahead. Laude's voice sounded farther away, but I didn't care.

Zichri is using me, and Milo resents helping us. These thoughts drove me forward. Hadn't I hoped to gather information? What was I thinking—trusting them? And why did it hurt so much to find out the truth? I picked up the pace, almost running across the muddied ground. Droplets soaked into my brown tunic.

What were Zichri's brothers doing? Did Zichri have plans with them? An ache crawled up my neck, hitting the base of my head. My legs slowed their pace, and I stopped to rest, drinking in the earthy fragrance. I had to find out more. I had to face him as if nothing had transpired. Like he had no secrets.

A growl echoed through the jungle. I darted glances at the crooks of the vined trees and stepped slowly in the direction I had come. Glowing eyes from above stopped me cold. A large catlike animal stared down from a thick branch and licked its chops.

Oh, Ancient One! I clenched my teeth to keep them from chattering. With smooth, calm movements, I trod backward, keeping the animal in my line of sight, only glancing down to make sure a jutting root didn't trip my foot.

The beast fixed its stare in my direction, still as a statue. My boots padded the forest floor. A verdant branch cut into my view of the creature, and I continued to walk until I could see it no more. I spun around. Thick blobs of rain blurred my vision as I shot through the forest like an arrow.

Why hadn't I been more concerned about losing my way? Had I secretly hoped I would stumble across the ruins, and the whyzer would bestow the gift with the wave of his hand? Had I been thinking at all? My stomach shriveled.

The forest held me in its clutches. I couldn't see mountains or much of anything. How was I going to get back? A flash of light tore through the sky. Thunder roared, and the ground trembled.

It didn't take me long to imagine a giant cat prowling in the canopy. I pumped my arms harder, looking over my shoulder, and slammed into something.

I screamed.

"Cypress, Cypress! It's me." Milo grabbed my shoulders.

My breath rushed out in spurts.

"Found her!" His bellow sent another jolt through my body.

In the distance, Jaime's voice responded, "Heading to camp."

Milo stuck two fingers in his mouth and whistled, piercing the air. Another person whistled from a good distance away.

"What are you doing so deep in the woods?" Milo's narrowed eyes told me his mood had not improved.

"I got lost."

He massaged his brow and tugged on his dripping hair before meeting my gaze.

His eyes rounded. He pulled out a dagger, knees bending in a fight stance. Was he going to attack me? He flung his weapon.

I gasped.

The blade flew past me, and a black-furred beast smacked the blade, sending it soaring until it collided against the smooth bark of a tree and dropped.

Milo slipped out another dagger from his boot.

The beast let out a throaty roar.

Milo stabbed its shoulder. The beast shrieked in agony but clawed at him with the opposite paw. A red gash opened on the beast's fur. Milo grunted, parried, lunged, but the beast continued to press forward.

Should I run? But Milo. Could I leave him behind? I dove for the dagger Milo had thrown and grasped the worn leather against my achy palm. I popped up. Feet apart. Ready to throw.

The beast caught sight of me. It pivoted in my direction and launched, claws exposed.

No time to think.

I slashed the blade in front of me, awaiting the impact.

Milo slammed into the cat's side and cut into its neck. Blood gushed onto my tunic. The body thudded to the ground.

My grip remained firm around the hilt of the dagger as I watched the black fur over the creature's ribs still. A metallic odor filled my nostrils, sickening in my empty stomach. My heartbeat pounded in my temples.

Bu-bum, bu-bum, bu-bum.

Milo took a long, slow breath and squared his shoulders. He looked at me with a hard glare. "Don't," he breathed. "Run off. Again." He reached for my sleeve but stopped before touching it. For a second, I thought there was something more he wanted to say. Instead, he tipped his head to the side and signaled for me to follow him. I dared not unlock my fingers from the handle of the dagger. Who knew what other creatures lurked in the shadows?

I stayed close at Milo's heels, adrenaline shaking through my body. I ducked under low branches and watched for roots springing high out of the ground. It surprised me how long it took to get back.

Milo slowed his gait upon reaching the pebbly shore. "Back off from my friend." His harsh words woke me from my daze. He gave one pointed look and stalked ahead in the direction of our campsite.

"Excuse me?" I jogged to make it to his side. "Were you speaking to me?"

"Yes." He glared in my direction. "You are trouble."

"Well, you all didn't need to come with us. I tried to part ways."

"Try harder." An intensity smoldered in his dark eyes.

No one had ever spoken so harshly or with such force to me in my life. "Why?" I stopped walking. "Explain. What trouble?"

He whipped around. His face contorted into a grimace. "Zichri will not lie if you press for answers. Ask him."

I lifted my chin in return.

He strode away. His figure grew smaller as he turned a bend. Was he truly going to leave?

Cold pins prickled along my skin. I said to myself that Laude remained my sole reason to head back to camp. That was not true. I desired to see Zichri again, to hold his hand just like the last two nights. He provided me the encouragement I'd not felt in years.

I recited words to myself, trying to be convincing: *Zichri's just a pawn ... a delightfully handsome one. He means nothing, just like all the other Himzos.*

Milo was right about me needing to ask more questions. Crunching noise came from behind me, and I whipped around, dagger at the ready.

"Whoa! There you are." Zichri's hand shot out and relaxed as I lowered the blade. "What happened to you?"

A warmth spread through my muscles, loosening my limbs. "I had a close encounter. I—I wanted to see if I could find the ruins myself. Here, take this." The lie slipped off my tongue before I had a chance to think it through. I bit my lip and held out the dagger.

"Milo's. Hmm. You should keep it."

"I don't have a sheathe. What if I hurt myself?"

"If you insist. We'll find you a sheath back at camp." He brought my hand up to his plump lips and gently kissed my knuckles. His smile dimpled his cheeks. "Next time, could you at least give us a chance to dissuade you from running off by yourself?"

"I understand."

A *crack* boomed near camp.

His eyes rounded, and a concern line deepened between his brows. "We should head back."

I bobbed my head, unable to process what could have made such a noise. We strode downriver at a quick clip.

"What do you think that was?" I clutched the front of my tunic.

"I'm sure all is well." He looked over his shoulder and across to the other riverbank. "One good thing came of you getting lost."

"Oh?"

"I know where we can cross the river without having to swim against the current."

"Good. I'm sure you and the others have been through many adventures before." I slid my most gracious smile in place.

Zichri interpreted my statement as an invitation to share near-death experiences. Blas had gotten lost in a cave once. Jaime had snuck into an enemy fort but was captured, and then the men broke him out. Gonzalo had tumbled after climbing a rocky wall.

He avoided any mention of Giddel or the worry tiptoeing the lines of his face. What would we find back at camp?

CHAPTER 23

UPON REACHING CAMP, LAUDE flung her arms around me. "You're here!" She squeezed my torso. "It was terrible!"

Charred wood laid strewn across the grass in the clearing, a tinge of fiery orange glowing beneath the blackened edges. Ash coated Jaime's hair, face, and clothes. Blas blew out his cheeks with hands clapped on his head. What had happened?

"If it weren't for you, miss, we all might have died." Laude swiped her cheeks and nose. "We went out searching for you." A tiny sob escaped her throat. "While we were gone, Jaime thought to prepare a meal, and if he had been closer ..."

Jaime squeezed her shoulder, offering comfort. "The fire exploded. I've never seen anything like it."

Zichri and Milo locked stares. Hard expressions settled on both their faces as some hidden message seemed to pass between them. Milo shrugged a shoulder, and Zichri twisted his lips to the side. A tiny flick of Milo's hand led Zichri to toss his head back in exasperation.

Blas collected the remnant of our tattered satchels. "I put the hammocks inside the bags. I guess we sleep on the ground from now on."

The markings on my arms itched intensely. I circled my shoulders, using the rough tunic to assuage the pain. Had it been the stress of today, or was it ... I pulled back the collar of my tunic, peeking at my skin. Metallic lines swirled to the ends of my designs. Had I run out of time? Would the ground swallow me up like it had Lord Pau's father when he broke his oath?

Milo groaned, still in some hidden conversation with Zichri. "Fine. We had enough action today. We'll cross the river tomorrow."

"No!" I shouted and cleared my throat. "We cross today."

Zichri's eyebrows drew together. Milo and Blas shared a look, then Blas shrugged with a mocking expression.

"Cypress?" Laude cocked her head and stepped in front of me, flitting her eyes toward the drying blood on my tunic. "Are you all right?"

I dropped my voice. "The blood is from a giant feline, but that's not why we need to move on. I'll explain later." I scratched my shoulder, observing her tentative head shake. "It's of the utmost importance that we continue."

Laude inhaled a long breath and nodded. "Off to the whyzer!"

And so, we all marched back upriver to the spot Zichri had discovered. Boulders formed a line through the river, water gushing over them. On one side of the boulders, water pooled into a wide gentle stream, and on the other, the stream narrowed and raced in a turbulent flow.

Laude clung to a sapling. "I won't do it."

"You can't stay here." I clasped my hands in front of my chest. "We need to get to the other side, remember? The smoke. The whyzer. All of them are across the river." Never had I begged a servant before in my life. But we could not have gone through all this effort to be stuck at the edge of a river. "What if Jaime carries you?"

Laude tapped her chin for a second and grabbed the trunk again. "Miss, I've done everything you asked of me on this trip, but I can't go in that water."

My eyes burned as I filled my lungs with a shaky breath.

And what should I tell Mamá if Laude gets hurt or worse?

Zichri dipped his head toward me. "She needs time. Gonzalo won't climb anymore, and a year has passed. We can still cross without her."

"I won't leave her alone, not with the creature lurking in the forest.

What if something happened?" My insides throbbed as if the wasps stung my insides. Was this also part of my time running out?

"It will be all right. Jaime can stay with her." Zichri pointed to his broad-shouldered friend.

Jaime gave a single nod.

"That's not enough. If more creatures attack, Jaime is one man. Sorry, Jaime, you appear capable, but ..."

Blas howled with laughter. "You hear that? She's calling you weak." He clapped Jaime's back.

I met Laude's gaze just in time to catch her roll her eyes. Blas had certainly lost her good favor.

Milo stalked to Laude's side. "I'll stay with them."

Zichri held my hand. "Then it's settled. Blas, Cypress, and I will cross."

I hesitated to step into the river. In my mind, Laude would see the ruins with me—that might have been a new thought, but it was what I envisioned. River water rushed up past my ankles, climbing to my waist. Each step weighed heavy from the water and my conscience.

Once on the other side, I waved, still not wanting to part from Laude. For the first time in years, she had become like a sort of sister. I wasted so much time pushing her away over one silly comment Lux made as a child.

"We can't stay at the river all day." Zichri pressed a hand to my back, encouraging me to continue. "I'm sure you want to make it there and back before dusk."

It did not seem right to leave Laude, but I peeled myself from the shore. Laude still held the sapling with one hand and waved with the other.

Blas led us deeper into the rows of trees. I trudged behind, and Zichri walked by my side. I should have asked more questions. But instead, I allowed my mind to wander. *Perhaps, my gift will be mindreading.* That would do away with all the pointless games I played to get to know a certain someone.

Sunlight peeked through the canopy of leaves. How odd. The

skies were gray on the other side of the river. A sweet aroma drifted through the air, inviting us to travel into a sparser part of the forest.

Blas picked dull, blue berries with little hairs from a bush I'd never seen before.

"Come now, don't tell me you're going to eat that." Zichri plucked the fruit from Blas's hand.

"I had the same instructor as Jaime." Blas lifted a cocky grin.

"As I recall," Zichri squeezed the fruit between his fingers, "the instructor removed you from his group because you nearly got another pupil killed."

"I was young. What can I say?" Blas popped the blue berry into his mouth.

Unease tensed in my stomach. I waited for him to fall over, but nothing happened. Blas strode along, shoveling a handful of the berries in his mouth.

"If they are poisonous, how long will it take to affect him?" I peered at Zichri, who examined a green leaf with orange around the edges.

"It depends on the berries. I've never seen these, but then again, I was also dismissed from that same class." He tossed the leaf to the side, and we continued to stroll along a grassy path.

"The instructor must have been very strict to toss out so many students."

"He was the most lenient of the bunch. And we all knew it." Zichri reached for my hand.

I hesitated but slipped my fingers in his. Should I even allow myself to get closer to Zichri? *Papá would never accept him—what am I thinking? There's no real possibility of him being a match. Play your role.*

My heart sank just a fraction as we walked along a grassy trail and swung our arms. Blas bounced along, merry to be in his own company.

"You've been distant this morning. I don't know this look." Zichri's deep voice soothed the tumultuous emotions sifting within me. One second, Zichri was irresistible, and the next, he was an enemy.

Zichri edged closer and relaxed into an easy gait. "Why didn't you want to wait to cross the river? No one would blame you for needing time to rest."

"Eager to get my gift, that's all." Glancing ahead at Blas, I enjoyed the light reflecting off his nearly black hair.

"You're nervous for Laude?"

"I suppose. Perhaps I take her for granted. She talks far too much, excites over the smallest of things, braids better than anyone else I know, and is beyond loyal." I pictured Laude blowing out her cheeks with moons for eyes when I told her about the ruins.

"More valuable than a high position is finding a loyal friend," Zichri said. "I know because I have four. I trust them with my life. I also have a sister back home who fights my battles when I am away."

"Why must she fight battles when you are away?"

He sighed and shook his head. "Our two older brothers make life impossible for the rest of the family."

This wasn't what I had expected to hear. Where did this information fit in with the threats Himzo had been sending Papá?

The sound of our footfalls mingled with the rustling and buzzing all about us.

I tucked flyaway hairs behind my ear. "Is that why you sneak into enemy kingdoms?"

He chuckled. "Is that what bothers you? I do what my superiors tell me to do. As of late, I think they prefer me away."

"Are you that bothersome?"

"Always." He gently squeezed my hand. The playful curve of his lips gave me the inclination to rise onto my tiptoes and kiss him. I fanned my face.

Why must I get distracted so easily? I tried to shake off this attraction, but giggles sprang out my mouth.

Zichri stopped. His eyes focused ahead. Blas laid on the ground, and I slapped my hand over my mouth.

"You dunce. Why did you eat those berries?" Zichri ran ahead, dropped to one knee, and rolled Blas over.

Blas's chest rose in short breaths. Bleary eyes wandered within their sockets.

"Should I run back to the others?" My breath caught. The edges of my vision blurred into shades of brown and green.

Something hard tapped my shoulder.

I startled and whipped around. A man with a long gray beard stared down his nose at me, but he continued past me and walked over to Blas.

Zichri squinted up to the old man. "Sir, can you save him?"

The man pressed his knobby staff against Zichri's chest, sweeping him away from Blas. In one quick motion, the man lifted Blas over one shoulder and strode through the line of trees. We ran to catch up. Though each tree line had a grassy walkway, the tall man's single stride covered more ground than several of mine. We almost lost him when he made a sharp turn. Zichri ran ahead, and I sprinted behind him into a clearing.

In the center of the clearing, a log cabin stood tall. This building, with its horizontal logs stacked high, thatched roof, and stone chimney, had appeared in my nightmares. A plume of smoke puffed out the chimney and swirled into the blue sky.

The old man burst through the front door of the cabin, leaving it wide open. Zichri stopped at the entrance, scanned the forest, and then stepped into the darkness within the doorway. I continued toward Zichri, slowing the closer I got to the cabin. We could be a meal for this man or his prisoners. Of course, we wanted to save Blas, but how could we know what this stranger would do?

Zichri searched my eyes. "Go back to the others. Tell them where we are."

I turned to leave when I heard the old man croak, "Come in. I've been waiting for you, Beatriz—or is it Cypress?"

CHAPTER 24

My eyebrows shot up. *Does the old man know me?* I took a shaky step forward into the dimly lit cabin. Sunlight peeked through the curtains of a small window, casting a warm glow over the bearded man who sat on a wooden stool and sprinkled herbs into a kettle. Behind him, a fire danced on the hearth, filling my ears with an inviting crackle. Blas lay on a sofa, rasping in uneven breaths. *He wouldn't be here if it weren't for me.*

Lured by curiosity, I continued forward and curled my fingers around the leather sofa. How did this man know both my real name and the one I created on this journey?

On closer inspection, the man's hazel eyes, a mix of green, gray, and brown flecks, reminded me of Papá's. Even the shape of his face and laugh lines resembled Papá. *Is this man from Giddel?* I held my tongue. Best not to risk sounding silly.

But what if he was my lost uncle? Uncle was the reason Papá would never let me pursue this quest, despite the command from my whyzer.

The door slammed shut as if by invisible hands, and my heart leaped into my throat. Zichri had not moved from my side.

Breathing hard, I said, "What is your name?"

"Uly. Whyzer Uly."

I flinched. My uncle's name was Uly. But Papá had never said his brother became the whyzer of Valle de los Fantasmas. "How do you know me?"

"I think you have an idea." Uly grabbed a clay jar from a shelf and sloshed a thick red liquid into a cup. He tipped Blas's head forward to drink.

A pungent odor attacked my nose. I cringed and forced my cheeks to relax, trying to maintain a semblance of ease. "Uncle Uly? You're alive? Why are you living in this forsaken valley?" Blood-colored liquid dripped onto Blas's tunic. "What is that?"

"Some say I am a blessing. Your father thinks I am a curse. Believe me when I say I do not wish you harm." Uncle Uly shifted on his stool. He pursed his lips and twitched his nose. "It was not I who withheld your gift. There is another whyzer in the valley."

Firelight danced on Uly's long, peppered hair. How should I feel about this man? His gaze reminded me of Papá's, yet softer. He even twiddled his fingers over his knee like Papá.

Blas groaned in pain. His eyes pressed shut and sweat beaded on his forehead. My insides twisted into a growing knot.

"Your friend will surely die if you do not get him the antidote. My ministrations can only keep him alive for a little while."

Zichri stepped forward. "Where can we get the antidote?"

"It seems you are destined for the ruins. The margus plant grows like a weed in that blessed land. I dare not go unless I am invited." He pulled out a red book from the shelf behind him and thumbed through its pages until he found a drawing scrawled in black ink. A castle was drawn near a waterfall, and a forest labeled Chupalma surrounded the ruins on the east side. "This slender-leafed plant will save his life. I must warn you, though, you have but a day, possibly two, before the red berry poison is irreversible."

"Blue. He ate many of them," I said. "And what are the Chupalma?"

"No. He ate a berry from the red trees. They lure their prey. If he had eaten more than one, he'd be dead." Uly slid a folded parchment out from between the pages and placed the red book back on his shelf, leaving no room for argument. "Everything in this valley is meant to keep all others out. Including the Chupalma."

Various questions spun through my mind.

"Then, how are you here if the valley pushes all others out? And you still haven't answered the question about the Chupalma." My voice sounded too small for a princess, so I lifted my chin. I had heard whispers of my lost uncle who had died in the wilderness. They said he went mad because of a dream that nagged at him. That's why I didn't want to tell anyone about my dreams—especially the ones where I wielded terrible power.

Uly smiled weakly. "You know what it's like to be called into the valley, don't you, my dear? I understand how you were desperate enough to make an oath."

My lips parted in shock. "How do you know this?" I asked.

"I've met your whyzer, and I have my ways of hearing about the world outside the valley." Uly smoothed his beard. He understood a piece of me I'd never shared with anyone.

"You should head west. Here's a map to guide you. The Chupalma reside in the forest of giant trees." With knobby fingers, he unfolded the worn parchment and pointed to scribbles labeled "Chupalma Forest."

On closer inspection, the scribbles had human figures in the shadows behind the trunks. I took the map. "Are there more people living in this valley?"

"Living? No. But yes, there are others in the valley. And they'd like nothing more than to ensnare you. Do not accept their help. Better yet, avoid them if you are able. Keep your head down and focus on your destination. The Chupalma cannot touch you if you do not engage with them."

Wood popped in the fire. Words formed on the tip of my tongue. Did I want to ask more questions about these Chupalma? Would I have the courage to get to the ruins if I knew more? Instead of speaking, I clenched my teeth.

Zichri raked a hand through his hair. "Is there anything else we need to know?"

"The trails are mischievous, but if you stay attentive, they will not trick you. You should head out soon if you want to make it there and back before dark." Uncle Uly whistled a tune as he wiped Blas's brow and served him more of the blood-red drink.

Something about Blas, limp and lifeless, sent tremors spiking through me. Did I even want to ask how a trail could trick a person? I whipped around and strode to the door, welcoming the outdoors.

"Don't engage the Chupalma," Uly called. "They're far worse than any other terrors in the valley."

Humid air hugged my body. Tallgrass swished as I made my way across the clearing. I spotted a tree trunk near a dirt trail leading into the forest beyond Uncle Uly's peaceful abode.

My arms tingled with the constant itch of my metallic markings. The oath brought me here, but I imagined trekking to this place for more than half my life. Would I still have wanted to come if I had known every tribulation I would encounter: the murderous hornets, Laude almost drowning, a cat nearly mauling me, Blas eating poison berries, trickster trails, Chupalma, and … Zichri? I opened the map, following the inky marks curving around the paper.

Zichri made his way through the tall grasses, a crestfallen expression set on his face, so different from his normal disposition. Memories of happy days with Lux flooded over me, and the thought that after this trip, I would have those days forever. I passed Zichri a sidelong look, guilt swarming within my mind. He, of course, looked stunning, even with those worries creased on his forehead. Why did I secretly hope to fit Zichri into my life beyond this quest? And not to gather information or to capture an enemy soldier.

"Could I see the map?" His voice sounded flat and disconnected.

I passed it to him. While he examined the drawings, sunlight peeked through the leaves, casting a dazzling haze onto the trail. The peace contrasted with our dire need to save Blas. "Do we have a chance of making it there and back in time?"

Zichri studied the mountains surrounding the woods. "I sure hope so."

"Always the hopeful one."

"How else does a person live?" A tired smile crossed his face as he examined the legend.

"Living my best life now," I said. "Good times and garnering the respect of others."

He folded the map swiftly and stuffed it into his pack. "I think I know the way, and what you described is only partially true. Without tough times, a person becomes haughty." He reached for my hand and kissed my knuckles. A happy tingle ran along my arm, but his words knocked an arrow through my chest. Princess Alexa was the haughty one, not me.

I yanked my hand free. "Are you calling me haughty?"

"It was a general observation, not an insult. Come now, we don't have time to stand around." He led us farther down the path.

"You must know that I've had hard times." I brushed a branch to the side and trekked next to him. "You heard my uncle Uly speak of how difficult it is to be called into the valley."

"I didn't say anything to debate that."

The way Zichri focused ahead without a glance at me stung more than I wanted to admit. Had he changed his opinion about me? I pouted, but he didn't notice. He had noticed the details of my moods and expressions until now. Logically, it could be that we needed to hurry. Blas should be our chief focus. I sighed loudly.

Zichri lifted a brow and peeked over. "I didn't say you were haughty." He tripped on a root. His eyes flew open as he threw his hands forward. He caught himself before he fell.

I giggled, not breaking a stride.

"You're possibly a little self-indulged." Zichri ran his fingers through his hair and continued forward.

"Self-indulged?" I marched by his side. "In Giddel, we don't outright tell people their faults. It is not proper."

"You laughed at me for tripping over a root that had been lower a second before. I could have rolled my ankle."

"But you didn't. You should have seen your face. Just admit it, you would have laughed if I tripped." I dodged a bush. Crashing into something would be more humiliating after laughing at him.

"No, I would have helped you." He picked up the pace. "You haven't told me anything about you and your family. It seems interesting that a merchant's daughter would have such a powerful uncle. I thought only the royal lines and noblemen wielded such powers."

I slowed my pace, realizing that he also had his doubts about me and for good reason. "Every person in Giddel receives a gift." As he turned his chocolatey eyes in my direction, I turned my face away, gnawing on my bottom lip. He didn't press for answers.

And I didn't want to lie. Every person in Giddel did receive a gift, but, as a general rule, the royal lines and noble people came into highstanding because of their powerful giftings. Padding boots and snapping twigs were our only form of communication for a long while.

CHAPTER 25

"WE SHOULD BE NEAR the river," Zichri said. "I would prefer to travel the edges of the Chupalma Wood."

I looked over my shoulder, and the dirt along the trail shifted ever so slightly. Had we been walking in the wrong direction? A terrible pain clutched my stomach.

The midday light grew darker. I walked under leaves large enough to wrap around my body. My markings throbbed as a constant reminder to hike faster. Push harder. The shiver of death chased me and wasn't far behind.

"Come with us," cried a voice.

Zichri and I stopped. His gaze darted about like eagle eyes scanning the landscape. Smooth tree trunks wider than a carriage stood in eerie silence. A carpet of foliage covered each side of the path. I edged closer to Zichri, heart pounding like a woodpecker stabbing at my breastbone.

We tramped ahead, air thickening. Silence fell over the land, and the leaves stilled.

"Zichri," I whispered, "do you think it's the Chupalma?"

"Remember what your uncle said. Focus on the trail. Don't engage."

My chin trembled, and I nodded. Our boots padded hard on the dirt, the only sound besides our breathing.

"We're watching you," the serene voice said again.

I clutched Zichri's arm. What would Uncle Uly consider worse than anything else in the valley?

Zichri held me close, keeping a firm grip on my shoulder. "Keep to this trail no matter what."

A pale face moved in a branch above.

His gaze shot up and around. I clasped his waist, pressing my cheek against his soiled tunic, and slammed my eyelids shut.

"I heard a voice. Did you see a Chupalma?" Zichri pulled my hands from around him and cupped my chin. His warm touch comforted me enough to peek at his achingly handsome face. "I can take you back."

"No!" I tugged on my sleeves. "I can't go back."

"Come with me to the land beyond," a melodic voice sung in a hushed tone. "Far is the reach of the Chupalma of Abismo."

We both searched the underbrush. Coils of leafy vines overtook the ground and trees. A wisp of cool air wrapped around my body, whispering in a gentle voice, *Lift your hands and squeeze until you become one of us.* The smooth words worked their way through me, like a song, carrying my thoughts into its melody. I crossed my arms over my chest, thumbs pressing into my throat.

"Let's keep going." Zichri turned his chin down. "Cypress?"

My thumbs jammed into my voice box. *What's happening?*

The serene voice spoke in my head, *Come to a place so divine. All is yours, and all is mine. You responded to our call, so we'll lead you there.*

Zichri yanked my forearms, but they wouldn't budge. My thumbs dug harder into my skin, and I gasped for air.

The voice continued to sing, twirling a chorus of the sweet taste of Abismo. How I longed for this place. But why did it hurt?

Flecks of light spun on the outer edges of my sight, spinning. Closing in.

A cackle pierced the skies.

"Cypress!" Zichri's call sounded so far off.

"She does this to herself," the serene voice hissed.

My vision blackened, and strong hands gripped my shoulders.

"Cypress! For the love of the Ancient One!" Zichri's voice was muffled. "Beatriz. Please."

The cool, wicked melody that had worked its way through me let go. My hands fell to my sides, and my knees buckled. Before I hit the ground, Zichri scooped me up with two strong arms. Leaves clapped as the air shifted into a sweltering heat. Why had I lost control of my limbs? Why couldn't I stop myself? Did Zichri call me by my real name?

My lashes fluttered with my efforts to open my eyes. I smelled a heady mix of healthy male sweat, sun-warmed clothes, and campfire. My body bobbed up and down with the steady pound of feet.

"Did you call me Beatriz?" I asked in a weak voice.

Breathless, he whispered, "I did. Are you all right?" He continued to plod along.

"Why did you call me that?"

"The Chupalma wood ends soon. We'll talk then."

"We'll be safe?" I snuggled to his chest and let my body relax until a ripple of some invisible current pressed into my body again. It twisted in my heart and whispered within my mind—*We have Laude, and we'll get him too.*

I shrieked and jolted, eyes snapping open.

Zichri grappled to keep hold of my legs and back, but I continued to scream despite my best effort to stop.

"Give her to us." The voice sounded from ahead on the trail. It had the same tenor as the Chupalma who had spoken before.

"Never." Zichri's voice resonated even above my screeching.

Hiss.

Dozens of blurry figures surrounded us. My throat burned. What could I do to help?

"Give up, you useless fool," a male Chupalma said.

I pulled my lips forward, trying to break the scream. "No!"

It worked. The invisible tentacle loosened its grip. Hadn't Uncle told us that it couldn't touch us if we didn't engage? But he never explained how forceful their prodding would be.

Zichri set me down, and I wobbled to an upright position. A Chupalma woman appeared only an arm's length away.

Zichri whipped out Milo's dagger, slicing the translucent body of the Chupalma. But it went through her, doing no damage.

She laughed. "You fool. Iron does not harm us, nor does your punch."

The ghostly Chupalma gathered close enough to touch, and a sneer covered each of their faces. All of them shone like dull moonlight. They wore the apparel of the people of a bygone era—long, dull-colored robes with ropes about their waists.

The Chupalma woman before me reached with long thin fingers, blackened cuticles, and cracked nails and took hold of my chin. "You will be one of us." She slid her tongue over her sharp teeth.

Zichri slashed at the Chupalma, attempting to overtake her, and I bit my bottom lip, swallowing the terror gathering within my chest. "Why not take me and be done with it?"

"Say you'll"—she jerked my chin—"come with me."

What can I do? My mind filled with the golden glow from the morning I made my oath.

"*Saalah kai hizzgezer revato,*" I called to the Ancient One. Warmth blossomed on my skin and lit my arms, shining yellow light shone through my sleeves.

Her hand flew back.

Words shifted in my mouth until they spilled off my lips. "Remove these evil creatures from our path that I may fulfill my oath to you."

The angry flesh on my palm shrank to its regular size, strength filled my legs, and my scratchy throat healed.

The Chupalma stepped off the trail and into the foliage, deep grimaces twisting into position. The one who had touched me opened her mouth to speak, but not a sound came out. Her nose wrinkled in disdain, and when she reached her talon toward me, her body began to quake.

I spun toward Zichri, but the Chupalma had roped vines around his body and tied him to a tree.

CHAPTER 26

THE MOMENT I STEPPED off the path, a male Chupalma blocked my way. His pale locks reached his shoulders, and his sneer crinkled across his translucent face. Through his body, I made out a stray ray of light coming through the tree canopy and illuminating a sliver of metal among the foliage—Zichri's dagger.

Now I had to evade the dozens of Chupalmas and free Zichri. Why hadn't I included him in using the words of power? I pursed my lips and tried to march around the stubborn Chupalma in front of me.

The dozen other wicked beings stepped back, but not this one. I edged as close as I dared to him.

The stench! Oh my. He smelled of something akin to soiled clothing, manure, and aging algae combined, but with a sharper burn in my nose. How had I not noticed it earlier? My mind must have been gone with fright.

Despite the stench, I ached to get the dagger in my hand, and the Chupalma refused to budge.

I dared a glance at Zichri.

He struggled against the green ropes that held him tethered to the tree. "Get out of here. I've been in worse bonds before." His eyebrows pressed low, and his lips pinched with strain.

A rivulet of sweat moistened my neck. How could he think I'd leave him? I wouldn't wish the Chupalmas on even the King of Himzo himself, and especially not Zichri.

I threw my hands up to shove the Chupalma but met a cool liquid feeling. Tiny lightning bolts sizzled within the being's body, and the Chupalma responded with a low growl. He stumbled backward. My eyes remained transfixed on my hands. What was I doing? I shook off my shock and snatched the dagger from the ground.

The Chupalma hadn't been scared of the blade or our fists, but now my presence sent them recoiling. The *revato* oath had worked better than expected.

I hurried to Zichri and sliced at his bindings. Even though the words of power had their desired effect, I didn't want to risk staying near these heinous beasts.

The vines took several jabs to loosen. My arm and fist ached, but I kept slicing, jabbing, thrusting. Coils sprang loose.

Zichri's arms broke free. "Give me the blade."

I handed him the dagger and swiped my sweaty forehead. Zichri finished breaking the cords. The Chupalmas watched from the crooks of trees above. Some remained a stone's throw away, while others paced, licking their pointed teeth. Their silence jostled my nerves just as much as the predatory stare chiseled on their faces.

"Let's get out of here." Zichri wove his hand in mine.

Both of us sprinted along the trail. I squeezed his hand so hard my fingers throbbed, but I wouldn't let go. The greater the distance between us and the Chupalma, the more my thoughts returned to the one holding my hand. We somehow had survived the beasts of legend. *What if we could be together like this?* The unbidden thought grew into a tiny bubble of hope nuzzled close to my heart. The trees grew smaller, and the trail took a sharp turn. The river came into view, and the trail ended at a bridge near a waterfall.

Water burst from the mountainside, collecting into a pool below, where it then separated into a river and a rocky stream. Mist hung in the air beyond the bridge. We continued to move forward, but Zichri slowed.

"We need to talk," he said.

"Not now." I tugged him along and finally let go when he wouldn't pick up his pace. A light buzz echoed in my ears and ignited a sensation—like the feeling of an army of ants walking under my skin. Something intangible drew me nearer the falls. Had I dreamed of this place before? Or was it something more?

I glanced back at Zichri, solemn and still breathtaking despite his tousled hair and stubbly jaw. My heart throbbed, but I ignored it. I wouldn't let doubts and hopes about Zichri ruin this for me. I crossed over the old bridge, moss filling in the spaces between the stones, and stepped onto springy grass. A thick fog whited out anything more than an arm's length away.

The music of a bird's pleasant song rang somewhere nearby. I tried to follow the sound when a breeze shifted in the air, and the mist thinned. Built into the mountainside, a roofless castle stood before me. Many of the walls crumbled at its feet. My breath caught in my throat along with a decade's worth of emotions.

Why did Zichri take so long?

"Come, Zichri! It's here!" I sprinted across the desolate grounds. *Will the whyzer be a boy, a young man, or someone like Uncle Uly?*

Two pillars made of white stone stretched toward a giant beam. I shuffled to a stop under its shadow. Designs twisted along the edifice and reminded me of the markings along my arms. I turned up my sleeves. The golden vines shone just as brightly as when I made my oath.

Are these ancient words? I touched the cold, grooved surface on the stone, and a pulse of magic brushed against my fingers, traveled within my body, and vibrated through my veins. Unlike the Chupalma's control, this renewed my energy.

Suddenly, pain began to race along my arms. A cry escaped my throat. My skin squeezed the metallic lines until slivers of metal pushed out the surface. Gold slices tumbled to the ground and plinked as they collided against each other. The weight of my oath lay strewn before me, and tender skin coated my markings. I sighed in relief, shedding worries and filling my lungs with glee.

Now the whyzer. Where was he? I walked through the pillars and toward the dilapidated castle, not waiting for Zichri to follow.

It must have been even more beautiful in its time. Stone steps led to an upper floor that did not exist anymore. Walls coated with vines and gashes hinted at a hidden history. Vegetation of all kinds jutted between the stones on the floor, including the margus plant. I yanked several by the root.

The deeper I went into the ruins, the more I expected to see the whyzer. I turned a corner and tiptoed through a large rectangular space. Grass and flowers replaced what was once a floor. Instead of a ceiling, a powder-blue sky stretched high above me. Still no whyzer, but something invisible filled this space, crackling through the castle and brushing against my skin.

More corridors extended into the mountainside until a stone wall marked the end of the building. I stared at the crumbling stones overtaken by vines.

What should I do? What should I do? We needed to get back to give Blas this margus, but the whyzer wasn't there.

I marched back through all the same corridors and halls, still searching. Could he be hiding? A tiny ache pinched between my brows.

What if I've been made a fool. Had the whyzer and all those dreams and nightmares been for nothing? Could the whyzer be somewhere else in the valley?

My footfalls padded the verdant ground as I rushed through doorways. I turned a corner and smacked into Zichri.

I yelped, heart pounding. "He should be here." I pushed the margus plant at him. "Take this to Blas. I can't return until I find him."

"It's too dangerous. I can't leave you here alone." Zichri reached for my shoulder.

I shrugged away from his grip and continued to search. "Blas will die if you don't get that to him."

He squared up in front of me, blocking my way. "You can't stay out here alone. We'll come back tomorrow."

"No, we won't!" I wrenched away from him. "The journey took too long. We won't come back tomorrow, and you need to get home. Or would you prefer to lie about needing to go home?"

He raked a hand through his hair. "How forthright have you been? You won't tell me your real name, yet you call *me* a liar." He shook his head, a wry smirk forming on his lips. "I am risking my friends' lives for you. I am risking my brothers' wrath for you. Please be reasonable."

I patted down the tunic that pouched out of my pants. How I had lowered myself on this quest, and no one was here. And for what? A hoax. Tears burned my eyes before cascading down my cheeks.

I let out a shaky breath. "My name is Princess Beatriz of Giddel. You assessed well." I met his unflinching gaze. "I am not a merchant's daughter. All my life, I dreamed of coming here. The little boy said he'd be waiting." I sank my face into my hands. My chest trembled, and I sobbed.

Zichri pulled me into his arms. A pool of tears and snot soaked into his tunic. I didn't care. What did any of this matter?

I sucked in a breath and continued, "I'm sorry for lying to you. You were so kind. Papá would never have let me come here. Mamá would never have spoken against Papá." This sent a fresh wave of tears gushing out.

"Beatriz, do you really need this gift? You are beautiful and brave. You're important to me."

I looked up at him. "Do you mean that?"

"I—I don't know how to tell you what I feel for you. Something about you struck me from the moment I saw you."

"I was in distress and needed saving." I tilted my head down to wipe my nose with my hand—where's a handkerchief when you need it? This is not how I pictured a man professing his love for me. I could at least try to hold myself together.

"Don't—"

"Do what?" I was caught. He must have seen the streak of muck I wiped all over my pants that really were his.

"You diminish what I saw. Where I come from, ladies throw themselves at me in an attempt to get my attention."

He ruined a perfectly good moment by bringing other ladies into this. I rolled my eyes.

"Please understand." He caressed my arm, sending a tingle through it. "I say this because I've never felt this way about anyone. I'm ... how do I say this?" He took a minute, eyes looking up and around. "I am the third son of Himzo."

"What do you mean?" My stomach squeezed. I perceived what he was about to say, but I didn't want to believe it.

"My father is the Himzo king, and I'm third in line for the throne."

My arms fell to my side. "You said you were a soldier."

"I am. That's not a lie." A muscle flinched on his cheek. "I get sent out all the time. My brothers, most likely, wish me dead. And I rather enjoy being away."

That small headache that pinched between my brows stabbed. "You didn't think telling me might have been in our best interest?"

His gaze locked on mine. "There's more."

I shook my head. How could I have been such a fool? Biting on the inside of my cheeks, I lifted my chin, remembering how a princess should act. "You may continue."

"The first time I saw you was not that day at the well. I'd heard rumors about the Princess of Giddel and wanted to meet you after we finished our mission." He ran a hand through his hair. "My men and I procured invites to your ball. Pity filled my heart for this beautiful but gift-less princess. It reminded me of how I felt among my brothers. When I saw you walking in that bright red dress, the color of a rose, I knew I had to meet you. You had that expression on your face, the same one you have now." He traced a finger down my jawline, and I flinched. "I'd been advised not to dance at the ball by my contact. But Blas dared a dance with you."

I gasped, unable to believe my ears.

"Blas said you were even more beautiful up close, but you didn't speak to him. That morning when you ran away, we saw you pass by dressed like a servant. So we followed as best we could. We meant no harm."

My lower lip trembled with fury. "You knew the whole time?" To think, I had enjoyed his embrace and company when all the time, he laughed at me. "Go away!"

"Let me explain."

"You've said enough." I pointed out toward the bridge. "Go!"

"Beatriz, please understand—"

"Princess Beatriz of Giddel," I corrected him.

Crestfallen, he reached for me, but I stepped back. "Princess Beatriz, I can't leave you here alone."

A rage rumbled up my spine. It would have been one thing if he just lied about who he was for self-preservation, but he had followed me.

"Isn't *Blas* waiting for you?" I clenched my teeth.

Zichri hesitated only for a moment before crossing the grassy ground leading to the bridge. Every so often, he peeked back. I crossed my arms, a dam of tears forming. Why did I ever meet him? The ache in my chest felt unbearable. He turned around and glided his fingers through his hair. Was he coming back? I held my breath and lifted my chin high in the air in challenge. He dropped his head and continued away. I couldn't believe I let him intrude in my life and shake things up so badly within my heart.

When I exhaled, sobs overtook me again. This time, it was the loss of new dreams rather than old ones. I cried out. My knees buckled, and I slammed my fists on the broken stones. How I wished to rip out the agony radiating in my body.

The whyzer duped me, and Zichri too.

I clutched a patch of margus and wailed. How could I ever show my face in Giddel again?

A shuffling sound echoed within the ruins. I swiped my cheeks, eyes shifting all about. A person stepped out from a shadow. Even with my vision blurred, I recognized him, the one who invited me here.

CHAPTER 27

THE BOY WITH THE potent blue eyes offered me a small loaf of bread, brown and ordinary. Compassion was painted on his face, yet anger coursed through each of my veins. This was no boy. No person stayed a child for ten years.

I ground my teeth. "How dare you offer me bread?"

Still, the boy extended the loaf to me with an innocent grin.

"I don't want your infernal bread. Give me what you promised." I smacked the bread from his hand.

Through pressed lips, the boy spoke to me, his voice calm and confident. *Why won't you take the bread? It gives life.* His doughy eyes, like those of a pup, wilted when I stood.

"Is this like the bread from when I was seven years old? Useless. Pointless. Inspiring nightmares. If that's what you offer, you wasted my time and energy." My voice trembled, and I willed it to be steady. "You said to come, and here I am."

The boy turned away from me, walking through what once was a giant atrium. The bread disappeared into purple smoke between the weeds.

What's going on? I stomped behind him. I would not let him go without giving me my gift.

He glanced over his shoulder. Again, he spoke into my mind, *Wait here, Beatriz.*

I halted. Goosebumps prickled down my legs and arms. A fog

emerged from deeper within the castle, and I stepped closer. Rays of light radiated through the mist. The nearer I got, the more the intense light stung my eyes. The brightest glow I had ever seen engulfed the boy, and he disappeared ... yet I heard his steps.

A voice called from within the light, "Beatriz, why do you reject what I offer?"

I stumbled backward. "Are you my whyzer? Will you not show your face?"

The shadow of a tall man floated forward. Long green hair blended into his ash-tinted beard and circled his angular features. His smoldering eyes glared down his nose and pierced me. It was closer to who I imagined I'd see—besides the green hair and the disdain radiating from him. But why should he disapprove of *me* when I had done what he asked?

I lifted my chin and took a tentative step in his direction. "When will you uphold your duty?"

His voice boomed. "What do you know about duty? I offer gifts for the good of society. You are less than worthy."

My heart leapt. All this time wishing and hoping, only to be punched in the gut by his words. "You haunt my dreams. You promise much and give nothing. You watch from afar, seeing the scrutiny I'm under, and do nothing to save me from it. Now, you call me unworthy. I loathe you."

The whyzer approached. The closer he got, the more my head tilted back until he stood right in front of me. I maintained my position with shoulders pressed back.

"I don't choose your gift, but everything else is under my control." The whyzer's baritone voice vibrated off the crumbling rocks. "I will not give such power to a selfish princess. I know your thoughts about what you will do with your gift. Even your father, who loves to wield his abilities, humbled himself the day he received his."

My fingers curled into fists. I devoured book after book of the ancient texts to understand this gift, to be ready to receive it. I thought I had been making myself worthy, yet the whyzer told me otherwise.

A memory dripped into my mind, and a ripple of hope grew within me. "You don't have a choice, old man." I raised my eyes to his. "Be rid of me, once and for all. Wave a hand or speak the gift into being. You must give me what is mine." I held up my arm to show the faint markings, a sign that I was destined for this.

"You are correct in saying I have no choice in the giving. But I will not make the same mistake twice. These walls stand to remind me of my past errors. I will never again give a gift that will be spent on a self-absorbed life. Until that *haughty* disposition of yours changes, rest assured I am content to withhold your gift until your dying breath." He whirled around, marching into the mist. Deep within the thick air, he shouted, "Your oath's curse is gone. I only offer you protection within the valley so you can get off my land." He waved a hand, and racing light flew around my head and shot into the sky. "Take everyone with you."

My eyes flicked wide in shock. Whyzers were considered kind and ready to dispense blessings over their subjects. The vapors dissipated, swallowing the shadows of my whyzer with it.

A yellow bird swooped across my line of sight, then up onto what once was a window in the ancient wall. I wanted to crumble to the ground, but like the wall, I remained standing—even if the life inside me drained. Water continued to spill from the waterfall outside. This memory would burn strong all the days of my life.

Would Lux still leave Alexa for me even if I was gift-less? I trudged back to the entrance, knowing the answer. Best friends or not, whatever match we made must be approved by our parents. His father would never approve of me now.

As for Mamá and Papá, they now had a rebellious daughter who ran away and returned with nothing. Would they consider me a traitor for traveling with a prince of Himzo? I swallowed hard.

The hum of magic still simmered through the air while I exited the castle. I placed a palm on the column with the ancient letters scrawled along the beam and leaned my ear against the stone. Magic had a melody. It reminded me of Zichri's campfire song and filled me with a sense of well-being.

Blas needs to live. Or should I wish for his death since he might go to war against Giddel? But I knew him and Milo, Jaime, Gonzalo, and Zichri. I could never wish for their deaths, and all of them had to feel the same way in return, right? They lied about who they were, but our time together hadn't been a lie. The grass cushioned my steps as I dared to move forward to face all those who risked their lives for nothing. What would I tell Laude?

I gnawed on my bottom lip and crossed the bridge. The trail, grass, and trees all grew fuzzy, with moisture building along my lashes again. From among the blurry scenery, a tall figure emerged around the bend.

CHAPTER 28

THE SHADOWED FIGURE DREW nearer, boots clomping the dirt trail. The lush, dark jungles were far behind him—a burbling river flowed to my left and a sparse forest to the right. As my vision sharpened, Zichri's smooth gait, broad shoulders, and muscular form became more distinct.

"Beatriz?" His voice pierced the air. "Did you get what you searched for?" Another question lingered in his eyes.

I swiped my palms on my pants as if wiping away the whyzer's insults. Years of humiliation and inadequacy swirled in my heart. Could I share that with him? "Yes, I did."

Zichri stopped an arm's length away. "Let's see. What can you do?" He smiled, but I detected none of the same excitement he had before doubts leeched into our relationship—before I knew who he was.

"Ehh … Why did you wait for me?" I bit my lip.

"I couldn't leave you alone."

A ball of emotion formed in my throat, and the whyzer's words began sinking deep into my soul. Was I really that selfish? Unworthy? Like haughty Alexa? Even she received an ability beyond the regular touch of magic. And then there was Zichri.

"Was it not because you'd encounter the Chupalma?" I tried to curb the accusation in my tone.

His jaw hardened. My heart thudded in my ears. It would be nice to lace our fingers together and pretend everything was just like before.

But I couldn't.

I stepped around him. "Don't worry. The whyzer offered protection for us to leave safely."

He caught my shoulder. "Did you really get your gift?"

Tears gathered at the corners of my eyes, and I blinked them back. Still, more hot tears sprung out, forming a steady stream down my cheeks. "No. I didn't." My voice quivered. "Please don't ask."

He wrapped his arms around me. I savored his strong embrace, feeling his hard chest against my head, warming my back, and steadying my erratic breaths. He pulled away with a sigh and showed me the wad of margus in his pocket. "We should make our way back."

And we left. Blas needed the lifesaving antidote. I couldn't wish him dead even if he was an enemy.

When we arrived at the cabin, purple and orange striped the sky. Zichri burst through the front door. Every muscle in my body ached as I climbed the last two steps into the candlelit room. My stomach had turned into a cauldron seething with every degrading insult I'd ever heard about myself, hollowing out my insides.

Zichri passed Uncle Uly the antidote, and he moved with the stealth and speed of a hummingbird, crushing the margus into a cup, adding boiling water from the kettle, stirring the mixture, and tipping the antidote into Blas's mouth.

Once Blas had drunk all the antidote, Uncle Uly got to work setting up two cots. Zichri tried to help, but Uncle insisted we were his guests.

Blas laid limp on the couch, glistening with sweat. His eyelids lifted a fraction and shut. He moaned like if he tried to speak but stopped.

After the cabin was set for the night, we had only to wait and see if the antidote would work. Zichri paced the length of the living room, and I sat on a stool next to the hearth, staring at Blas's chest rise and fall in a steady pattern.

"You should get some rest," Uncle Uly said. "I know of an easier way for you to get out of the valley, but it's another long trek."

"Does it involve swimming?" Zichri asked the question perched on my tongue.

"No." Uncle Uly crossed the room and entered the doorway at the end of the cabin. "We'll talk more tomorrow." He yawned again. "Goodnight."

I laid my head to rest on Uncle Uly's cot and sunk into a deep slumber.

The next morning, light peeked through the curtains onto the blood and dirt on my tunic. A dull headache throbbed. Yesterday clung like a stain. The little boy from the ruins did not visit my dreams, and I hoped he'd never come again. I rolled off the squat cot and tiptoed across the hardwood. Blas snored on the sofa, mouth hanging open, while Zichri slept on another cot across from him. I escaped the cabin and tapped the door shut behind me.

A thick fog draped over the trees, giving off a haunted appearance. I supposed that was fitting since a haze loomed over my future. A few stumps circled a fire pit, and I sat on the tallest one. The sun chased away the night and reminded me of the promise I made the Ancient One. Why didn't the Ancient One intervene and force his whyzer to give me my gift? I did what I promised.

"Beatriz," Uncle Uly rasped.

I startled and whipped around to see him coming from the forest. "I didn't know you were awake. Good morning."

He leaned heavily on his staff, making his way through the grass. "I heard about yesterday."

I dipped my head.

"Don't look so glum. A friend told me about your trip, and I also heard about what happened at the ruins."

How embarrassing! I tugged at my collar.

He sat on a stump next to mine. "All the burdens you carry won't matter."

"You live alone in a valley. What would you know about my burdens?"

He nodded his head. "Yes, I live here, but I'm not alone. You, my dear, *think* you need the gift and that people need to see you as some grand princess. Enough. Let yourself be at peace. You need nothing special to form a betrothal. You don't need this gift to earn people's good favor."

"I don't have a betrothal nor anyone's good favor." I rubbed my arms, loathing the day I was born.

"Those two things are easy to change. Find a man who will love you no matter what and marry him. Perhaps that part's already done." He cleared his throat at my sharp glare.

"Zichri is a Himzo prince." I enunciated each word then bit my lip.

"Why does his origin matter to you?" His eyes fixed on mine, so much like Papá's.

"Giddel and Himzo are on the brink of war."

"Do you prefer to choose a suitor from a line of men at a ball instead?"

I jerked my head back. "How do you know about that?"

A smile spread under his mustache. "Like I said, I have friends who gather information for me. Don't dodge the question. Is Zichri better or worse than those who lined up to dance with you?"

"That isn't a fair question." I glanced over my shoulder to the cabin, where Zichri and Blas slept. What would it be like to choose him?

Uncle Uly clicked his tongue, drawing my attention back to our conversation. "Regardless, your father gives you a choice. Not every young lady can say that. As for favor, consider others before yourself. It really is simple, but not easy." He tapped his staff on the ground.

"The problem is that I can neither choose Zichri nor change who I am. If you spoke with the whyzer, you'd understand I'm a lost cause."

"Is it because you still want to marry that Prince Lux?"

I stilled. "How—how do you know?"

A bird swooped down and perched on Uly's shoulder. It tweeted a sweet melody. Uncle Uly whispered back to the tiny creature. The bird chirped in response. "You'll go back through the caves." Uncle Uly turned toward me. "I promise you will get the answers for which you search."

Did the bird speak to him?

From several paces behind us, I heard the cabin door creak open. Zichri appeared in the doorway and rubbed his bleary eyes. Why did he have to be so handsome? And why a Himzo prince?

"He's not so unpleasant. And doesn't the Ancient One call us to love our enemy?" Uncle Uly winked. "This might be your chance to not be such a lost cause."

I tucked stray hairs behind my ear, suddenly aware of how I must look and what my breath must smell like. Zichri's boots brushed the grass as he joined Uncle Uly and me around the fire pit.

I rolled my shoulders back. "Thank you for heading on this journey with me."

"It is my pleasure." Zichri bowed his head like a gentleman at court.

How I wish I could have seen Zichri that day at the ball. He must have been breathtaking, dressed in noble attire. I had been so caught up in how everyone saw me that I didn't bother to pay attention to anyone else.

Uncle Uly leaned heavily on his staff as he got to his feet. "Forgive me, but I need to check on Blas." He walked around Zichri, and when he reached the cabin door, he fixed a knowing gaze on me. The playful way he wagged his overgrown brows reminded me of Laude. Heat rushed up my neck. He tapped a hand over his heart before disappearing into the cabin.

"Uly supposes much." Zichri took a seat on the stump next to mine. "I'm sure you need to get back home to your family."

"I do."

"We can escort you, but I must speak to my superiors first."

"How? Messenger hawk?"

He laughed. "No. I'm not that gifted. We have friends"—he cleared his throat— "waiting for us just beyond the Himzo border."

My brows furrowed. Was he lying?

"It shouldn't take too long." His sad smile cocked to the side.

"Don't worry about it." I stilled at his knee brushing against my leg. Trying to refocus, I pulled away from him. "Tell us the way, and I'm sure Laude and I can manage with the wagon and horses." Would my words come back to haunt me?

He reached for my hand, lacing his fingers with mine. "I'm sorry for not telling you the truth."

My heartbeat quickened. "I'm sorry too. I really should not have been so hard on you. I lied, and I didn't consider you and your friends. I wish I could make it up to you, but that's quite impossible." Aware that I sounded like Laude when she was nervous, I filled my lungs and exhaled before continuing. "You may have been right in thinking I wouldn't have talked to you if I would have known about you being a Himzo prince. Let's enjoy the rest of the trip." I ran my fingers across his rough knuckles.

Zichri massaged the now faded markings on my hand. I needed to think of anything besides Zichri, but I allowed this intimate moment, enjoying his warm touch. There was no chance of us meeting again in any cordial fashion since we were on the verge of war. Even if Papá met to discuss trade, Papá would never allow Zichri to court me. We couldn't sit in the woods holding hands and bantering the days away. This wouldn't last. But I wished it could.

CHAPTER 29

"PRINCESS BEATRIZ, I WAS so worried about you! We've been waiting close to the river." Laude pulled me into a tight embrace. "What is your gift? Let's see it!"

Judging by how she addressed me, she found out that the men knew my identity. "I—I'd rather wait until we're alone." I met her sapphire eyes with a meaningful look.

She bobbed her head and winked, beaming. "I have so much to tell you."

A pace from Laude and I, Milo and Jaime patted Zichri's shoulder in greeting. Blas winced when Milo and Jaime did the same to him. Questions arose about the lamps, food, and maps given to us by Uncle Uly.

Laude's eyebrows rose and furrowed in question.

The Himzos, Laude, and I hiked through the forest midmorning, entering a cave hidden by a boulder near the falls just before noon. Uncle Uly told us the exact location and gave directions on how to get out through the mountain passageway. Many booby traps set by bandits in a bygone era waited for those who might wander into the cavern.

"Oh, Princess!" Laude said. "I was so angry at Milo and Jaime when they told me how they attended your ball. I swore to tell you as soon as you got back, and I chastised them for leading us to believe that they knew nothing about us."

Laude continued to prattle on about the same topic over and over again. Pinching my mouth shut, I kept silent. I knew she did not exaggerate her reaction. The poor men must have been rolling their eyes when Laude first found out. I kept my focus on the rocky floor of the cave.

Zichri and Milo led our caravan from several feet ahead. Jaime and Blas trailed behind us. Blas still held his gut with a twisted expression as we tramped through the dark places in the earth. Lamplight caught in Jaime's eyes. He watched Laude intently. She glanced back with a flirtatious raise of her brow before continuing her story again.

"Laude," I whispered, "they can hear you. You needn't go over the grueling details about how upset you were at the men. Zichri got an ear full from me already." I dodged a protruding rock in the cave.

"Oh?" She squeaked. "But you shouldn't be so mad at Zichri."

"You just said that you were angry. Now you say I shouldn't be mad at him. Which one is it?" I descended a narrow portion of the cave that Zichri and Milo ducked into a second before. They must have heard every word we said. What did it matter if they heard us anyway? *They'll be gone—back to Himzo—soon enough.*

Laude peeked back and crouched through that part of the tunnel. Leaning in, she whispered, "Jaime says he's never seen Zichri so taken by anyone. You and I both know that you've never felt this way either."

I glared at her. She supposed much. What of Lux? She must have known how much I adored Lux, but I could not correct her out loud. Better to change the subject. "You seem to favor Jaime still."

The dim light reflected off her bubbling cheeks. "He likes me."

"I gathered that much. Did anything happen while I was away?" Stooping low to avoid hitting a rock, I noticed Zichri and Milo stop at a fork in the path.

Laude glanced back, and smacked her head against the rock and yelped. "Ai-yi-yi!"

I rushed to her side and reached for her shadowed head. My hand came back dripping with warm liquid. "Speak to me. Are you all right?"

"I think my nose is bleeding."

Relief flooded through my body. Blas stumbled forward, passing us.

Jaime rushed to her side, bumping into my shoulder, and he gave her his handkerchief. She covered her nose with the fabric, blood coloring the light material—noticeable even in the dim lighting. He scooped her up.

Something about Jaime carrying Laude released a yearning inside my heart right in that moment.

My intention was always to get married and hope I could have some semblance of what my parents had. The way they always addressed each other with respect. The way Papá kissed Mamá's hand, inspiring a blush to creep up Mamá's neck.

Jaime and I lumbered toward the fork in the cave while Laude swayed in Jaime's arms. Seeing Jaime dote over Laude brought about a sinking feeling because I couldn't imagine that ever happening to me with the person I married. Lux could never be mine now. Though, I suspected even if we were to marry, we'd never romance each other like Laude and Jaime.

And Zichri? He waited for us at the fork alongside Milo and Blas.

I drank in the sight of Zichri, who met my gaze with a tender smile. *He, too, can never be mine.* My heart thumped wildly, but I pushed feelings aside. I still needed to bury fanciful dreams. We continued to move, and my mind searched for a way out of the troubles that awaited me back home.

Jaime held onto Laude, guiding her and whispering in her ear. She giggled. At times, they strayed so far behind the rest of us that we had to stop and wait for them. Zichri slowed to walk next to me, but I kept my gaze ahead on Milo's lamp.

"What are you going to do now that you're heading back home?" Zichri kicked up a pebble. "Before you left, you were choosing a husband."

A moan vibrated low in my throat as I imagined a life with Marden, the suitor of Papá's choice. Siding with Papá would surely be the prudent thing to do after running away, and he'd be pleased with Marden's ability to change the water currents to be in our favor. A sourness filled my belly. I would do nothing exciting ever again. Mamá warned me that stealing Papá's personal sailboat and going out to sea with Lux would not be appropriate for a betrothed woman.

I answered, "Perhaps, I could stay lost in the woods forever and learn how to fish and wander from town to town."

"If you do that, then I'm going with you." A mischievous grin played on his lips.

For the first time since the encounter with my whyzer, I laughed. What would it be like to wander with him? Threats lurked behind every turn as we walked the dark caverns, yet I let myself forget my worries.

Zichri leaned closer and grazed my side. "Of course, we'd also need to make you some better clothes. You can't go around dressed like me all the time."

"Why not? I kind of enjoy wearing pants." I lifted my belt, which had slipped down to my hips.

"You can wear pants if you like, but at least let me get you something nice."

I considered his proposition. Stars above, a campfire at night, singing until sleep befell one of us. "I'll let you make my clothes *if* you dance with me while singing that song. The one you sang so beautifully."

"It would be my pleasure. I never got my dance at the ball."

"So, you wanted to dance with me at the ball?" I lifted my chin and held my breath. My heart devoured this little game. Part of me wished he'd say *no,* so I could easily walk away.

"More than anything in the world."

Biting my bottom lip, I looked away, trying to be reasonable, but the conversation moved into murkier waters.

The path flattened, though we still descended. Zichri's expression sobered. "We weren't going to go to the ball that day, but curiosity got the better of me. I watched you dance with every one of those suitors, wishing that was me. Something about you, Beatriz, drew me in."

His sweet words drizzled over me like melted chocolate. I wanted more, but I didn't want to seem desperate. "You may get your dance and several more after all."

He slipped his hand in mine again, and I smiled. Lux and I never ever shared these tantalizing moments. Lux, the ever-faithful friend whom I talked to for hours, never sent me floating into an imaginary world.

Zichri continued, "Just so you know, we'll sleep in hammocks if we wander the forests."

"Prince Zichri, I don't want you getting any unwholesome ideas. No man will share my hammock until he commits to me for life in the presence of many witnesses."

A hearty laugh slipped out of him. "I was just trying to say that you need a hammock of your own. Believe me when I say I wouldn't want less than the best for you."

My cheeks burned. Thank the Ancient One for this dark cave.

We decided that I'd gather fruits. He'd catch fish and hunt. I'd get the wood, and he'd stoke the fire. On and on we went, imagining this life where I'd have no worries.

A light reflected on a rock down the path, revealing the way out. Milo and Blas slipped out of the cave. Laude and Jaime trailed way behind us, too caught up in their own conversation.

As we drew closer, I covered my eyes to block the light. Zichri stopped at the opening. The pinched expression on his face let me know he didn't want the daydreaming to end either.

Once we walked out into the daylight, our dream of living in the forest would evaporate into the wind. He was a man of his word, so he would go to his kingdom. I needed to ease my parents' worry over me. I loved them too much to do any less. I also loved my brother, who I imagined may have shown signs of concern about me after so many days away.

I slid in front of Zichri, brushing his arm. He followed one step behind me. The light stung my eyes as my vision adjusted from the darkness to a blue sky. A tree-laden land stretched before us. Blas leaned against a boulder, and Milo paced with hands on his hips. Water slurped and swooshed nearby where Gonzalo would be waiting, but we didn't move yet. Jaime and Laude tarried in the cave.

I curled my fingers in between Zichri's, considering asking him if we could wander a bit longer. But I was no fool. I knew this charade had to end ... eventually.

CHAPTER 30

GONZALO DANGLED HIS FEET off the side of a cliff, singing to himself. He lifted his bald head. "I was hoping you'd arrive soon. Everything in order?"

Zichri squeezed my hand, and I squeezed back. A sobering expression trickled down his profile. He opened his mouth to speak.

But Milo cut in, "We need to get back today. Where are the horses?" He puffed out his chest, hands on his hips.

Standing, Gonzalo towered half a head over Milo and boasted a wide torso. No wonder Milo couldn't beat him in a wrestling match. Milo arched his back in challenge despite his rather precarious position under Gonzalo's dead stare.

There must be something I can't see between these two men. Gonzalo flared his nose and lazily pointed down a path. If only Gonzalo would have knocked Milo out of his cocky disposition.

All Gonzalo's features relaxed when he shifted his gaze to the rest of us. "Did you get what you all were looking for?"

Zichri answered for me. "She found who she meant to find and more." He kissed my knuckles and led me behind Milo.

My stomach wriggled with butterflies. But the shadow of Gonzalo's question stilled my fluttering belly like a spider wrapping its prey. He wouldn't be the last person to ask that question. I wouldn't always have Zichri with me to give such easy responses. What would I do when I faced my parents? They deserved the full truth.

The tiny trail led to the three horses and the wagon with all our things in it. A large bag of assorted fruits waited in the wagon bed beside a pile of nuts. Gonzalo had prepared for our return. Gratitude swam in my heart.

Milo hopped onto the driver's bench. "We're headed straight to camp. No argument this time." He passed Zichri a challenging look. His selfish manner snapped something within me.

"You may do as you please." I stepped around to get on the other side of the driver's bench. "This is my wagon. Laude could do just about anything, so we have no need for you to take us all the way home. Show us to the road. We will follow it to Giddel."

Milo had a condescending purse to his lips.

Laude and Jaime strolled along the path holding hands. Without thinking, my gaze shot straight to Zichri. I needed to get away before I forgot myself and lived out our forest fantasy. The longer I stayed, the harder it would be to leave him.

Gonzalo cooed in Carmel's perked ear and patted his neck. "Take us the last leg, won't you?"

Zichri remained tight-lipped, watching from a distance.

"You, Princess, are not lord over us." Milo narrowed his eyes. "We need to get back. The wagon and horses will get us there faster. You could stay in a nearby meadow. After we are done, we'll march you to the road. Do you understand?" He remained in the driver's seat, clasping the reins.

"You will do no such thing." Zichri scooted next to me on the bench. "We'll take the ladies to the main road and part ways there."

"The back lane is much faster." Milo shook the curls from his eyes. "And what of the wagon?"

"What of it? Even if we showed up with it, we'd need an explanation. I don't plan on telling my brothers more information than necessary." Zichri climbed on the wagon bed and extended his hand toward me. "Princess, would you do me the honor of sitting on the wagon bed?"

Milo grunted, then tipped his head back. I climbed out of the driver's bench, triumph filling my lungs, and plopped on one of my trunks. Zichri's cheek dimpled. A stained white tunic never looked so impressive on anyone else I'd ever met.

Poor Blas tottered down the trail, pushing between Jaime and Laude. He threw himself on the wagon, stuffing a margus leaf into his mouth. Uncle Uly said it would take a day or so for him to heal.

"Thank you for helping me with Milo," I said.

Zichri grabbed some fruits and nuts from the pile Gonzalo gathered for us.

Milo mumbled foul words under his breath. He turned his wrath on Gonzalo. "Get on your horse already, old man!" He whipped his head to the lovebirds. "Jaime! Haven't you had enough of her yet?"

Jaime snapped his head up. "You could spare us your bad company and ride the horse instead of Gonzalo."

I suppressed a chuckle, but Blas chortled and snorted. Laughter erupted from Zichri, then Laude and Gonzalo, and then Jaime. Milo harrumphed.

At least I'm not the only one disturbed by his snappy attitude.

Jaime and Laude sauntered over, still lost in each other's company. He sang a line from one of the Himzo's songs. Laude beamed and wrinkled her nose in delight. I'd never seen her this happy. She always exuded joy, but this was so much more. Jaime lifted Laude into the wagon bed and leapt in after her. They cuddled in a corner and continued to whisper to each other, unconcerned about our stares.

Milo snarled at the two giggling lovebirds. "Take the back trail and prepare for our arrival," he called out to Gonzalo.

An unguarded scowl crossed Gonzalo's face for just a second. I'd read in the ancient script that a fool gives full vent to his anger, but a wise man silently holds it back. A deep respect grew within me for Gonzalo that hadn't been there before. He trotted ahead of us and sang a happy Himzo tune.

Milo clicked his tongue and snapped the reins. The horses pulled us along as we bounced in the back with every dip and mound on the trail.

Zichri passed me a bag of nuts and a prickly, yellow fruit. "Should I hang Milo by his toes when we lose ourselves in the woods?"

I giggled. How I wished to hold on to this moment but staying here would only prove the whyzer right. "Could you be serious now that we're heading back to our *real* lives?"

"All I can see is bark, leaves, and a fine young lady. This, my dear, does not look like home yet." He passed a melting look that warmed me from the inside out. "But you're right. Let's talk real life before you make me regret ever leaving that cave."

I bit into the prickly fruit. The skin tasted sour and did not come apart easily in my mouth. My lips pinched together.

He cupped a hand over his mouth. "You're not supposed to eat the skin."

"This is why I need to go home." I turned to the side and spit the sour fruit out. "Although, I'd love to go back to our cave."

"We can still go back to the cave if you like. I didn't want to leave either. We could even marry and have children in there."

I flicked his shoulder. "Have a little respect."

"A man can dream." He shrugged.

"Zichri, that *is* only a dream. Tell me something real, like what it's like being a Himzo prince." I fluttered my lashes in the same flirtatious way Laude had with Jaime.

"Is something in your eyes?"

My voice lowered an octave. "Just answer the question."

"All right. Like I said earlier, my brothers fight for the throne and send me away on errands for the kingdom as often as possible. My father is a stern man but reasonable. He loves his people, my mother, and all four of his children. He groomed each of us for something different. My eldest brother will be king, and my brother behind him can't get that through his thick head. I was groomed to be a ranking official, and my sister has the most freedom of us all."

I considered this for a moment and watched something veiled slip behind Zichri's eyes. What isn't he saying? "You said your father is fair, but he lets your sister do as she pleases."

A soft smile played on his full lips. "She's trained in many arts, including archery. She is already betrothed to a nobleman and need not win the favor of our people because she already has it."

"Is her betrothed as generous as your father?"

He rubbed the stubble on his chin. "Milo is very generous."

My mouth fell open. "He's a nobleman *and* your future brother-in-law?" The pieces came together in my mind. That would explain why he was the only one speaking back to Zichri and the cocky air he let out from time to time.

"Yes. This is why we put up with him," Zichri's voice rose.

Milo yelled back to us from his seat, "I aim to please his royal pain-in-my-rear."

Zichri leaned in, his breath tickling my ear. "He calls me that because he can't beat me in a good wrestling match."

I turned to him, his face mere inches from mine. Why must my heart cling to the impossible? Catching my breath, I dragged a finger over an old scar on his eyebrow and grazed my fingertip down his cheek. No one would know about this. We wouldn't even see each other again unless ... I let the thought trail.

Recoiling, I remembered myself. "I'm sorry."

"Don't be sorry. There's much I regret and wish I could change." He pulled away and pressed his back against the side of the wagon.

I couldn't stay silent. "Why were you in Giddel?"

He glanced in my direction. "I can't say. Just know that I wish Himzo and Giddel were on good terms." His fingers slipped through his wavy locks.

My heart throbbed. "What would that change?" I swallowed hard, anticipating the response. I was far too attached, and his answer could be anything but good.

He fixed those dark eyes on me, revealing a well of emotions. That was answer enough. "Everything. I'd be in line with all those suitors fighting for your hand."

My breath caught, imagining what it would be like to marry Zichri. Each day I would awaken to his handsome face and kind heart.

We'd get ourselves into all sorts of trouble. But, like all my dreams, a shadow cast over it. Zichri brushed his knuckles against mine. Instead of speaking, I leaned back against the wooden side, letting my thoughts sway with the wagon.

Before I knew it, Milo called back to us, "We're at the road."

The wagon jerked to a stop on the east trail, ending my daydreams. Gonzalo was long gone since he had turned up a lane an hour ago. I should have bid him farewell. Blas and Milo stood up. Deflated, Jaime and Laude stepped off the wagon. I tried to think fast, but my mind muddled.

I went through the motions of getting up and lowering onto the gravel road, hoping to stall somehow. "Thank you, from the bottom of my heart. I never expected even half of the help you gave us." My words sounded hollow.

Blas dipped his head while holding his stomach, exhibiting no trace of his previous ease. Jaime hugged Laude. The tender way he wiped stray tears from Laude's face twisted within my gut. Then he offered her his black and gold dagger, reminding me of the possible dangers ahead. The sky grew gray, adding to a foreboding that seeped deep into my bones.

"Princess Beatriz." Nothing sounded more beautiful than the way Zichri said my name. He placed the handle of his sheathed dagger into my palm. "You will need this. Keep it on your belt."

I nodded.

"Good. I wish I could have run off with you, but it seems we must part." He gestured to the northern side of the trail, which looked just as lush as the forests to the south.

"So it seems." My throat thickened.

"You needn't say more, my dear." He traced my jawline. "Which window should I stand under if I ever sneak into Giddel again?" He pressed a hand to my back and lifted one arm high as if he meant to dance.

"My balcony can be seen by the road and is the closest to the sea. Is this an invitation to dance?"

He beamed at the question, leading me in the traditional Paso Giddelian as he hummed the same tune Papá and I danced to at my ceremonia. Always the one to notice details. His strong hand guided me easily into a half-spin. My feet moved through the steps on their own. His melody slowed. He spun and dipped me with a firm grip.

Rather than bring me back up, he whispered, "How many balconies are there?"

I flinched but answered, "There are three in the front and three in the back. Mine is closest to the sea near the watchtower." Why in all the seas was he focusing so much on these details? Sneaking into the palace was impossible.

He lifted me in one smooth motion. "I promise to always be your loyal guard."

I stared up at his tousled hair—letting seconds pass between us. "Goodbye, Prince Zichri of Himzo."

He bowed his head, looking up at me through his thick lashes. Like all good things, whatever *this* was had ended.

Milo shouted, "We're pressed for time. Come now, you two knuckleheads."

Who does he think he is, calling me a knucklehead? Jaime and Zichri plodded toward Milo, and oh ... he hadn't been referring to me.

I looped my arm through Laude's. She whimpered and waved. "This is the worst day of my life."

"Ai-yi-yi, Laude." If she only knew about the idea nudging in my mind.

Jaime turned back to wave at her every so often. As they turned the curve up the road, Zichri waved one last time. Something about his look, the tense posture, and the stillness in his gaze confirmed a suspicion that nestled in my stomach. I knew what we must do. It would save me from my parents' reproaches.

Laude slumped her shoulders. "I guess it's time to head back home."

"No." I kept my stare fixed on the empty forest road ahead.

She squeaked. "We can't stay here forever because, as you saw, not all the men in this forest are so kind. If only we could enjoy another day. I know how you feel." She swiped at her cheeks and climbed to the driver's bench.

"No, no, that's not what I mean. We aren't going home yet."

She gasped. "What do you mean?"

The horse whipped its tail.

"Turn the wagon toward the mountain—to the road Gonzalo used. Milo said something about a meadow being near their campsite." I hopped next to Laude. "We need to follow them now. Trust me."

CHAPTER 31

DROPS OF RAIN SOAKED into my tunic and pants—the last bit of Zichri I kept. From here on out, I was a spy for Giddel, at least that's what I told myself. A glob of water plopped on my nose. If the heavens down-poured, the wagon might get stuck. We needed to hurry.

The wagon wheels thumped and bumped, hitting more dips along this back road than the entire trek to Valle de los Fantasmas. This path followed the curve of the valley's mountains and bordered Himzo territory. *Is this a mistake?* If I was right about my hunch, then I'd be a hero. If I was wrong, I didn't want to consider the consequences.

"Miss, I see a meadow up ahead." Laude clutched the leather reins with a white-knuckled grip.

A cool breeze swooped into our faces, hinting at an incoming storm. It blew a rush of doubt straight into my heart. I reminded myself, *If I succeed, then I can go home with my head held high.*

"Pull over the wagon," I said with all the confidence I could muster. "Let's get our cloaks and walk the rest of the way."

"But, miss! I still don't know what we're doing. Are we going back for Zichri and Jaime? Don't tell me! We will steal the men and take them home." She squealed with delight. "Do we need the daggers, or are you going to use your gift?"

I wrinkled my nose, ignoring her exuberance. Did she not pay attention the whole time we were with the Himzos? One look at her, and I supposed the silly grin on her face meant no. "Bring your dagger, and"—my throat tightened—"there is no gift."

"No gift? What do you mean? We went to the valley. You saw the whyzer. I'm confused. You have all those markings—and large ones. You have to have a gift."

I dipped my head. I couldn't meet her gaze. "The whyzer refused me."

"Ai-yi-yi! I'm so—"

"Don't. I don't need your pity." I wrung the stiff fabric on my shirt. If something went wrong, Laude and I might never see another day again. Everything in my body quivered. *Zichri will protect me if all goes amiss. After all, he said he was my loyal guard.*

Laude stopped the wagon at the edge of the meadow near the tree line. I strained to hear beyond my heartbeat thumping in my ears. Beyond the clapping leaves, the tip-tapping rain, and the tree line across from us, I could just make out deep voices on the other side of the meadow.

"Please tell me what we're doing," Laude pleaded in a low, urgent tone. "How will we find them? We can't walk up to each person we see and ask them where Jaime and Zichri stay. Oh, and if anyone finds out you're the Princess of Giddel, we're dead or worse." Laude tilted her head back and slapped her face. "Ai-yi-yi!"

"Calm down." I climbed to the back of the wagon and opened a trunk. How Laude switched between pure joy and terror astounded me. Digging through the material, I pulled out two black cloaks. "We're already dressed like men. We need to walk like we belong at the camp. The sun has just set. Let's use that to our advantage."

With a shaky hand, Laude took hold of the rough cloak and slipped it over her clothes. I adjusted my dagger and wrapped the cloak over my body. A cooler current rustled the loose hairs that had escaped my braid, and dark clouds swirled in the sky. My body shook like one of the leaves rustling around us. A steady sprinkle of rain continued to flow from the heavens.

Laude untethered the horses while I took one last bite of a prickly fruit from Gonzalo's pile of food. I'd need energy. The tangy fruit slid down my throat and burned in my stomach, most likely because of my nerves. I hopped off the wagon and tossed the fruit into the woods.

"Laude, you are strong and fierce and completely calm," Laude said to herself, then solemnly nodded.

"Are you ready?"

"If I die and you live, tell your mother that I love her."

"Of course. But we're not going to die." I patted her shoulder. "Let's go."

We trudged through the field with long yellowed grass up to our waists. The moment we reached the thin tree line on the other end, gruff voices carried from tents standing only a stone's throw away. I hid behind the tree trunk, and Laude did the same. My heart drummed louder and harder with each passing second. We could turn back. There was still time.

Someone trod down the lane, huffing. "The Prince is back."

I peeked around the trunk. Shadows cast by lamplight revealed the silhouette of several men standing in a tent. Their voices overlapped, each one with an accent far thicker than anyone in Zichri's group had. A man shouted above the rest of the voices, "What news did he bring?"

"I don't know. I ran straight away when I heard he was back."

Grunts followed. A slight figure popped out of the tent and strode between the row of tents. We needed to follow him. I snapped my fingers at Laude for her to come alongside me and marched into the camp. Her boots splashed a few steps behind me, but I didn't check. I tried to imitate my brother's wide gait but gave up when a heavier flow of rain dropped from the heavens. Mud stuck to my boots. More soldiers approached, so I pulled my hood over my eyes. The men ducked into a tent before reaching us. By the time I looked forward, I couldn't find the scrawny man. How could I have lost him?

Hairs rose on the back of my neck. A haze of rain made it impossible to see the size of the encampment, so we wouldn't have that information to share when we got back. We moved ahead, unsure of where to go when a melancholy song wove through the tents. I recognized it. One look at Laude, and she mouthed the name: *Gonzalo.*

Will he be for us or against us? There was only one way to discover the answer. I waved for Laude to follow. Water cascaded off the front of her hood while the cloak clung to her slight figure. It's a miracle no one stopped us to ask what two ladies were doing in the encampment.

I turned toward a large tent at the end of the row, suitable for housing an entire garden party. Gonzalo's deep voice grew stronger during a long, passionate note, drawing us near. Lightning slashed the blackened sky. Keeping low, I pulled back the flap to the tent and gagged at the stench of the muck. But I tiptoed deeper to peek around the corner of a horse stall.

Gonzalo tended a steed, his back facing us. "When do we move?"

"We'll find out soon enough," Jaime responded. "Blas won't be coming. He still hurts from whatever he ate. He should have known better."

"Don't blame the poor lump. He still believes his failed year with your tutor went well." Gonzalo chuckled.

Laude stepped on my toes, and I did everything to bite back a screech of pain.

Jaime spoke again, "He needs to control his impulses before he gets us killed."

Laude clapped a hand over her mouth, her cheeks bubbling. I mouthed for her to keep still. Despite my reminder, she peeked around the first stall and turned back toward me, so overjoyed I thought she might rush into Jaime's arms. I clamped my fingers on her arm.

"That's something interesting, coming from a man who makes a fool of himself for a *servant girl.*" The contempt in Gonzalo's voice hit Laude like a slap across the face.

Jaime sighed. "I'd take the march back from Giddel over again if I could."

Laude's eyes shot open wide. Thank the Ancient One we were hidden by a tent wall and for Jaime's sincere heart. In her excitement, she danced on her toes.

"Did you hear that?" Gonzalo said.

A rustling of hay kicked up my already clamoring heartbeat. I pulled Laude out of the tent, dragging her around the corner. The heavens unloaded a torrent, soaking down to my underclothes. I glared at Laude, who bobbed her head, making it difficult to see if she was upset or beaming. Lightning cracked through the sky, and then came a rumble. I tried to listen for Gonzalo or Jaime, but all I made out were muffled sounds.

A man raced around the corner, and we turned away to hide our faces. Judging by his form and the way he walked, it was Jaime. I guessed he didn't notice us. With a slight jerk of my head, Laude and I bounded in pursuit. We followed a short distance behind him so we wouldn't lose him like we had the other soldier. Other men moved to and fro, but thankfully all of them seemed focused on their destinations.

Jaime halted. He whipped toward us and pulled out a dagger. I jolted back, and so did Laude. The point of the dagger hovered so near my nose I dared not breathe. Raindrops splattered on the blade, rushing down to the hilt.

After a second, recognition flashed across his face. "What are you doing here?" He slipped the dagger under his cloak and leaned in. "You should be halfway to Giddel by now." Like a mother hen, he lifted the corners of his cloak over our shoulders and ushered us away.

I'm not sure what he hoped to achieve by covering us. We had already been soaked, and his cloak didn't cover more than a fraction of my shoulder, but I appreciated his gesture. Men passed by with mischievous grins on their faces. Those smug smiles could not come from anything decent in their minds, and I seethed with disdain.

Jaime led us into a dark tent. He picked up a lamp and tipped it toward Laude. "Only Gonzalo, Blas, and I share this tent. You should be safe here. Let me go see if Prince Zichri is still meeting with his brothers."

Laude took the lamp and lit it with a glowing finger.

I seized his forearm. "I want to go with you."

He shook his head.

Another flash of lightning illuminated the space outside the tent.

Thunder boomed. Jaime glanced over his shoulder, unintentionally flinging droplets from his drenched hair. "You cannot. It's not safe." He passed a poignant look at Laude.

I understood that he didn't want anything to happen to her. He wouldn't negotiate. So, I dipped my head, letting him go. He tromped out of the tent flaps.

I whispered to Laude, "You stay here."

"But he said for both of us to stay. It isn't safe, miss." Lamplight cast deep shadows over Laude's pinched face.

"I don't do safe anymore. Be brave, my dear friend," I said to myself as much as I did to her.

Running out of the tent, I glimpsed Jaime's back, turning a corner. This time, I stayed farther behind to amend my previous error in following him. This section of the encampment had more people bustling about, even in the rain. Men sang within their tents. Black and red flags flew high on poles. Jaime darted past soldiers, guarding a tent that looked the same as any other. Of course, I found it difficult to gather details in the dim light cast by lamps and distant fires. I scurried around the corner to listen through the tent walls.

A man barked, "Did he say when all would be ready?"

"A week ago, he said that entrance would be ready in five to seven days."

Zichri. Hearing his voice awakened a longing in my heart.

"How long will we have?" Another man asked in a tight voice.

"We're guaranteed a few weeks if we're lucky—" Zichri got cut off by a person coughing, then continued, "But he believes we can have up to a month."

"Why did you take so long to relay the message?" A man shouted. "You could have sent a messenger on the horse. Isn't that why you took four others with you?"

A din of voices erupted. I exhaled slowly, but not much came out. The wind had been knocked from my lungs. The Himzos planned an attack against Giddel within the month.

The plan reminded me of my brother's friend, who walked me

back to the stairs the night of the ball. I couldn't remember his name, but he cast wards, and many had been disappearing rather than fading.

"I didn't," Zichri shouted over the arguing men, "because we were nearly caught by the enemy. They ... cast a spell over us, and that took time to resolve. We arrived as soon as we could."

"Cast a spell over you?" someone asked mockingly. "You haven't gone soft, have you?"

"Enough of the banter!" Another man interjected. "We're ready to march. The portal could be open tonight."

Several voices overlapped.

A commanding voice said, "In two days, we attack."

Thunder rumbled so loud it shook the mud under my feet. We needed to leave immediately to warn my family, my kingdom. The nerve! If I could, I would have cast a very nasty spell over Zichri right then. Of course, there was nothing I could do except listen.

More clamor arose within the tent as my cloak grew heavier. A female voice spoke, but her words sounded muffled. I stepped forward, touching the rough canvas edge of the flap. Though rumors had reached my ears about this threat, it never felt real when I tasted sweet coconut treats, collected flowers, or lived my daily life.

Stray soldiers clomped through the mud and darted into tents. The attack was imminent, and Giddel had a traitor. Who could have brought down the wards or given Zichri information? I needed to go home.

I trudged back to Jaime's tent. How could Zichri have been the kind man who saved his enemy *and* a conniving spy arranging an attack? He could only be one or the other.

I knew it, too—the explanation about them trading didn't piece together. I should have pressed harder once I found out they were soldiers. Somewhere deep within, I knew it, but I wanted to believe he was all good.

Whatever I thought about him didn't matter as much as getting back home to warn Mamá and Papá. The rain stuck to my lashes, blurring my vision, but I still managed to remember the path Jaime and I had taken from his tent. I peeked within the flaps. Blas lay on a small cot, fast asleep. Laude stopped mid-step. Had she been pacing the whole time?

Words stuck within my chest. *How do I tell Laude?* At least Zichri hadn't shared that he traveled with the Princess of Giddel. Salty tears dripped on my lips. I had let my heart grow too fond of him. This was embarrassing.

I slogged deeper into Jaime's tent. Dollops of rain splattered from a hole in the canopy.

"Just tell me the bad news." Laude fanned her face with her hands and breathed short, choppy breaths.

"We need to go now." I swiped my cheeks and rushed outside.

Laude didn't protest and followed close behind me through the rain.

We walked back to the tent where Gonzalo had been tending the horses. Gonzalo was brushing a steed's body when I tapped his shoulder.

"Which horse is Zichri's?"

He startled, hand pressing to his chest as he caught his breath. After a pause, he shook his bald head and pointed to a tall, dark steed.

"Thank you, Gonzalo, for your kindness on our trip." I dipped my head in respect, even after overhearing his horrid comment about Laude. I could not blame him for thinking Laude was a mere servant, especially since I had thought the same for so long.

The steed's soulful eyes stared down at me. "What's his name?"

"Muck." Gonzalo entered the stall and fastened a saddle on Muck's back. "Take good care of the beast."

I smiled warmly at Gonzalo's kind gesture and whispered to Muck, "Will you fly me to my people?"

Muck tipped his head in my direction.

"Laude can take Jaime's horse." Gonzalo grabbed another saddle. "You two ladies need to get off this land soon if you want to get home." He placed the saddle on another dark steed with a white patch between his eyes. "Where did you leave *your* horses?"

"In the meadow." I petted Muck while Gonzalo helped Laude into the saddle. How will Mamá and Papá respond when I tell them about the Himzo invasion? Their faces flashed through my mind. *They'll be so proud of me for protecting our home. My kingdom will finally love and embrace their princess.*

Then it hit me. Papá could squash any attack with his ability to control others' bodies. How would they subdue Papá? There was more to the plan than what I heard, but we were already set to leave. Why hadn't I listened longer?

Gonzalo walked the steeds out of the tent. "Follow the east road to the junction. Your patrol should be there."

I climbed onto Muck and tugged on the reins. He wasted no time dashing forward.

Hooves clomped in the mud behind me. I startled. Had the Himzos caught me? But it was Laude's slender figure in a cloak racing to catch up.

Tiny droplets splattered onto my skin as I bolted toward the road. One thought hammered through me: *The Himzos threaten everyone I love.*

CHAPTER 32

MUCK'S HOOVES POUNDED THE path. I had no idea how much farther we needed to go. My thighs burned, and I could sleep sitting up if I didn't fear falling off the steed. Laude fell far behind on the trail. I slowed my speed. So long as we kept moving, we'd make it in time. That was the hope.

Laude groaned. "Please, miss, can we stop? I need another break."

I hesitated but agreed, knowing she would never ask unless necessary. We pulled over. She hastened behind the high grasses on the side of the road, and I did the same, the drizzle chilling my bones. A strong wind rustled the trees, making it difficult to listen for the patrol or unsavory characters.

Once done, I stood on the muddy road. Moonlight peeked through the clouds, casting deep shadows in the forests surrounding us, and clouds overtook the skies again.

I lifted my voice to the Ancient One. "If you care, please make the road straight. If you hear, will you give me an ability to protect my people?" A rush of cold wind flapped around my cloak, hurrying me to Muck's side.

Laude raced to the horses. "Miss, we should rest. You look just as exhausted as the horses. And I'm sure you have good reason to rush, but I'm a little confused."

Her tender voice reminded me she served in love rather than obligation, and she showed implicit trust in my judgment. Those thoughts warmed the walls of my heart.

"We must continue," I patted her arm, "and pray that these steeds can endure. I'll tell you as we ride."

Dark semicircles sat beneath Laude's eyes. She looked more like a wilted flower than a lady on a horse.

I maintained a trotting pace while working up the courage to vocalize my thoughts. "I overheard Zichri speak …" My throat thickened. I glanced over my shoulder, still expecting a Himzo rider to crest the road. Surely, Zichri would be upset about me stealing Muck.

"Tell me, miss. I am brave."

Hadn't I told her to be brave? A nervous laugh escaped my mouth. "Yes, you are, indeed. It's not you. It's that Zichri and the others met with a traitor of Giddel to arrange an attack on our kingdom."

"No! That can't be. But Jaime and all the men were so kind. No, miss." Laude shook her head, disbelieving.

I pictured the candlelight shining over the sea of faces at my ball. Anyone could have slipped in if they had the right connections. A memory of dancing with Blas shot into mind in that instant. No one else had such potent blue-green eyes besides Lux. And hadn't strange men been watching and laughing when Blas danced with me? Lux had intervened, so I had no time to process my misgivings.

"Consider all that time they were with us," I said. "They didn't share why they went to Giddel. Did Jaime tell you anything contrary to what I say now?"

"He didn't, but…" She gasped. "He did say they'd met with someone at the ball. And now that I think of it, he said that they barely made it due to the wards. Ai-yi-yi! I must have been so blind. Jaime even warned me to stay in the palace with all the problems between the kingdoms." She drifted into thought for a moment and widened her eyes. "He was trying to warn me!"

"Zichri was keen on knowing the exact location of my room." It occurred to me that he would not be certain of my whereabouts in the palace unless I was asleep. "They'll attack at night. If Papá sleeps, he can't stop the Himzos. The wards are down. No one will expect an attack either."

Laude shrieked. "How can the wards be down? The scoundrel who betrayed us must be powerful too. Oh, Princess! We need to move faster. It would have been nice if you had received the gift of quick travel."

How dare she mention the gift! I stifled the quip ready to roll off my tongue. Pulling on the reins and pressing my legs into Muck's sides, I shouted, "Pick up the pace."

Laude was right about one thing. A regular person could not have brought down the wards. Whoever betrayed us must have attended the ball. That person must have been able to manipulate wards. *Could it be my brother's friend? What's his name? Yes, I remember. Sir Lucas.*

Twisting anger stormed through my blood. A turn in the path nearly caught me off guard. I balanced myself, panting. Since the treaties in my grandparents' days, no one had dared threaten the eight allied kingdoms. Even the least-liked and most southern kingdom, Aldrin—from which Princess Alexa hailed—would not dare to break away from such a strong alliance.

Unless … these plans were the machinations of a few kingdoms. No, that was absurd thinking and would require too many mouths to stay shut. People were far too eager to share secret information for a pretty coin. No, the betrayer was most likely someone like Sir Lucas who dealt in wards.

The path slithered along, rattling my nerves. My fingernails dug into my palms as trees flew past us.

Bu-pum. Bu-pum. I shot a glance over my shoulder. The clomp of distant hooves pounded the road. Did I imagine this?

Sore in mind and body, I pressed forward. Laude sat up a bit, slowing when a fork in the road required us to choose a path. No marker indicated where each led. I bit on my bottom lip, holding in a scream.

"Do you know the way home?" Laude brought Jaime's horse to a steady jog.

Gonzalo and Zichri had mentioned a road. Did they say to go left or right? Where were the patrols? The men made it seem like the patrols waited nearby. We didn't have time to wait. I pulled on Muck's reins, slowing him to a halt, and I heard Laude's horse come to a stop behind me.

My palms sweated, making the reins slippery, so I wiped them down on my damp pants. Both roads appeared similar with scattered trees. A forest loomed in the distance ahead on the left while hilly grasslands cut into the landscape on the right. An ache fired from the back of my head toward the front.

"Do you hear that?" Laude lifted an ear to the sky.

I stared at the snaking path behind us. Leaves rustled almost thunderously, and branches snapped overhead. Then, I registered the sound of horses galloping toward us.

"It could be the patrol," I said.

I glanced at Laude, who sat upright like a statue. The moonlight caught on her fiery curls whipping in the wind.

Two horsemen appeared around the bend, and I wanted to cower. Their cloaks billowed behind them. The closer they got, the more my entire body tensed with doubt. They wore dark cloaks, and dull light illuminated white tunics underneath. The patrol wore green.

I called to Laude, "We can outrun them."

Laude didn't budge.

"Laude! Come now, they aren't the patrol. Don't you see that?"

Instead, she guided her horse in the direction of the two figures speeding toward us. I could have wrung her neck for such foolishness. There was no time to hide anymore, so I pressed my shoulders back and moved my horse next to hers. I hoped whatever hunch motivating Laude proved true.

"Princess, trust me. I heard it on the wind."

I'd heard this phrasing a million times by those who hoped to convince me to do as they bid. It always chafed against my will.

But Laude said it with such conviction. I daresay she believed she heard the wind speak.

The galloping of the horses meshed with the beat hammering

in my temples. It was Zichri and Jaime. I'd recognize Zichri's face anywhere. *What could they possibly mean by chasing us down? Are they upset?* Each muscle coiled tight enough to crack a bone.

Zichri came to a stop and dismounted in one swift movement. A glimmer reflected off the hilt sheathed at his side. *Is he here to detain me?* He drew nearer, and the forest blurred in my peripheral. I held my breath, keeping my head high.

"Princess Beatriz." The breathy way Zichri said my name awakened goosebumps all over my skin. He petted Muck, nuzzling up to his neck. Muck wrapped his head around Zichri in a hug.

I ground out between my teeth, "I overheard everything. About how you helped plan an attack. About how the war is imminent. Did you follow me to take me captive?"

"Yes. Would you have me betray my father, brothers, and people? I am a man of my word." Zichri massaged his brow. "What did you hear? Gonzalo said you looked distressed."

My throat thickened. "You came all this way to ask me what I heard?"

"I came because I did my duty, and I said I'd come for you." He placed his rough hand on mine.

Unsure if I should yank my hand free, scream, cry, or ride away, I swallowed a lump blocking my throat. "I didn't want ... Why did you follow me? You saved me from those unsavories, won my heart, then you broke it." I blinked back tears, upset at myself.

"Do you truly mean that?" He tipped his head to the side, trying to get me to meet his gaze. A pleading marked his eyes.

My bottom lip quivered.

Something inside me snapped, and guttural sobs trembled out. I plunged my face into my hands. It was all I could do to hide this raw emotion.

"Beatriz, come down." Zichri's fingers grazed my knee.

My fingers pressed into my forehead and my thumbs into my cheeks. Slick palms remained in place. I inhaled a quavering breath.

"I'm sorry, Beatriz." Zichri's voice grew huskier. "I'm sorry for not being forthright. I'm sorry I hurt you."

An ache swelled inside my chest and crushed against my rib cage. Would this pain ever go away?

"Please, put yourself in my place," he said in earnest. "I had been doing my duty. I went with you into Valle de los Fantasmas because I believed you were called to it. I wouldn't be here chasing after you if the last week hadn't meant something to me. Please, come down so we can talk one last time."

My hands dropped partway down my face. I so badly wanted to believe him. Did it even matter anymore? Zichri and I would never court, and he proved that he would never cause me physical harm. He had such a sincere expression on his face that I decided to trust him.

I brought my leg around and hopped to the ground. He gathered me into his arms, and we hugged so tight his warmth melted into mine. The heat reached deep into my soul. An invisible something sprouted out my skin, and I shivered. It was foreign, yet a familiar impression. *Is this love?*

"Tell me what you'd have me do?" Zichri's chest rose and fell.

Warring emotions tugged in my chest. A strange sensation sizzled along my arms. I jerked away, confused, and looked up into his doleful gaze. "Could you stop the attack?"

He tucked a frizzy puff of hair behind my ear. "Even mentioning it could be considered treasonous. Would you have me forfeit my family?"

I wet my bottom lip, wishing I could say yes, but I said, "No. You wouldn't ask that of me either." I sensed his understanding just as strongly as I felt his hands pressing against my back.

Him letting me go could mean failure for his people, yet he nodded, resigned. "I guess I knew all along. I cannot hold you captive. My reasons for wanting to keep you are different now than before. Do you hate me?"

I searched his dark eyes and glanced at Laude, who spoke with Jaime. What would I have done or thought in his predicament? I felt my eyebrows crinkle and turned back toward him. "I want to hate you, but I can't. How could I?"

He squeezed my elbows affectionately, brushing his hands along my arms before releasing me from his embrace. His touch lingered on my skin, and his inner battle tugged in my consciousness. But that was impossible. It must be the tension marked on his drawn brows giving me that impression. He ambled to his horse—no possibility of returning to each other.

"Which road should we take?" I lifted my chin out of habit, swiping my cheeks.

"Take that one, beloved." He pointed to the path on the right. "You have little time. We have ways of getting there faster."

That could only mean a powerful, gifted person helped them—a portal maker. I climbed on my horse's back. We needed to speed away.

Jaime cupped Laude's face, and her arms were around his torso. Laude whispered in his ear the last words they might ever exchange. The look in Jaime's eyes spoke of devotion, pain, and dreams that would never come to pass. Zichri's whistle pierced the sky, hurrying his friend. Jaime kissed her forehead, and they parted.

I positioned myself on Muck, and my heart tightened. *My last words to Zichri will be a practical question. What if he goes away not knowing what I still feel for him?* I called out, "Prince Zichri of Himzo." I tightened my grip on the reins when he turned his gaze on me. "If things were different, I'd choose you."

CHAPTER 33

THE SEA REFLECTED THE light of a thousand stars and two moons. It was usually a good omen when the second moon rose. I hoped it proved true. Laude and I galloped across the countryside. When Giddel appeared, an overwhelming feeling stirred within me. Somehow, the stone walls, twisting roads, and palace felt different than before I left.

The villagers slept in their tiny houses scattered along the hillsides, ignorant of what our enemy planned. The slopes challenged Muck, but he was willing to go on. How did I know this? A new sensation trickled into my mind, something like feeling, seeing, and hearing all at once. There was no name for the change in my body, but I tried not to overthink why this happened.

The closer we got, the more my urge to see Papá swelled. The windowless city walls grew more imposing, especially since the soldiers welcomed Laude and me with arrows pointed at our hearts. We slowed the steeds and stopped before the main gates.

The arched doorways towered over us like a giant mouth set in stone. A strange sensation emanated from the soldiers, appearing like tiny whispers in my mind.

Be still, you fool.
Who might this be?
What small men.

My heart pounded. Was I going mad or imagining things? By the grim expressions on the soldiers' faces, they weren't going to let us in unless I revealed my identity. I pursed my lips and dismounted to calm the tension. "Will you not let your princess into her own city?"

Soldiers held their arrows notched back. The tautness in the air vibrated down to my inner being, whispering, *Is she telling the truth? How do we know it is she?*

I glanced down at the markings on my hands. They glowed. That had only happened when I said words of power. The air rushed from my lungs. I traced the swirling lines, and strange prickles flowed into my finger and up my arm. Did anyone else see my skin illuminating? "Here are my gifting marks. Now open the doors."

Though the archers loomed over us a good distance, they trembled with confusion.

One soldier's eyes snapped open, and he let down his bow. "It is she!"

Others relaxed their bows while some soldiers maintained their positions.

Sounds of unbolting and clicks echoed. The door scraped along the cobblestone. Laude shrank back on her horse, looking like she might faint. I whispered to myself, wishing I could push the words at her, *Be of good courage, my dear friend.*

She took the reins of her horse and puffed out her chest, preparing to walk through our entrance.

A stern-faced man, clad in a green uniform, marched toward us but stopped short of exiting the city gate. "Get off your steed." Upon closer inspection, the glint of the moon reflected off colorful embroidery on both his shoulders, indicating his high rank. Disbelief rolled off him. It murmured in my head, *This is no princess.*

Am I losing my wits? What am I hearing?

"Bring them in." Stern-face's gruff voice cut through the night.

The whyzer did not give me my gift, yet something within me *had* changed. Heat burbled through my veins. I led Muck through the gates and inside the city walls. "Good sir, we need you to take us to the palace as quickly as you can manage or let us ride through." In reality, I hoped a carriage awaited next to the entrance, ready to go. My achy muscles would have thanked him.

His tight-lipped expression told me I'd have no such luck. I lifted my chin high despite the obstinance woven through the aura around him. If I hadn't been so emotionally spent, it would have been no effort to maintain the regality a princess should always possess. But it was an effort.

Laude walked her steed next to mine. "Sir, could we not speak to the head of His Majesty's service to confirm our story? I am a loyal servant to Princess Beatriz, and it would be no inconvenience to wake Lady Myla. If we lie, you may do as you wish to us since we would be committing a crime against the throne."

A grinding noise dragged our attention toward two soldiers pushing the entrance doors shut behind us. They slapped the bolt shut with a loud clank. Stern-face maintained a twist to his lips, his grayed mustache unmoving. In fact, his annoyance, though apparent, lapped through me, like water washing on the shore before pulling back to the sea. Mamá always encouraged me to be perceptive about how a person looks and their movements, but I had never been able to *feel* how another person wrestled with their emotions. Laude had pricked his pride somehow with her suggestion.

Laude continued, "Come now, good sir. Lady Myla might even be awake. The birds sing with the coming light." She had a confidence in her posture. It reminded me of Mamá on her throne.

This whole time, I'd been so focused on getting the gift and saving my pride. How did I not see the change in Laude? Before we left, she would not have dared tell anyone what to do, and now my Laude spoke boldly.

"I'll escort you to the servants' entrance." Stern-face pointed toward our horses, signaling for us to mount again.

The slow and intentional way Laude climbed up suggested that she also ached from the ride. My body screamed at me for even considering climbing on Muck's back again, but what could we do?

Muck stomped the road in protest.

I leaned forward and whispered to him, "My dear friend. You will get the break you desire soon enough. Only a little more to go."

Muck huffed, walking despite his need for rest. We continued through town, following closely behind three soldiers on their horses. The shuttered windows lining the buildings watched us make our way through the barren town center. The horses clomped down the cobblestones, shaking my already buzzing nerves.

I played with the new pulsating sensation in my veins. It was invisible, yet tangible. I stretched it out from my body, and the transparent force spread out like tentacles. It flowed over a woman popping her head out a window, and she bubbled with curiosity and anxiety. Whispers about soldiers escorting two scrawny men vibrated down the invisible line. I couldn't blame her for thinking we were men.

"Remain calm," I whispered to myself. Confounded, I massaged my forehead, and those invisible appendages wrapped around her like they had in my nightmares. *Remain calm, remain calm.* The transparent appendage uncoiled, knocking the lady's chin as we rode past her. All her features widened in shock and then relaxed into a smile. She closed the shutters, and I focused on the road ahead.

This reminded me of my dreams. But not all my night visions had good results. My clammy hand slipped down the leather rein a bit, and I gripped it tighter. Whatever invisible thing was extending out my body needed to be contained. I would never forgive myself if anything happened to anyone.

We veered down a lane where the road narrowed. The invisible force surrounding me brushed against the souls within their houses. Many people slept soundly in their homes, while others were startled awake. There was no way of seeing this, but I knew. In my dreams, I could change how people reacted, and I gulped. All my dreams turned into nightmares. I brushed the thought aside and focused on Stern-face. The soldier gave me a sidelong look, and I extended the invisible tentacles toward him. I exhaled, "Trust me." But the wind swept away my words.

The palace appeared larger the longer we clomped through town. All the stones on the east side glowed orange from the morning light, my favorite time to sit on my balcony. A shadow fell on half the palace. My heart filled with longing. Even the jagged stakes my brother added to the entrance appealed to me. It was home. I hadn't realized how much I missed it.

As the horses continued to walk, a red building blocked the way, so I clicked my tongue to quicken Muck's pace. Even with this tenseness roiling within my belly, a hint of relief spread through me when I gazed upon the familiar town square and marketplace on the main road. It led to the front entrance. Laude furrowed her brow. Perhaps she shared the same concern that we weren't going through the side entrance.

I tightened my grip on the leather cord, ready to pull on Muck's bit, but two soldiers followed behind us, leaving no room for us to backtrack. The cloak latched at my collarbone grew heavier, choking my neck. *No! They can't trap me.*

The two soldiers bristled—that revelation came to me through waves of heat flowing into my body. *Oh, Ancient One, what is this new sensation?* I swallowed hard, trying to sympathize with the soldiers. How it disturbed my soul when people disliked me. What would I think of me if I were them? I'd probably put myself in jail.

If Stern-face turned left, we'd be sent to jail. If he went straight, he believed us. *He may not want to insult my good name.* We couldn't do anything more to convince him.

I inhaled, getting a whiff of the sea air mingled with fresh bread. Not even the Giddelian morning air calmed me. Instead, sweat beaded on my nose. I didn't want to consider what it would be like if we were in jail when the Himzos attacked.

Muck trudged behind the soldiers. I pleaded with Stern-face in my head. *Order for the palace gates to open. Come now.* Stopping at the entrance, Stern-face peeked back at us and set his jaw. Not good. My blood simmered with his disdain. He maneuvered his horse forward and lifted a hand.

Relief flooded through me, but then he made a sharp left turn. My stomach clenched. I couldn't breathe. We passed the sealed front gate.

We needed a miracle. This could take a long time to sort out if we were in jail and we didn't have time. We could try to outrun the soldiers, but how would we get into the palace? The soldiers ahead of us stopped in front of the windowless stone facade—all stone and no style.

Stern-face bounded off his horse and commanded, "Detain these two."

"You are making a mistake." I clenched my fists.

"And gag her."

Two burly men came out of the jail. I scooted off my horse to make this whole situation smoother. *There must be a way to show them I am Princess Beatriz.*

I rolled my sleeves up. Everyone knew about my markings, and they had been glowing upon entering Giddel. "See the marks on my hand. Look at my face." My teeth ground and I said, "Please see reason. You'll regret this."

Stern-face tilted his head toward me, unimpressed by my words and my gifting marks. When I lifted my arms, the marks stared at me with their regular dull lines, difficult to see in this light. But ... they had glowed.

Strong hands clamped around my arms. I kicked and protested. One of the soldiers who had been following us squeezed my wrists, sending a violent surge of pain sizzling throughout my body. My arms fell limp to my side, and my legs gave way, making it easy for one of the bald jailers to snatch the dagger from my belt and lift me over his shoulder. He must have had a gift that left people incapacitated. I caught a glimpse of another soldier dragging Laude into the jail. Her cheeks drooped compared to her normal bubbling smile.

I tried to scream at the head soldier. "Unhand me. I come with a message for my father, the king." The words came out garbled even to my own ears.

Stern-face crossed his arms. A smug smile tugged at the edges of his lips. I tried to extend the invisible force out of my body, but I couldn't even feel my toes. Had I imagined it?

The jailer tied my wrists so tight I thought my shoulders might break. I held back a yelp. A princess needed to keep *some* dignity. He jerked me forward through the jail's dark doorway and down a long, stone hall. The front door of the prison framed the silhouette of a soldier as he slammed the door shut.

CHAPTER 34

Mamá always said that the Ancient One could use even bad things to do something good. She was wrong. The bars jailing Laude and I squeezed every drop of hope from me. I planted my palms on my forehead, a headache throbbing from temple to temple.

"At least, we're together." Laude's thin voice did nothing to ease the lump in my throat. But us together in the same jail cell had kept me from melting into the stone floor that reaked of filth.

I swallowed hard, trying to wash away my guilt at her being here. If it weren't for me, she'd be in the palace, the safest place to be when the Himzos attacked. Why did I ask her to accompany me in the first place? How I wished to go back in time and be satisfied with choosing a husband. She wouldn't suffer. Mamá would have let me travel to see my aunt in the north, and Zichri may have followed me there anyway. My imagination ran wilder than Laude's unruly hair. Regrets jailed me in just as much as the gray stone on each wall.

One of the jailers plopped bowls of gruel on the floor, then marched down the hall without acknowledging our presence. The indignation of the whole thing churned in my stomach.

Laude ran to the bars and shouted at him, "You can't keep us here. It's a matter of life and death for all of us in Giddel."

But the man continued to stroll down the hall and slammed a metal door without so much as a grunt in return.

"You will regret not listening!" Laude stomped her foot. "When the king finds out about how you treated Princess Beatriz, you will find yourself watching an ax fall on your head—*if* you survive the Himzo attack!" She kicked a metal bar and howled in pain.

"Stop that, Laude. He can't hear you." My voice sounded weak.

"But how do they not recognize you? You are their princess. It's not like you hide yourself in the palace for no one to see. Even if they are unsure, why not look into our story? They should be interrogating us."

Even in the dimness, I noticed red blotches blooming on her neck. A weak smile turned up at the corners of my mouth. Her passion was so contrary to my sulking. It reminded me of Lux's remark about how I whined all the time. Now that I thought about it, he had called me a whiner. Only he could have done that without me lashing at him. *Am I still that person?*

Silent minutes stretched, leaving me trapped in my own abysmal trenches—recalling every foul word I'd ever spewed, every terse look I ever glared, every judgment I'd made. Lux and I used to laugh at other people. It made me feel so much better than those in lower stations, and it elevated my own position when I longed to be esteemed and made worthy of a gift.

The door at the end of the corridor rattled. A slender man strutted in front of our bars and sneered. "I was awakened to attend to you. Speak quickly before I lose my temper and send you to the stump."

My mouth grew dry. It had never crossed my mind that we could be sentenced to death on our arrival. Pushing off the ground, I worked up the strength to combat this. *Will he believe me? What other evidence do I have besides my face?* I pushed back my shoulders and lifted my chin—all that time practicing Mamá's dignified expression needed to come in handy right now.

"Good sir. Your sovereigns are waiting to hear from their daughter. Bring in Myla, the head lady's maid, and she will identify me. But if she finds me a stranger—which will not happen—send us to the stump." I puffed out my chest, hoping beyond hope that he'd listen.

"That's a mighty large request you make since our highness will require her closest maid." His pale eyes bulged over his pointy nose.

"But I will do as you ask when I get a chance. And she will come when she's available." He shifted toward the door.

"But sir! This is a matter of life and death." I clasped the bars of my cell.

The man scowled. "You will not die if you are who you say you are."

"You are transgressing against the king's family. You will not get the luxury of the stump. Instead, my papá will pour out his wrath on you. And believe me when I say, your end will not be quick." I inhaled a quivering breath, thankful that each word came out more forceful than the next.

He clenched his fists and turned toward the door.

My words hadn't made an impact. I flashed an apologetic look at Laude. She touched my elbow, but instead of being comforted, I was mad. *There must be something else I can do.*

I trained my eyes on our jailer, who was one boot out the door. A flow of energy rattled up my spine, and I focused it on him, squeezing it around him like an octopus's tentacle. He audibly inhaled. I said to him through pressed lips: *Say yes. It's but one word.* Still quiet, he wagged his head.

"For the kingdom's sake, will you not check to see if I'm telling the truth?" I reached beyond my physical self again. This time whispers of rage screamed in his mind. *Something about her reminds me of the queen. So does her arrogant manner. But what a dirty-looking thing! I can squash her with my pinky. Fitting for a giftless princess. I even have a gift. Why shouldn't I weld the rails shut with my touch?* A cruel laugh escaped his mouth. I stiffened at this, but I didn't relent.

Through my mind, I commanded, *Get Myla, and I may be lenient. Do nothing, and I will crush you.*

He flinched in disbelief, but his face quickly contorted into a scowl. "I will burn you alive if Lady Myla doesn't recognize you." He slammed the door shut.

Had any of my outbursts ever looked so ... foul? How I loathed those memories. This time, my heartbreak was not about my lack of gift but what I'd done.

I leaned in toward Laude. "Have you any reason to believe Myla would lie?"

Laude threw her arms around me. "Don't be silly, Princess. We're going home."

For once, her squeals filled me with hope. Even though it lacked any decorum, and it might not be allowed ever again, I was happy for her show of affection. Back home, I only received kisses and hugs from Mamá, Papá, and my brother. Yes, there were the diplomatic greetings from other queens and princesses. Lux sometimes stole a handhold. But nothing like this ... or being held by Zichri. My chest squeezed.

My tangled thoughts wouldn't stop. The way his strong arms wrapped around me. The way his touch lingered—that one dance. My heartbeat kicked up to a gallop in his presence and swirled my insides into sweet nectar any time he looked in my direction. An ache radiated all over my body. *Lock up the memory, Beatriz. Lock it up.*

CHAPTER 35

THE DOOR UNBOLTED WITH a metallic clang. I held my breath. Did they send for Myla, or were we dead?

The jailor's meaty hand reached through the crack first, and he swung the door open. A woman stalked to our cell, her hooded cloak brushing the rough stone floor. Once in front of us, she swept her hood back. Myla's blond hair was pulled tight into a bun, and her small, brown eyes narrowed over a gaping mouth. The jailer fumbled for his keys.

"Release them at once." Myla tapped her foot, waving her hand at him.

The man, though a head taller, squirmed under Myla's scrutiny.

"How dare you lock up your princess? Her mother and father will not take this offense lightly." Myla continued whipping her words at him.

The jailer clinked through his belt with rings of skeletal keys and stabbed one into our door, exuding a sickly yellow feeling through his pores. Laude's cheeks bubbled in delight.

Thunk. The cell door swung open. Laude flourished for me to walk first and curtsied. It reminded me I boasted a title again. I tipped my chin up high and pinched my lips into a pout. That gesture no longer felt as dignified as I had thought it looked—especially not after Zichri's comments. But habits were hard to break.

The jailer bowed his head. "My most sincere apologies, your Highness."

Myla dropped a quick curtsy. Her eyes quickly locked on my filthy clothes. "What. Are. You. Wearing? No wonder these stumps don't believe you're the princess. Is that grass in your hair? Laude, do something about those locks of hers—now!"

"We haven't the time." I brushed off Myla's hand and shifted a meaningful look toward the exit. More important matters needed handling—like an enemy invasion.

Myla strode ahead, and I followed close behind. Laude's footfalls scurried close at my back. Two burly men in green livery bowed their heads when we passed them.

Tension pulsed through the air, so I reached out, feeling with that invisible tentacle. It was more like swatting with a limp napkin. There had to be a better way to work with whatever flowed through me. The men's foreheads beaded with perspiration, and a small twinge of pity poked within me. Passing them, I whispered, "Be at peace."

We exited the hall, and I took one last glance back, seeing the burly men wearing confused smiles. There was something satisfying about helping them—even if they were brutes. I strode to catch up with Myla.

"Put your hood up." Myla stopped mid-road until I obeyed. "We're taking you to Laude's room to change. No one should see you like this."

I pitched my voice low. "I need to see Papá now. It's an urgent matter."

Myla grunted. She had known me since I was a baby and had heard this phrase before for trivial concerns. "You will do as I say, or else you will cause your parents more reason to worry. Furthermore, your father and brother sailed away yesterday."

"What do you mean? Who protects the city?" A familiar ache throbbed in my skull. No one could overcome Giddel because of Papá's gifting—the kingdom needed him.

"What do you call the men who captured you? Pull the hood down to your eyes." Myla continued in long strides and turned into the servants' entrance. Palace guards unlocked the gate for Myla and let us pass through.

Laude nudged my side. "Miss Myla, could I ready Princess Beatriz on my own?"

"Ha! You will do no such thing. A good lashing awaits you. Blanca told me how you asked her to help Princess Beatriz escape." Myla pushed open a small back door into the kitchen. "Hurry behind me."

Laude dragged her feet and hung her head. A string of dread pulsed from her to me as if our hearts connected. I reached for Myla, but stares from all sides bore holes into my cloak. The servants murmured behind the counters, yet even from a distance, their judgment plumed around them, overwhelming my senses. *How do I shut off this connection to others?*

We hastened across the cinnamon- and yeast-scented room. The chef stirred the caldron while another servant chopped vegetables at the counter next to the chef. At another counter, a servant rolled out dough. That person lifted a questioning eyebrow. Recognition crossed her expression, and instant disdain flooded her being. It was like someone plunged a dagger into my soul.

Myla turned a corner, and we entered a long, dreadful hall with doors on each side. "Get in this room. Blanca, come here to help." From down the hall, Blanca rushed in behind us. White walls, two small beds, and one wardrobe filled the plain room. Laude scuffed the floor next to me. Mud clung from her knees down. Her appearance sharply contrasted Blanca's clean clothes and neat hair.

I rolled my eyes at seeing Myla throwing towels and a basin at Laude. "How long is this going to take? Just let me speak to Mamá or one of the advisors."

Myla slammed the door when she exited, leaving Laude and Blanca stripping my boots off and undoing my ratty braid. Helplessness threatened to overtake me, and I sensed Laude drowning in it too. Tear droplets coated Laude's lashes.

I tipped Laude's chin up. "This is too important. We must be brave."

Laude nodded and worked a knot out of my hair with her fingers.

"Enough of this." I grabbed Laude's wrist. "You're coming with me."

I shoved my feet into my soiled boots, stood, and headed for the door, leaving Blanca holding a wet towel. She stepped back, wrinkling her face like an angry pug. A wave of her sentiments crashed into my body.

Laude led me out the maze of halls and up a stairway. She stopped to ask a male servant for Mamá, and he directed us into a meeting room on the second floor. It was hard not to notice how he quirked a brow up at the sight of us. A tugging feeling pulled my attention from one person to the next. They exuded derision. I chose to ignore the servants on account of the message we carried. Climbing another set of stairs, we ran into Myla, who lugged several dresses over a shoulder.

"Where do you think you're going?" Myla said in clipped tones. "Young lady, consider your mother for once."

I raised my chin in challenge. "Get behind me, Myla. As princess, I will do as I please. Only my family will hold me back."

A venomous coil wound in her gut, and I interpreted bitterness and a sense of ruffled pride. That stabbed at my heart even more than regular servants hating me. She had read to me and played games with me when I was a child. Never had I imagined her harboring ill feelings toward me. I wanted to cut off this string that connected me to people. It had already turned into a curse—knowing all the judgment people carried within.

Stay calm. Keep moving. I pressed my shoulders back and slid a mask of indifference over my face, hiding my hurt. Laude followed me up the stairs and down the hall. Two soldiers from Pedroz, Lux's kingdom, guarded the gold-plated door. Were Lux's parents meeting with Mamá? How odd.

I burst into the meeting room with Laude in tow. Mamá sat behind Papá's desk wearing a pursed-lip expression, as always. I wanted to run over and throw my arms around her body, but a man with cropped sandy hair sat across from her. My heart raced. *Why is a man speaking privately with Mamá?*

The man turned his head. It was Lux. His turquoise eyes widened, and a tight smile settled on his lips. I smiled back, but something heavy lay between Lux and me. We hadn't argued before I left. With my gift blooming, he was a plausible suitor, even with him being betrothed. My heart was constrained.

I breathed in and out, slowly letting the gift pulsate from my body. An instant attachment formed between Mamá and I. Worry clung like leeches, draining the lifeblood from her. But Lux and I made no connection. Some sort of barrier wedged between us. I tried again with the same results. His gifting had something to do with changing the perception others had of him. *Maybe his gifting runs deeper than he explained.*

"Prince Lux, it is good to see you here. Mamá." I rushed in to kiss her cheek. "Could I have a minute to speak with you? It is a matter of great importance."

Mamá tipped her chin high. "So is this, my dear. I would prefer if you go up to your quarters and wait for me to finish." Something in her voice sounded strained. This was not like her.

What could it be? Lux wouldn't be cause for worry. A pang struck my forehead. Mamá stared intently. Could she be causing the pain?

Trying to think past the throbbing, I said between gritted teeth. "Mamá, stop that! You don't understand the importance of my message." Speaking proved difficult. "Himzos attack. This week."

Mamá showed no sign of shock. "Darling, I need you to go now." She screwed her lips shut like she does when there's no chance of me winning an argument.

"What's wrong with you?" I shouted in frustration. "We need to contact Papá. I know for a fact ... that our enemy comes with a large army. And that the wards are down." The pain spread behind my eyes, throughout my entire head. I massaged my temples, unable to think. The door creaked open.

"Myla, take Princess Beatriz to her room. I will be there once I'm done speaking with Prince Lux." Mamá sounded distant and stern.

I stepped toward Myla when Lux touched my wrist. In an instant, an insatiable desire vibrated up my arm—from him to me. I stood still, desperate for information, but he let go.

"Bea, I'm glad you came back. Your mamá and I were just speaking about the news you bring. Everything is under control." Lux winked to comfort me like he always had.

The gesture that used to turn my stomach into a hive of buzzing bees now left a trail of unease. I had never felt that before in his presence. My head throbbed too much to think, and I bit back a yelp. Myla pushed against my back and guided me out the door.

My head lightened the moment my foot hit the hall. We went up another flight of stairs to my bedroom, our boots tapping the marble floors in even beats. The ache that immobilized my thinking vanished. In its place, heartache made its home. Could Lux be the traitor? I could never believe that. The oncoming attack must have stirred the tension in the room.

Mamá worried. She never would have caused my head pains otherwise. I hadn't realized she had the power to cause bodily pain. She always worked with the healers to refine her gifting and said she'd made no progress.

And why hadn't Lux told me he could block the power others had over him? A memory came to mind. Once Cosme tried to levitate Lux when we were playing as kids, but my brother strained as he lifted shaky hands with no success. Cosme had been able to raise a grown man off the ground. Lux laughed at Cosme's attempt. From that day on, my brother hated Lux. I always thought their rivalry had to do with who had more power. Was there more to the story?

Myla turned the knob of my bedroom door. The hardwood seemed darker, and the powder-blue walls no longer welcomed me with an open hug. I hadn't expected home to feel different though nothing in it had changed.

Light poured in through the windows, and the plush comforter invited me to jump into bed. Myla spoke in hushed tones to Laude before calling out to the servants outside my room to bring the water summoner and water heater. Laude tapped my door shut and headed straight for my closet. No one said a word.

An undercurrent of emotion circulated in the stale air, and I stared at the back of my hands. A hint of gold flecks ran along the pale lines. My jaw trembled, considering when the sensation began. This had to be my gift, and it felt just like my dreams. I gulped, remembering how some of my night visions took sour turns. If only I had better control. The trip may have been worthwhile after all, but my whyzer had been adamant about not giving any gifting. Had the Ancient One taken pity on me?

I opened the double doors to my balcony and stepped out into the sunlight. A melody soared, horses clomped, music danced through the town, and the people bustled about. Nothing seemed out of the ordinary, like Himzo soldiers. I squinted to make sure I caught details on the hillside, but no prince in black attire rode on the thoroughfare to whisk me away.

I should think about practical things, like hearing that conversation between Lux and Mamá. When Cosme and I were younger, we'd spy on Papá through secret corridors in the walls. Our parents introduced us to these hiding places in case of an enemy attack. Few of the servants knew about them. If I could keep Myla out of my room, Laude could stay here to make sure no one tried to enter while I snuck down through my closet. Mamá might not sense me like Papá had.

"The bath is ready." Myla's stern face told me I had no room for argument.

I stretched my practiced smile in place. "Thank you. You are dismissed. Laude will stay and help."

Myla heaved a sigh. "When your mother becomes aware of the situation, you will not get such liberties."

"Until then." I waved a hand of dismissal.

CHAPTER 36

"PRINCESS, I'M ALREADY RECEIVING lashings for our time away. Please have mercy on me and take your bath." Laude clasped her hands together, scrunching her nose. "I will be in more trouble than you know if you don't get in the tub."

"I'll get in the bath when I return. No one will found out I disappeared. I'll only be gone a short time." I pulled on the invisible connection to Laude and spoke to her through it. *Be at peace.*

Laude unclasped her hands. "But what if your mamá comes here? What do I say?"

"Blame it all on me and cry. She likes to spoil you." I chucked Laude's chin. "Mamá loves you like a daughter. She may even hold back Myla's hand from all those lashings."

The edges of her lips snapped upward with delight. "Be quick about it and tell me everything that happens." She lit my bedside lamp with the tap of her finger and passed it to me.

"Thank you." I placed the lamp on the table again. Opening the entrance to the hidden passage would require both hands. I strode into the closet and shoved a giant chest along the floor grooves. Underneath, a staircase led into darkness. I ran back into my room for the lamp. Laude leaned on the balcony railing, looking out at the road.

I rushed into my closet, determined to save my kingdom and prove the whyzer wrong. The candle flame flickered, causing a tremble of apprehension through my bones, but I descended the stairs anyway. I set the lamp on a stair and yanked on the handle beneath the chest. It clunked along the grooves until it shut me in.

Spider webs lined the corners of the stone corridor, and a stale scent permeated through the darkness. The few servants who knew about these corridors cleaned and repaired the passageways each year, but not often enough for my liking. I continued to make my way through the stairwell, boots scuffing the stairs until I reached the bottom. A shadowed passageway led deeper into the palace.

My stomach squeezed as though a spider had captured my stomach and wove its sticky cords around it. Every shadow marked an unknown danger, possibly readying to attack. An intersection crossed ahead. I turned to the right. At each doorway, I climbed a ladder set in stone, with one hand holding the lamp. My body bumped the stone more than I would have liked.

Papá used to say that we made so much noise that he didn't need to use his gift to sense us. I doubted that. *Only two more doorways.*

I climbed and counted the doorways. *This should be the room. Please, let them be here.* Tiptoeing to the chimney hole between the walls, I stopped to keep myself from falling three stories down.

Mamá spoke in a neutral voice. "Our kingdoms have a long history. What changed?"

"Father believes we need a new order to ensure all the kingdoms get equal resources." Lux's voice remained steady. It held no emotion or bitterness. His father always wanted more power, as Papá always said after each visit with the King of Pedroz. But Lux was nothing like his father.

"Forgive me, but I disagree with you on your assertion that Giddel unfairly distributes resources. We allow commerce among our kingdoms without interference. Our alliance has always been a peaceful one. You leaving the alliance will cause strife between more than just our two kingdoms. I beg you to reconsider."

Someone shifted in their seat. I leaned my head toward the grate to peek into the room. Mamá maintained a dead stare, and Lux walked toward the window behind Mamá. That broke societal rules. No one should ever cross the desk of another unless invited. I let out a shaky breath. What an insult.

"Queen Cottia, you misunderstand me," Lux said without turning toward Mamá.

Neither did Mamá turn toward him when she said, "We speak in circles. If I didn't know better, I'd believe you hold me hostage in my own office. Himzos will arrive, and the confirmation is in my daughter's words. One might assume you had something to do with it, though you claim you merely will not assist us in battle."

Lux ignored her statements and continued to peer out the windows toward the sea. His eyes scanned the horizon in such a way I imagined that he waited for someone to arrive. But who?

"I also assume you had something to do with my husband attending to matters across the sea. We both know that if he were here, he'd squash any skirmish before it even began." Mamá said it as a matter of fact.

My tongue stuck to the roof of my mouth. Lux would never betray us. He simply could not be Zichri's contact. His father yes, but Lux no. He loved me and Mamá. He even told me he aspired to be like Papá one day.

If I could speak reason into Lux, he'd even go against his father for me. I know it. He was willing to break ties with Alexa to form a betrothal with me. That would have caused much strife between him and his father. Without reconsidering, I kicked open the grate.

Mamá howled. "What are you doing here?"

I crawled through and ran toward Lux. His mouth hung open in, and his eyes grew playful. I grabbed his hands. "We've known each other since infancy. As a best friend, would you reconsider your plan of action? I'm certain we could come to an agreement that will leave us both happy."

"Bea, you know me. I don't have that much influence over my father. He makes decisions as he pleases. I am but a loyal servant to the crown." He searched my face in the same way he always had done. "This is nothing personal."

While his gaze twinkled with affection, I felt something different through our touch. A pulse of something malevolent swam in his heart. He must not have known that I had a gift to sense others. Was this what Uncle had done when he distinguished truth from lies? He had never told me how it worked.

Trying to smile, I said without considering my words, "Is this why you sent me away?"

He pulled his hands out of mine and looked out to sea. "Do you accuse me of leading you astray?"

"No, I'm asking if you had other motives for having me seek my gift." I bit my bottom lip. All this wasn't going the way I hoped.

"Did you get what you desired?" His mouth tipped to one side.

"No," I lied.

"Oh?" He lifted a brow and peered out the windows. I reached for him through invisible means. Any attempt to grab hold of him deflected. He grinned in my direction. "You lied to me about your gift."

My heart raced. How did he know? I shrunk back. "What do you mean?"

"I can feel you trying to use your gifting on me. Like I just finished telling your mamá, I cannot be manipulated by others." He looked past me.

Mamá pushed her chair back, scraping it along the hardwood floor. She stood up and flipped out her train. "Beatriz, you need to leave this room. I said I would be with you as soon as I could. You see that we wait for someone. We will not get anywhere with Prince Lux until his ship arrives."

A sharp pinch took hold of my ear and dragged me to the door. "I want to stay here."

Mamá opened the door and called for a servant. She scowled at me while we waited for a person to scramble up the stairs from the main floor. "Take her to her room by whatever means necessary. Make sure two guards stand at her door. They may use whatever is in their power to subdue her."

My eyes snapped wide open. "Mamá, please don't do this."

She pulled me in for a hug and said over my shoulder to the servant,

"I want guards at her door. Get Myla." She hugged tighter, watching another set of servants sprint down the stairs from the third floor. "I know about the Himzos. They still cannot defeat us without support from other kingdoms. You will be safer up in your room than with our enemy. Myla will lock the secret passages connected to this hidden corridor so you stay put. He can use you against me, and I won't have that." She let go.

Strong arms dragged me backward. Mamá nodded in agreement with the guard's method. My boots slid along the floor. I wiggled to get out of the man's clutches. "I'll walk on my own."

He released me, and I raced up the last flight of stairs, up to my room. There was no doubt in my mind that this man would do exactly as Mamá requested. Orders directly from the queen would not be disobeyed.

I sprinted ahead. The guard's feet pounded the steps trying to catch up. Upon reaching my room, I hammered my fist on the flower-carved surface.

Laude cracked the door open. "She is indispose—"

I wedged through and slammed the door shut in a guard's face. The man's stunned expression reflected my sentiments. Thrown out of the meeting room by my sweet mamá. Jailed and expected to sit by and do nothing. That may have been me before, but it was not me now.

CHAPTER 37

I DIPPED MY FOOT into tepid water. Goosebumps spread from my legs to my scalp. Hot or cold, Myla would have dunked and scoured me herself if I didn't bathe willingly. The water turned a nice shade of grayish brown. I scrubbed hard. It was a wonder Zichri hugged me with so many unpleasant bodily scents flying off my skin. I could have called Laude to get me the maid with the gift to heat water, but the other servants hated me, and maybe—just maybe—I could win them over by not being so needy. Why did I care what maids thought of me? I inspected my arms and stood.

Laude pulled out a thick robe and covered my body the moment I stepped out of the tub. She then waited for me behind a cushioned stool in front of my vanity. Using long strokes, she worked out the snarls knotted in my hair. My head jerked back.

"Sorry, Princess."

Tears gathered at the corners of my eyes. "The knots must come out."

Laude used smaller strokes, and ideas sprang into my mind. She braided a headband made of hair that swirled into a low bun. It made me look older, which could work in my favor if I followed through on the plan bubbling to life in my mind. "Thank you, Laude. It's perfect. Could you call on the male servants to dispose of the slops and summon fresh boiling water?"

Laude dipped her head with pinched eyebrows. I didn't explain myself, and she didn't ask. If she knew that the water was for her, she might not have done as I asked. My slippered feet clapped the tiles, and I stepped out from my bathroom onto the hardwood floor.

Two dresses lay on my bed. It was just like Laude to lay out two dresses. Both choices were covered with bold floral prints, screaming for others to notice me. I lifted the red one, about to put it on, then reconsidered. My plan wouldn't work with these gowns.

I rushed into my closet and searched for my riding pants, boots, and tunics. It was one rebellious luxury Papá allowed—for training purposes, of course. I plucked my undergarments, beige pants, and a white tunic off the shelf. Sliding each piece on, I whispered to myself, "You are bold and will not stand back."

The bedroom door clicked. I tiptoed to the closet door and peeked out. Laude entered with an army of servants. When would Mamá come to see me?

The servants marched out of my room without glancing in my direction. While they exited, the soldiers became visible, four guards. Laude shut the door, and I slipped behind my small desk, shifting papers.

Her round eyes took me in. "Princess, you did not choose one of the dresses. What would you have me do next?"

"I've grown accustomed to trousers." I tucked wispy hairs behind my ears, hoping she wouldn't guess what I devised.

"As you wish, Princess."

I hated the formal way Laude spoke. It didn't sound like her, and it aggravated me. I pulled her in a side hug and walked her to my bathroom. "I want you to bathe. Take as long as you like. Afterward, put on one of my dresses."

She squealed. "You can't be serious. Myla would rip the dress off me on sight. Please, miss, let me call for a servant's dress to spare myself the embarrassment."

"Whatever you choose. We are sisters at heart."

Laude clapped and skipped to the door to get a message out to another servant. I waited at my desk while she hopped into the bathroom, lining up the soaps and oils, squealing with glee. Someone knocked at the door. She bounded to it, frizzy curls bouncing on her shoulders in the perky way Laude exudes happiness. Blanca shoved a bundle in Laude's arms, a jealous frown on her face, and I waited back with arms crossed, suppressing a smile.

Laude tapped the door shut. "Thank you for bestowing such a gift. Could I use any of the soaps and oils I'd like?" She squeaked in delight at my nod. "Even the rose one and the creams?"

"Use any and all of it. Take as long as possible." I waved for her to go into the room. The moment she was in, I dashed to the edge of the balcony.

Across the horizon, the sun touched the flat rooftops, city walls, and the hilly grasslands beyond, revealing a perfectly golden day. Playful music mixed with the typical bustle on the narrow roads below.

Just as I pulled away from the edge, a smear of gray appeared in my periphery, and I gripped the balustrade. Far down the road, we had traveled early this morning, a group of soldiers marched. In a blink, more gray-clad soldiers appeared behind them, materializing from thin air. The Himzos had arrived. *So soon?*

Fear hammered in my chest—the extravagant plan I had concocted unraveled, leaving me with only desperate choices. I spun toward the stone on the palace. *Something must be done.* One large ledge traveled from my room all the way to the main balcony where announcements were made, and the other side of the ledge led to the watchtower.

I removed my boots and climbed up barefoot, facing the wall—gripping for dear life. Any misstep, and I'd tumble to my death. Concentrating on placing my feet, I scooted along. Left foot, right. I gripped the stones with sore fingers.

The world teetered. Nausea rose in my stomach. A gust of wind brushed at my back. I was halfway there. I persisted, even though a stitch of pain shot up my side. All the people I loved would die if I didn't keep going. With one final step, I swung open the watchtower window and climbed into a small round room with a rope at the center, which led up to the tower's warning bell.

I yanked the rope with all my might. Above me, the giant bell rung, vibrating the floor. I ran out the watchtower door and sprinted down a spiral staircase.

Sunlight poured in through a wall of windows along the lengthy corridor to the other tower—used as a lighthouse to indicate something was wrong at the castle. I pumped my arms. Time was short. A green-clad soldier blocked my way, but I picked up my pace. He wouldn't harm me. Moving out the way, curiosity seeped out his skin. I panted, climbing the spire of steps, eager to make it up to the other watchtower before anyone intervened. The man rushed just a step behind mine, and it hit me. I should have set the flame first and then the bell. It was too late to do anything about it now. A giant pile of wood sat on top of a high stone ahead of me. A tiny flame danced within an oil lamp hanging on the wall.

"What are you doing?" The soldier shouted, but he didn't dare intervene.

I smashed the lamp onto the logs. The wood caught alight, and the mirrors behind us reflected the blaze out to sea. Sweat beaded on my forehead. "Did you not see the Himzo soldiers across the way?"

"No." Doubt marked the wrinkles on his forehead.

"Don't you dare douse these flames. I wouldn't want the reputation of a soldier of the throne marred by how he could have helped his kingdom." I patted my hand on his chest. In an instant, I knew his heart raced at my touch. He tensed. Two fronts warred within him: one wanting the pride of saving his own people and the other appalled at the idea of not following protocol.

Satisfied, I rushed down the stairs. What to do next? I had completed my mission. I should head back to my room.

A strong pulse of energy surged through my blood, throbbing ... suffocating. I stuck my head out a window and sucked in a breath of fresh air. Trees jutted from the ground like spears, threatening to impale me should I fall. I leaned back into the corridor.

It was like a poisonous, invisible fog dropped over the empty space. Dread wriggled through my insides. *I can't stay here.* Do I walk to the front door of my room with all the soldiers standing guard? Surely, they would insist on remaining within my chamber when they find out I escaped. I gulped, realizing the ledge had become the only way back into my quarters.

"I see you've been busy," Lux called from behind me.

I twisted around. Lux clutched Mamá in his arms with a dagger pointed at her neck. Two of his soldiers followed behind him. The world I thought I knew shattered.

CHAPTER 38

"ODDS SEEMED IN MY favor of you not returning from your quest," Lux said. Mamá squirmed, and Lux held her tighter.

I tried to swallow past the lump in my throat. All the years I spent daydreaming about marrying him, and here he was before me. We'd been inseparable last summer. Mamá had been like a second mother to him. He had said so himself. Had I been blinded by my affections?

"I didn't go searching for a Himzo alliance," Lux said, voice calm and assured. "The king of Aldrin came to us with the idea, and since I am betrothed to Alexa, I felt obliged to listen." He whipped his head toward a scuffling of feet.

The young soldier came down the stairs, eyes widening. One of Lux's Pedrozian soldiers flung a dagger, and it landed with a thud. The only sound after that was a gurgling from the dying man's throat. I slapped a hand to my mouth and gasped. The soldier never had a chance.

Lux continued in the same placid tone. "All their reasoning struck me as true. Giddel thrives while Aldrin suffers want. Even my very own Pedroz would do well trading with the northern kingdoms. What stops us from trading with them?"

Heat vined up my face, and I fanned myself. "What if I can arrange a way for us to open up trade?" I knew Zichri could help me in that regard. *Imagine us in constant contact. Focus, Beatriz.*

"The only problem with that is they don't want anything to do with Giddel. I met with them right here at your ball." He heaved a sigh. "Himzos hate you more than you hate them. Everything about you is vile." The twisted expression on Lux's face transformed him into a stranger.

I wanted to slap him. "Lies. All lies. Is that why one of them danced with me?" I paused to observe his jaw slide from side to side. "There's something you're not saying."

He fixed a dead stare on me. "You know me too well."

"We're friends, aren't we?" I stepped closer in the hope of connecting with him. *It may still be possible to reach him, even with his overinflated ego.* Aldrin's king must have spoken sweet words of how he should lead the alliance rather than Papá. Power had always been Pedroz's undoing.

My crush made me blind to Lux. He and his father had always been two different sorts of creatures to me. But I was wrong.

Lux jerked Mamá back, and she yelped. A drop of blood dripped along her neck. If it weren't for him still having her in his arms, I'd batter him myself, even though I didn't know how to fight. Mamá lifted her brows in a way that got my attention. She closed her eyes, lips smashed together.

Lux yelped, and the dagger clattered on the floor. The two soldiers fell to the ground, writhing.

I inhaled sharply. *What in all Giddel?* She darted toward me, her blue dress billowing around her, and grabbed my wrist. One cock of her head sent us running up the bell tower steps. We slammed the thick wooden door shut, and I bolted it. She plunged a reinforcement plank in the brackets, locking Lux out and us in. Mamá and I panted.

Thoughts poured into my mind faster than I could speak. "What did you do? Did you cause my headache? I thought," I caught my breath, "you were a healer. Look, I'm shaking." I lifted my hands to show her.

She dragged me away from the door. "The two soldiers won't recover, but Lux can't be reached unless we have skin-to-skin contact. Yes, I am a healer, but there are some things I need you to know." Mamá's fingers dug into my sleeves.

"I can handle whatever you have to tell me." I put on a brave face. At least, I'd like to think I kept my expression neutral.

"Your papá's betrothed passed, and he had to choose another to be his queen."

"I know that story." *What does this have to do with her gift?* I rubbed my palms against my pants.

"Your papá did not meet *me* in court. I wasn't eligible to be in court, but I had taken a different route because I had no control of my gifting." Her dark eyes pierced with their intensity. "He found me sneaking around the palace. I knew who he was, so I used all my female arts to try to get myself out of trouble. He was amused and begged me to come to court so we could formally meet under no pretenses."

I considered her story for a moment. "Why would you sneak around the palace? He should have jailed you instead of *marrying* you."

She pressed her lips in a firm line, inspiring further questions. Good-standing noblemen and women have no need to sneak about unless she had less than reputable reasons for being within these walls.

She tossed her head back, unwilling to meet my gaze any longer. "Could we talk about the why later?" She let out a sigh. "I wanted to see what it was like to be accepted. Even after marrying your papá, I worked ceaselessly to garner the people's good favor, to make them forget he married a weakling."

My mouth fell open. Lux betrayed me, and Mamá wasn't accepted? My chest tightened. "You have such good standing now, and you heal wounds."

Something slammed the door. Lux shouted, "All will know that you slaughtered my guards. Our attack will be valid. No other kingdom will support you unless you come with me, Beatriz."

"And what about you holding a knife to Mamá's throat?" I hugged my midsection.

"That's hard to prove, and she started the violence," he said.

Mamá stepped toward the window with hunched shoulders. She never hunched. All those years putting up a strong front. "I did try to subdue Lux, but I lack control. Even now, I have more strength in harming people than in healing. Am I a beast?"

Should I try and use my gift to soothe her? I released my invisible tentacles, and Mamá's pain washed under my skin, making me feel how she felt. Shame swirled within her. I could give her a happy thought. The memory of me jumping off the boulder and into the river outside Valle de los Fantasmas came to mind. Joyfulness tingled out my skin. She darted a glance at me, clearly aware of my intrusion, but said nothing about it.

I reached for Lux, forcing the invisible tentacle through the door. Nothing.

"Nice try, Bea. You have a distinct way of pushing in. I'm curious, Bea. Did the Himzo prince and his band of miscreants chase you down?"

My ears perked up. Nothing good could come from admitting the truth.

"Yes, they must have," Lux said, playfulness touching his voice. "How else would you have known one of them danced with you? If you believe you can form a truce, that means you got *cozy* with them too." The way Lux said "cozy" insinuated something less than savory.

I balled my fists tight. My nails dug into my skin. Mamá put a hand on my shoulder, and I released my fingers. When I thought about it, she may have opened my fists for me.

"I assume your silence means it's true. I'll let you in on a little secret. The day after your ball, I thought to terminate the plan since you didn't seem all that convinced to leave. You still mean more to me than you know."

He had to be lying. Yet his words started stitching together a gaping wound inside me. I wasn't sure I believed him, but I wanted it to be true. Still, we could not trust him again.

"Say something, Bea. I could never have broken a betrothal with Alexa, but you seemed set on staying. I had suspicions that you desired more than friendship for years now. You leaving confirmed it … Do me this one favor?"

One of my legs bounced even when I tried to keep it still. Mamá's grip on my shoulder tightened. The worse part of all this was that a small part of me wanted to say yes to his favor, even still.

"Promise me you'll leave Giddel. It is under my authority to release prisoners of war. Let me see you, and you'll know I'm sincere."

I shrugged Mamá's hand off and stepped toward the door.

"Don't you dare," she said.

"Trust me." I reached for the rope dangling in the middle of the room, pulling as hard as possible.

The room quaked with the gong of the bell, and the doorknob shook. Lux shouted, but his words sounded muffled. Mamá covered her ears. I slapped my hands over my ears also. Time seemed to stretch into a thin piece of thread as we waited. Waited for Lux to break in? Waited for help? I couldn't say.

A hum of bugles sounded in the distance. I flew to the window, and Mamá pressed behind me. The Himzo soldiers had made it to the city gates.

I shouted, "Does your gift work like Papá's?"

Mamá shook her head.

If Papá were here, he could immobilize an entire army of soldiers with a wave of his hand. Even with my gift, I was helpless to stop the incoming attack.

CHAPTER 39

FROM AFAR, I COULD see the flow of Himzos into Giddel. Our soldiers attacked the line entering, but we had small numbers. Where were the rest of our soldiers? Once the bell stopped ringing, the clash of swords and the clomps of hooves rang through the streets.

"Why hasn't anyone arrived to help us? Someone *must* have seen Lux dragging you up here." I leaned heavily on my elbows at the windowsill.

"I let all the soldiers go off to the front lines and had all the male servants protect the palace gates. I sent Myla to hide all the guests and women below." Mamá drew me into a tight hug and stepped back. "We could hope that Lux would mend his ways."

"Why didn't you cripple him from the start when he had his hands on you?" I shook my head, still not believing Lux to be this monster.

"I hoped for him to change his mind at seeing you. We had gone to your room, but you weren't there. He insisted on seeing who set off the bell. When we entered the tower passage, I noticed a change in his demeanor." Mamá poked her head out the window.

I followed her gaze. Soldiers in gray made it to the palace gates. Himzos. Some climbed the wall around the palace. Others clashed swords with the guards. The Himzos lugged a giant log and banged it against the front gateway.

I wiped my sweaty palms on my tunic. "What do we do?"

"When they come within range of my gifting, I may be able to knock them out as they enter the palace grounds. You, my dear, will need to practice using your gift. Follow your whyzer's instructions."

I bit my bottom lip.

"Just try to see what you could do to stop them." Mamá focused her attention on the gray soldiers. Many fell to the ground with the point of a finger.

I backed away, not wanting to see how easily she dropped the men, possibly killing them. Ships from the sea cut through the still waters. My heart fluttered with hope but stilled upon seeing red-uniformed men climb out—Lux's people. Another ship crested the horizon, but I couldn't see the flags from this distance. Is this why Lux stopped banging on the door? There was no time for wonder.

I turned my attention to the enemy soldiers at the gate. Mamá had already knocked out several dozens of them. A horse galloped to the gate with a rider dressed in golden-trimmed attire. Four other Himzos trailed close behind. It had to be Zichri and his men.

"Mamá, stop! Not those men." I pointed to the palace entrance.

Mamá crinkled her brow in confusion. "Many could die if we don't stop them."

"No. They are here for Laude and me." In a desperate attempt to save our servants, I stretched my hand out toward the gate, feeling the pulse of fear within our soldiers.

Go hide, hide, I whispered in my mind, infusing the words with the urge to keep out of sight. Hoping beyond all hope, I reached deep enough within them to quell the battle at our gate. Zichri and his men raced into the palace yard, but other enemy soldiers made it in with Zichri. I let go of my grip on our servants the moment Zichri entered the palace. "I don't care what you do with the rest of them."

Mamá continued to dispatch soldiers quicker than a skilled archer. Sweat dripped along her hairline.

I strode to the other side of the bell tower to see what happened at the coast. Soldiers in red streamed onto our grounds. How long had they been pouring in? I breathed heavily from the exertion it took to calm the soldiers at the gate.

Lux must have left to meet with his countrymen and the Himzos. Even if we got out of this tiny room, where would we hide? Myla closed off access to many of the hidden passageways. Lux also knew about them because of me. I groaned at myself. *Thoughtless, thoughtless girl!*

Would Zichri save me amid the battle? My breath caught, and a sharp thud banged against our door. I glanced at Mamá.

"I can't hold off the soldiers in front of the palace and the ones on the other side of the door. Try harder to subdue them." The desperation in Mamá's voice coiled my muscles into tight balls.

I hadn't been trying. The little bit that I'd done helped the Himzos and not our own people. Using my gift left me weak in mind too. Nevertheless, I needed to try something. I closed my eyes like I'd seen Mamá do earlier and extended the force farther and farther out of me.

An invisible current of force released from me—rolling out in weak waves. It flowed out the door and down the stairwell. I concentrated harder—a throbbing pulsed at my temples. Hitting a person and another person with my new sense, a connection formed. Invisible cords continued to form until my sense quivered to a stop. No matter how hard I reached, my gifting wouldn't stretch any farther. Could it be that I was spent or that there were no more people?

No time to think. I whispered through pressed lips, *Be still.*

The thud of the door stopped. It worked! I continued to whisper into each soul that walked into my invisible waves. One empty spot waded in the current I sent out. I had no control over him. A sharp thud sliced through the wooden door.

"Do something about that!" Mamá shouted at me.

"I can't. It's Lux."

CHAPTER 40

Mamá waved her hands out the window like a music conductor. My mouth hung open—soldier after soldier toppled to the ground. Even so, streaks of gray uniforms raced into the palace.

"Bea?" Lux's voice held the same loving tenor as always. "I tried to warn you with the pocket watch. Didn't you get it at the garden party?"

Yes, I remembered the beautiful pocket watch and the strange tune it played. How was I supposed to know it was a warning? Then the cogs in my mind aligned. Myla had understood his warning. I thought I had displeased her when she stormed out of my room.

If Lux was the one who had given me the watch, that proved that he wouldn't hurt me. Yes, he threatened Mamá, but he still had affection for me. He said so, and we had always been best friends. Why is Lux doing this?

Only if Papá were ... That's it. I massaged my forehead, fighting off a headache. Lux and I were like family. But there really was one logical conclusion. Why else would he need Mamá and I to come out of the watchtower? "He wants me to be his hostage."

Mamá continued to swoop her hands out the window. "Did you say something?"

"No one could bring down Papá. You were his first choice, but he didn't know about your gifting." My head spun, and nausea gripped my stomach.

Thwack.

I startled.

Thwack. Something pierced the door. I tugged on Mamá's silk gown. "Should we climb out the window? That's how I got here in the first place."

The ledge seemed thinner now that I looked at it from this angle. Another *thwack* ripped me from my thoughts.

"No, I won't see you fall in your haste." Mamá cupped my cheeks. "Give me strength to do what I must."

"What do you mean?"

She lowered her gaze. A tremor of fear trickled through her body and bristled up my back. There was a crack, and I flinched. A hole opened in the door.

Mamá straightened her back at the next hit on the door. The ax pulled out and landed again.

A bubble of fear bulged in my chest, and I spoke to it. *Be at peace.* A sensation burst in my ribs and oozed like the flow of blood rushing into a sleeping limb. Mamá's tension seemed to be easing without me. She moved her lips as if she spoke silently, and her palms glowed a fiery red. The aura growing within her went beyond personal gifting.

I drew closer, straining to make out her whispers.

"All things hold together in you. Let me be willing to do what I must for my people and family." She pulled away from me, nodding. "I dread personal encounters."

An arm reached in and removed the plank barring the door. Lux's face disappeared back into the dark stairwell. Mamá waited, her fingers splayed out in front of her face. She readied to fight. The door swung on the soundless hinges. Silence. A dark passageway gaped before us.

At once, Pedrozian soldiers flooded into our room and surrounded us. One soldier thudded to the ground. Then another. Mamá did it with a simple flick of her wrist, but more Pedrozians poured into the tight space.

I flung my arms up like Mamá, motioning my hands. I pictured the creature from the valley licking its chops. Every bit of the horror I had experienced trembled out of me. Mamá was on to something with this hand thing. I had better control of the invisible. Many soldiers hesitated to enter, but not Lux. Unlike the others, he got all the way through and grabbed my arm.

Mamá continued to flick her wrists, rivers of perspiration traveling the worry lines on her face. She started after me, but a soldier almost reached her. Crinkling her brows, she continued to knock out man after man—a mound of bodies formed at the door.

Lux and another fellow lifted me over the bodies. My legs fell. The soldier holding my legs had gone limp, but Lux clung tight. I flailed my arms and tried to drop to the ground, but Lux continued to drag me. More arms clawed at me, pulling me down the stairwell. I breathed short, quick breaths. Reaching for anyone or anything, my finger smacked into someone, and I pulled my throbbing finger back.

Sunlight poured in as they moved me out the stairwell, revealing the long corridor to the other watchtower. A soldier hoisted me over his shoulder. I reached deep within, trying to spread my gift like a current again, but the jostling and pain prevented me from any semblance of control.

A long line of red-coated men waited to get into the bell tower. It moved forward, but almost no one came down the stairs. Did Mamá kill the men, or would they recuperate? Maybe that's why she needed strength. *It's best not to think of those things now.*

Turning a corner, the burly man holding me ran through a maze of halls, passing paintings and statues I had forgotten existed. I twisted to get away, but the man's fingers dug into my legs. We neared the balcony floor, where Papá gave announcements.

Suddenly, I imagined them throwing me off the front of the building, which sent another burst of energy racing through me. I rolled my body, hoping to catch him off guard. He lost his grip. I hit the floor hard and landed in a heap. The soldier's boot knocked into my rib. Pain spread along my side. A short man took hold of my legs and continued to drag me. I twisted my hips, ready to race into a meeting room to get into the secret passages.

The burly soldier swept me over his shoulder again. I kicked and screamed. He raced into the balcony room with me pounding my fists into his back.

A line of Pedrozian soldiers stood against the wall in front of portraits of my ancestors. Himzo soldiers stood against the opposing wall. It seemed fitting that the Himzos would stand in front of my great-grandmother, Iris. She was known for constantly being on the move and also for killing a Himzo dignitary by mistake when she sneezed. It worsened political tensions. They didn't believe us when we explained that it was a mistake.

The soldier unloaded me from his back and set me on my feet. Himzos and Pedrozians stood at attention, staring. I rubbed bruised skin on my arms and legs. Two other men lunged at me, throwing cords around my wrists and ankles. Panic swelled within my lungs, but I swallowed it back down.

The men whispered amongst themselves. Stray words like *Prince Lux, new reign,* and *a ship* echoed through the hall. My stomach cramped, and the cord bit into my wrists. *Be brave, Beatriz.* I squared my shoulders but wilted at seeing all my enemies' gloating faces.

I whispered to the Ancient One, "Why did you give me my gift if it were to be so useless? I can't do anything." I inhaled deeply. My mind's eye filtered an image of the sea in a storm. Water crashed against the shores and took with it anything it touched. I exhaled, "Is this the image I'm to use?" I licked my lips. *Am I silly for thinking I am like the sea?*

The force within me burbled out, reaching for anyone around. I dragged back a slew of gaiety. Then, I crashed another wave of magic, and it pounded into the soldiers. They couldn't see it, but I knew they felt it. The moment I dragged away their joy, their foreheads wrinkled, and a frown settled on their faces. *What good does this do?* I didn't know, but I needed to try something.

The double doors from the palace entrance opened, and the men snapped upright, chins up and chests puffed out. The door frame made Lux appear like a walking portrait. His sandy hair tousled around his face, and his potent eyes fixed on me. His boots knocked on the floor.

"Your mother fights well." Lux chuffed and patted my arm. He continued to walk out the balcony doors. "Bring her out here."

The same soldier who lugged me from the watchtower lifted me again in the exact same undignified way. It ruffled my pride, being seen by all the sneering faces. I lashed out an invisible whip at one man who guffawed. He jerked back, touching his cheek. I couldn't take my eyes off the soldier's crinkled face and the red streak marking his cheek. What in all Agata?

"We waited for your father," Lux said. He pushed back wayward hairs from his face. "Your father will comply or lose his darling daughter."

I gritted my teeth. "You said that you wanted me to go free."

Lux's lips curled into a smug grin. "I would have said anything to get you out of that room. Your mother was my first choice, but she hid a very powerful gift. To think, we thought she could only heal a scab."

I spat at Lux's face. One droplet dribbled down his cheek. He wiped it, flashing narrowed eyes at me. I clenched my jaw.

Sets of footsteps stomped toward us from inside the room. When I looked over my shoulder, my heart stopped.

Zichri, Milo, Gonzalo, Blas, and Jaime swaggered toward us in a V formation, like ducks sweeping in from the north. With their attention fixed on Lux, I willed Zichri to look at me. The suspense squeezed my heart. Will he ally with Lux or save me like he said he would? Zichri threw out an arm in front of Lux, and Lux held fast to Zichri's forearm in a gesture of comradery.

CHAPTER 41

Lux's back faced me. He stood like a pompous peacock behind Papá's lectern on the balcony that overlooked Giddel. A red-haired man in uniform amplified Lux's voice by placing his hand, palm up, in front of Lux's chest.

"Good soldiers of Pedroz and Himzo, I declare our victory over Giddel."

Cheers erupted from the crowd below. I shuddered. Though I couldn't see who gathered because of how far back I stood, I heard the echo of gruff voices—a multitude of soldiers.

Lux pointed out to sea. Ships floated to the port, flying the green and blue flag of Giddel. "When King Ezer of Giddel arrives, he will bow to my will because he cannot touch me. He will not force his will on me like he does everyone else."

He spoke only of Papá like Cosme didn't exist. A bolt of dread struck my heart, realizing that Cosme and the Dotados could be dead. But Cosme had disappeared on secret expeditions many times before. *I hope he makes it back soon.* His power could send a spear straight through Lux's haughty heart.

Lux glanced over his shoulder and tilted his cocky chin high. He extended a hand out to the crowd below. "People of Giddel, remain under my rule, and you will see just how much this region will bloom, aligning ourselves with Himzo. Aldrin takes our side. Akkub takes our side. Uzen takes our side. All others will join us in their own time."

The ropes chafed my ankles and wrists. When did all these kingdoms meet to betray us? Had we been so blind? Cosme and Lucas must have had a clue with all the wards disappearing.

Lux looked over his shoulder with a contemptuous smile. "Your father has arrived."

I lifted to the balls of my feet, trying to see the shoreline. It didn't help. *What will Lux do next?*

"Prince Lux of Pedroz, I know you are up there." Papá's voice thundered through the air—someone amplified his words with their gift. "You will regret breaking our alliance. Leave now, and you may live—unlike your father, the *former* King of Pedroz."

Lux yanked the cord around my wrists. I started to fall, but he caught me. "Release her feet," he snapped at a soldier.

As the soldier sliced the bindings around my legs, I felt Lux's pain seep into my senses through our skin contact and grip my heart. With so many violent emotions sloshing through him, he had to have understood Papá's meaning all too well.

He set me upright, and our faces were only a breath away from each other. He still had those turquoise eyes, but they had grown dull and worn. His thin lips, which I had dreamed of kissing, now pinched with disdain. His glare swept over me as though I were a cockroach.

I should practice my gift on him and try to flick his pain into an agony. Could I physically harm him with my gift like I had the soldier? How had I done that?

Lux twisted me around before I could do anything. His roughness made it hard to concentrate. He pressed a dagger to my neck. "What say you to losing your daughter?" He spoke to the crowd as much as to Papá. "As I recall, you haven't had a chance to see her since her trip with the Himzos."

The words shrouded over me like the trees had in the Chupalma Forest.

"Good people of Giddel, she betrays you more than I." Lux flourished toward Zichri. "Did she not spend her time away with you, a prince of Himzo?"

I fixed my gaze on Zichri in disbelief that he would betray me less than a day after professing his love. His placid brown eyes examined my face before turning to the people below with a hardened set to his jaw. Zichri said, "Yes."

This dug at my heart just as much as Lux's betrayal. Why should Zichri lie about us being together this week? He told the truth. We hadn't known each other long. His main allegiance was to Himzo, not to me. Dreaded tears burned as I held them back. I couldn't let anyone see how his complicity hurt me.

"Face me like a king," Papá demanded.

Lux widened his malevolent grin, satisfied with himself. "You may enter. If you use your gift on even a servant, I will push your daughter off this ledge, and then I will do the same to the queen."

A deep-seated fury burned in my stomach. How could I have considered him a friend? His presence repulsed me. We waited in silence, a salty breeze whipping stray hair into my eyes.

I tried to concentrate like I had before, envisioning the sea, tentacles, anything, but everything distracted me. Voices in the crowd heckled Papá. Gonzalo cleared his throat, and Lux blinked more than usual. Blas tapped his boot and hummed a song we had sung many times on our trip together. The cords rubbed the skin on my wrists all wrong. How was Mamá holding up?

Boots scuffed within the room, followed by a soldier shouting, "The Lord of the Gifts!"

"All-powerful of Giddel, where is your sting?" Lux dragged me by the arm and entered the room to meet with Papá.

Every breath took effort. A force pushed on my spirit. Was this Lux's gift or Papá's? Stumbling to keep step with Lux, I remained docile so as not to incur wrath on myself in front of Papá.

"What do you want, Lux?" Papá marched up to Lux with hostility burning from his glare to the tips of his trimmed beard.

"You've come far enough, old man. Bow to me, and I will make your execution a quick one."

I snapped my head toward Lux. It never occurred to me what he had planned for Papá. Footfalls gathered behind us. I snuck a look over my shoulder. Zichri and his men drew near like fawning subordinates ready to fight Lux's battles. I twisted back toward Papá with my chin raised high. Those Himzos didn't deserve even a glance.

"Oh son, you are weak," Papá said. "Your reign will end poorly for you. All those in this room take note that I said these words." He lifted a brow, daring Lux to kill him on the spot.

Lux tightened his fingers around my bicep. He pointed the tip of his dagger at my neck. "Say it again, old man."

Papá's dark mustache twitched.

But Lux yelped in pain and released his grip. The dagger sliced into the flesh of my arm as it fell, and I screamed. Rivulets of blood trickled to my fingertips and splashed on the white marble. The sound of metal rang through the room. I whipped my head toward Lux, who arced his sword to strike Zichri, but Zichri parried the blow with his blade.

What just happened?

The air thinned, making it easier to breathe. I was certain Lux blocked our gifts from being used. Papá lifted his arms to each side of him, forcing the soldiers to stand against the walls like statues. Red anger raged out of his body. The clang of metal against metal filled the space. I stooped toward the forgotten dagger and sliced the cord wrapped around my wrists, hoping no one saw.

Lux glanced at his unblinking soldiers and lunged toward Papá. I shot to my feet when Blas and Gonzalo darted in front of Lux but froze mid-stride. Papá must have taken control. Lux wound his arm back for a killing blow to Blas, but Milo blocked it. Jaime appeared at my side, blade out and ready to defend.

Lux and Zichri continued to spar, moving toward the exit until they disappeared out the double doors.

"Why do you not help Zichri and end this fight now?" I turned to Jaime, but he was unmoving.

"Papá, these men are my friends. Let them help Zichri."

But Papá kept his arms up while stepping toward me. "Dear

Beatriz, you should not assume their friendship with you. This all may be a ploy to garner power for themselves."

I hugged Papá tight, realizing that he could execute each man in this room without differentiating my Himzo friends from the enemy. "Please, Papá. You could do as you please with the rest of the men, but do not harm these four and Zichri, the one who fights Lux." I placed a hand over Papá's heart. My skin shone like a gold coin in the sunlight. Had it been happening this whole time? It wasn't like when I made my oath or when I arrived in Giddel.

Papá's loving eyes filled me with hope. "I will do as you say. Where is your mamá?"

"She fights in the bell tower. Soldiers lined up to attack her, but she makes all of them fall."

Papá smiled with pride. "That's my queen."

"Should we get her?"

"I can't move from this room unless you want all these soldiers after us."

I considered for a moment. "Could you release these four Himzos? We can retrieve Mamá together."

Father examined my Himzo friends under his dark brows, seeming unconvinced.

I tapped Papá's heart, releasing the trust I felt for them.

Papá exhaled loudly. "Only because you ask."

Jaime blinked, Blas shook his head, and Gonzalo grunted all at once.

"Thank you, Papá." I flew to the doors. "Come now, good Himzos."

Milo raced toward me without the slightest hesitation. All the other men followed close behind him. The corridor was empty, but clashing swords echoed through the corridor. No one had won yet.

CHAPTER 42

PRESSED AGAINST WOOD PANELING, I allowed myself a breath before entering the tower corridor.

"You said you can feel the numbers we are up against," Milo murmured in an accusatory tone.

"I'm new to this. Give me a moment." I glared at Milo, who grabbed two handfuls of curls at the top of his head.

Growing waves of energy surged out of my body. I reached farther and farther from our spot outside the watchtower corridor. The invisible waves crashed into my small band of friends and away from me, but it stopped sooner than expected.

Blas grunted and gestured to Gonzalo, Milo, and Jaime. The fellows all nodded, and Blas led the charge, his companions in tow. The clashing of swords filled my ears. I stayed back. Within a matter of minutes, ten Pedrozian soldiers groaned on the floor. My mouth dropped open. It was one thing to know my companions were soldiers but quite another to see them in action.

"Mamá should be in the east tower. I need to go so she won't put an end to you on the spot." I sprinted, skipping over bodies strewn on the floor. Racing up the stairs, I shouted, "Mamá, it's me. Are you in there?"

At the top of the stairs, bodies mounded to my shoulders. Mamá stood in the bell tower, leaning on the wall for support.

"Beatriz." Mamá's voice sounded weak.

"I'm here with four Himzo friends. Come with us to save Papá." I pushed a body with all my might. The man flopped over, glazed eyes staring heavenward. I cringed, realizing I touched a dead body. Did the stain of death linger on my palms?

Blas and Gonzalo shoved the fallen soldiers to flatten the mound. Mamá stabilized herself with the wall as she stepped on the fallen Pedrozians. Each footfall sank down a bit, but she continued forward, pursing her lips and keeping her chin high. She hopped off the last body, almost tumbling down the stairs.

"Papá is in the balcony room," I said, reaching out to help her in case she stumbled.

The vulnerability displayed on Mamá's face made her look more beautiful than ever.

Without a single word more, we moved. Mamá stopped at the sight of the groaning soldiers over the hardwood. She waved a hand in front of her, ending their groans.

Blas whistled. "Whoa! I thought your father was the powerful one."

Gonzalo backhanded Blas's chest.

Mamá shared none of Blas's awe. She bent down and shut a soldier's eyelids while tears streamed down her face. I offered a hand to help her up, but she didn't budge. She let out a shuddering breath. Without me attempting to use my gift, a connection formed between us. A hollowness sank in my chest. I knelt and placed my arm around Mamá's shoulders. I pulled her into a hug.

Her warmth comforted me, providing hope that somehow, we'd survive today. She cupped my cheek and fixed her gaze on me. Her brown eyes sparked with a new flame as she wiped her cheeks. She stood and nodded, whispering something to herself. Stepping over the fallen, she pressed her shoulders back.

My connection to Mamá's sunken emotions began to shift with each tap of her boots. I rose to my feet, watching the blood-stained hem of her golden gown drag over the hardwood.

Blas arched his brows in shock. "Do you need us to assist you, or should we just stay out of your way?"

"I have a hunch that she doesn't need your help," whispered Gonzalo.

Mamá disappeared around a corner.

A clang drifted from deep within the palace walls. I turned down a different passageway to where I suspected Lux and Zichri fought. "Let's find Zichri."

We marched forward, corridor after corridor, hunting for Zichri. If he led these men and they fought off the Pedrozian soldiers so easily, he must be of equal skill to Lux. I hoped. But Lux had always been praised for his sparring skills. A fresh current of dread twisted within my gut. Our steps became a rhythm of stomping boots and my slapping feet, and we listened for any sign of swords crashing.

I imagined us charging forth like a storm marching across the sky. It descended, spreading its cover over all the land. Without thinking, an invisible string formed, tethering me to my Himzo friends. I inhaled the new information. A pulse of Milo's love for a woman pushed him forth. It made his stern face seem softer, even though he still furrowed his brows. Blas' brotherly affection for these men ran deep, Gonzalo's loyalty could not be broken, and Jaime was filled with anticipation and hope. I guessed his hope was for something to transpire between him and Laude.

It occurred to me that she may not be as safe in my room as I suspected. I pushed that thought to the side. After all, there were four guards outside the door, and Myla would have surely come for me first once she knew something was amiss.

I shuffled down the marble steps. Clashing and shouting grew louder the closer we got to the throne room. I pumped my arms and lifted my knees, racing toward the sound. Pushing open the arched doors of the hall, I entered a giant empty space. Sunlight poured in through tall windows, highlighting Lux's golden locks. Lux pressed a boot on Zichri's chest. Blood gushed out Lux's brow, but a puddle formed beneath Zichri.

Milo, Blas, Gonzalo, and Jaime stampeded across the ample room, but they wouldn't make it before Lux plunged his sword into Zichri. My feet stuck to the marble. Time slowed as Lux lifted his sword over his head, ready to sink it into Zichri's chest.

My mind's eye pictured a hurricane.

I threw my hands in the air.

Rage and desperation flowed out of me like flashes of lightning slashing a blackened sky.

Lux flew through the window and crashed somewhere outside. My heart stopped. Blas jerked his head toward me.

What had I done? I raced toward Zichri. His eyelashes fluttered as if he struggled to keep his eyes open, and I sank next to him. I placed my fingertips against his neck, and a weak pulse bumped against my skin. Blood continued to pool beneath his leg, too much blood.

"You can't leave us." I cupped his cheek, willing him to live, but my markings didn't even blink to life.

Cosme rushed into the hall, his Dotado companions close behind him.

"Get Mamá now! She's in the balcony room!" My voice came out forceful and desperate.

Beyond Cosme, Giddelian soldiers raced into the palace corridor. Cosme whistled to a Dotado next to him, and the fellow darted out the doorway. My brother hurried next to me, ripping his sleeve. He exposed the bloody wound, wrapped it with his sleeve, and tied the fabric tight. Blood soaked through the fabric.

"He needs a healer," Cosme said in a low tone.

"Mamá can heal him." I exhaled a quivering breath.

Dark strands of Cosme's hair flopped over his forehead. Dirt smeared his cheeks. A worry line deepened between his eyebrows as I sensed the pinch of doubt tethered between him and me.

My mouth grew tight. "Yes. She. Can."

Footfalls pounded at the doorway. My gaze flew in that direction. Mamá shot to Cosme's side and dropped to her knees.

Searching her face through a torrent of tears, I begged, "Please save him. Don't let him die."

Mamá placed a glowing hand over Zichri's wounded leg and closed her eyes. I'd never seen her heal more than a scrape or a nick, but today she had shown her ability to be far greater than anything I'd ever seen her do.

Zichri closed his eyes. The world around me spun. Did he faint? Was he dead?

I leaned in and pressed my lips to his. "Stay awake just a little longer. Healers can fix you. We still need to roam the forest together." Tears gushed, and snot ran down just as fast. I didn't care about propriety. "Just a little longer, Zichri."

He breathed out, "I love you."

I sighed in relief. "Save your breath. You are going to live." I plopped my head on his chest. "You will live. You must live."

Warm blood continued to soak into my trousers.

Mamá pressed her hand over Zichri's chest. Her touch glowed with orange heat that warmed my face. I gnawed my bottom lip, watching no change in Zichri's blanched face. He'd lost so much blood. Mamá trembled with strain.

Someone gripped my shoulder.

I flinched but didn't bother to see who it was, afraid to miss Zichri's final breath.

CHAPTER 43

"LET ME HELP," PAPÁ said in a steady voice.

I turned my gaze up. Papá squeezed my shoulder in a tender gesture. A string connected him to me, letting in waves of gentle sunshine that matched the compassion glistening in his hazel eyes. When had he arrived? A half dozen more Giddelian soldiers also stood among my Himzo friends in the grand hall. Beyond the doorway, Cosme's friends marched captured Himzo and Pedrozian soldiers, who kept their hands woven over their heads. Perhaps, I shouldn't have judged Cosme so harshly.

Lucas ran into the hall, disheveled, muddied, bloody, with a gash running across his forehead. He crouched beside my brother. "Cosme, they're retreating."

Zichri wheezed, and it drew me back to our situation. Mamá shook, her hands glowing a fiery red over his chest.

"Mamá ..." I didn't know what else to say. Deep inside, I wanted Zichri to live, but I didn't want it at her expense.

Papá placed a steadying hand on Mamá's shoulder. She still trembled, but not so vigorously. Cosme clasped Papá's shoulder. A second later, Mamá opened her eyes. Lucas patted Cosme's back, and the effect was immediate. Mamá pressed her shoulders back. Another soldier I'd never met before joined, and a chain formed.

I had never seen anything like it. The room flooded with power—a sensation of gentle warmth. I held Zichri's hand, and a current pulsed through my body, which I shifted to flow into Zichri. His breath steadied. The beat of his heart strengthened. I brushed his hair from his forehead. Caressing his cheek, I whispered, "See, you can't leave us, not like this."

When I raised my gaze, Gonzalo, Blas, Milo, and Jaime had joined the chain. Blas connected and disconnected his fingers from the soldier in front of him. He had the look of a boy receiving his first real sword as he watched the bright current, rushing like mini lightning bolts from his fingertips. Gonzalo swiped his cheeks with his free hand, and Milo yanked on his curls with moons for eyes. I'd be surprised if Jaime saw much of anything beyond his tears. The whole room illuminated with the brightest, glistening light I had ever seen.

"Beatriz," Zichri whispered.

I turned my gaze to his face. I swiped my cheeks, unable to contain the deluge pouring down.

"I told you I'd come back," he drawled. "The forest awaits."

I clung to him, laughing.

Mamá cleared her throat. "Darling, Cosme needs to take him to the hospital room. He's going to need recovery time. His wounds are deep."

Cosme lifted a hand, levitating Zichri from the floor. I followed close to his side, blood splashing on my bare feet. A soldier clapped. More followed. Invisible strings tethered to my senses, pouring over me the warmth of their jubilation.

I glanced back and slipped on a patch of blood. Mamá steadied me, nearly slipping herself. However, Milo and Gonzalo swooped in, holding tight to our arms, while Blas and Jaime followed closer than a shadow.

We crossed through the bustling main corridor with vaulted ceilings and grand paintings of the Giddelian city and countryside. Several men gasped. Himzo soldiers slowed their pace as they watched their prince levitated. Milo and Lucas stopped to talk with a Giddelian captain when we turned into the back corridor. After several paces, we entered the infirmary hall.

Beds lined the outer walls, and servants erected a center aisle with squat cots.

Cosme lowered Zichri onto a plain bed. Nurses raced to Zichri's side. I reached for his hand, but Mamá barred my way with her body. He seemed so defenseless and unawake to the world.

"Let the nurses and healers work on him. There was much I left undone." Mamá's tired eyes saw through me like they always had. "But nothing."

"Is he going to make it?" I sensed her trembling spirit weaving into my own anxiety.

She sighed. "Healing hands don't bring back the dead, and he nearly died." Tucking a stray hair behind my ear, she added, "But, he's strong."

"I can't leave his side."

"You must." Mamá flicked a look past me at Blas, Jaime, and Gonzalo. "All of us must leave the room. Many more wounded will be brought in, and we mustn't be in the way."

Three healers and a nurse touched and prodded Zichri's body. Blas climbed a window sill on the outer wall to get a better view. The others stayed back, watching small bruises disappear at a simple touch. Zichri winced at each new healing, sometimes groaning in pain.

"Could I at least say a parting word so he knows I'm not leaving him? Please?" I leaned my head on Mamá's shoulder.

She cupped my face. "Make it quick." Then she signaled to Cosme, who stood with Zichri's group. "Himzo boys, come with me."

Blas argued from his spot at the window, but one stern look from Mamá, and he shut his mouth. They weaved past dozens of hospital beds before exiting. I waited for them to leave. It felt more private this way. Only a few servants stood against the wall. I tapped a healer's back, and he moved to the side without me having to say a single word. Zichri cracked open his eyelids.

"You're in good hands. I need to leave, but I will be back. Mamá says it will take time for you to heal." I squeezed his hand and laced my finger with his.

One cheek dimpled. "You bring me back to the cave." The drowsy way he spoke concerned me.

"We gave him something so he can sleep," A frizzy-haired nurse said. "No worries. He should be fine. I have a good eye for the survivors." She flapped a hand toward me, then back to Zichri. "I know we don't like to promise anything, but things are looking good. Sorry for reading your thoughts, it was impertinent of me, but your mind is racing."

I unlaced my fingers from his, observing the wild-haired nurse with her bright eyes. The idea that she could see what I was thinking made me squirm inside. I had only read about people who had that gift. Could she be lying?

"No, dear, I'm not lying. It's a weak gift because most people learn how to block me out. Just so you know, this fellow thinks about you a lot. I'm enjoying his little daydream about sitting next to a campfire."

Heat burned in my cheeks. I turned around, trying to hold back my thoughts, if possible. I took one long look at Zichri while standing at the exit door. The nurse grinned in a way that plumped her cheeks. It reminded me that I needed to find Laude.

CHAPTER 44

THE MOMENT I LEFT the infirmary, I had one thought drumming through my mind: *Find Laude.*

A line of soldiers in gray attire sat outside the infirmary, some with gaping wounds and others with desolate gazes. It was as if guiterna strings were latched to my chest. Invisible cords connected me to each man and played a bleak song. Ruffled pride. Twisting pain. Confusion. The sheer number of connections left my head spinning. I longed to rip the gift from my body and focus again. I took a deep breath and exhaled.

Blas, Gonzalo, Jaime, and Cosme turned into the main corridor, disappearing around the corner.

Mamá stood, hands clasped in front of her stomach. "Are you well?" Her knuckles grazed my forehead.

"Where would Laude and the other servants hide?" My heart raced, waiting for Mamá's response.

The corners of Mamá's lips lifted. "She's most likely in the servants' quarters below. If she's not there, she may have escaped the palace grounds."

Oh, Ancient One, let her be here and safe. I strode around her, determined.

"Take my shoes." Mamá removed her leather slippers. "Your feet are much more exposed than mine."

"But Mamá—"

"Say nothing more." She shoved the pair into my hands and kissed my forehead. "Your skin glows."

I flinched, taken aback by her random comment. My skin didn't radiate like Laude's or Mamá's, but it glistened along my markings like water on a sunny day. With all the rush, I hadn't taken the time to observe the gentle way my skin revealed my gifting.

I stuck my dirty feet into Mamá's shoes. My toes curled to fit into the small slippers, but this would do. "You're sure you won't need them?"

"Go find Laude." The earnest spark in her brown eyes and the urgent flow of worry washing through my senses let me know she was just as concerned as I.

"Thank you, Mamá."

Every step past sweaty and bloodied bodies frazzled my nerves. I crossed Gonzalo and Jaime carrying a dead Himzo soldier. Blas helped a healer hold her supplies as she put a radiating bright hand over a man's chest. Milo, Cosme, and an older man yelled. Milo held a hand full of frizzy curls, pointing at his countrymen. I escaped into a servants' stairwell before I could make out what they said.

Down, down the stairs I went. Servants raced up, forcing me to move to the side. A metallic odor mixed with sweat grew thicker the farther I descended. I turned a corner into the servants' quarters. It was a beehive, filled with wounded servants tending to other wounded servants.

Myla appeared in a doorway. She looked around at the chaos before her eyes landed on me. She swept toward me. "What are you doing here? You should get some rest. I'll walk you to your room." She dabbed her forehead with a handkerchief.

"No, I came to find Laude. Is she here?" I found my eyes darting glances through each doorway.

My breath stilled at my old maid's inquisitive stare. I imagined my emotion feeling tentacle reaching out to her but pulled away. How could I use my gifting after seeing what it could do?

Myla sighed. "Laude's at the far end of the corridor, tending to injured servants." She pointed to the rooms beyond the kitchen nearest the exit to the beach.

My feet moved of their own accord over the rough stone flooring. The beach door, now missing, yawned open to the outside, which fell in heavy shadow. Sand stuck to the crevices beneath me and gritted against the leather soles of Mamá's shoes. Servants raced back and forth carrying pots of water and another with soiled linen. I continued to peek in each packed room, every time seeing beds holding bloodied bodies.

Servants pressed their hands to water kettles, heating the metal. Their powers cast light over the edges of the room, reflecting off the sweat and grime coating their bodies. One water summoner fanned herself while slumped against the wall. I seemed to float past the kitchen area in my haste.

Only four more servants' rooms remained. A moaning man lay in the first room. Blanca prayed on her knees over a lifeless body in the next. *Two more.* My palms slickened. Should I use my gifting? I hesitated, remembering Lux's body flung through the window. I tightened my fists and peered into the room on the right. Two women slept in beds. Darkness covered their features since no candles had been lit. I turned to the left, to the last room, half expecting to see just some other ragged maid.

Fiery curls sprang out a rather shabby braid. Laude sat next to an injured man and tipped a cup to his lips. Besides a few bruises on her body, she appeared intact.

All tenseness left my muscles. "I worried about you. What happened?"

Laude whipped her head toward me. Her eyes sparkled. "Princess!" She set the cup down, sprang to her feet, and skipped the three paces between us. Her arms flew around me, and she squeezed so tight my back cracked.

"I'm sorry." She pulled away. "So sorry, but I didn't know if you died or if you were stolen or if you'd done something rash again. When I got out of the bath, I saw that you were gone, and I didn't know what to do. Myla came in through the hidden passages to get you, but she got me. And I worried so much about you, but Myla insisted I go with her down the passages. We did what we could to stop the soldiers, and—"

I hugged Laude to cut off her rambling, and at the same time, loving that she hadn't lost her joyful spirit. Nothing kept Laude down for long. "Could another tend to this man?"

"Yes, I suppose."

I dragged Laude by the hand.

"Princess, where are you taking me?" She giggled.

We dodged out of people's way, almost crashing into the cook.

I grinned at Laude but said nothing. She might not know about Jaime and all the Himzos being heroes. We shuffled up the stairs and into the main atrium.

The space had emptied. Only a dozen or so Giddelian soldiers remained.

My heartbeat quickened. "Come on, Laude, I want you to see one of our heroes."

We dashed to the infirmary. Many more beds had been filled with bloodied soldiers from the Himzo and Giddelian lines. I steeled myself from any connection to them, already sensing waves of sorrow and pain crashing over me.

Zichri's sleeping form came into view.

Laude gasped. "What happened? Is …" She trailed off, chin quivering.

"He's safe, but I don't know what happened to the others. They were all here."

Laude bit down on her bottom lip. Her eyebrows pinched together with worry. Even with me attempting to put a barrier over my gifting, a shrill note pierced my soul, and a single word echoed in my mind: *Jaime.*

How I wanted to see Jaime and Laude reunite. I would not let her out of my sight until then. "Come now, we should figure out what happened to everyone."

CHAPTER 45

"SISTER, YOU MUST REST." Cosme blocked me from entering the grand hall. Candlelight danced in his eyes, and a heavy shadow fell on half his face as he stood in the doorway with his hands on his hips. Two more of his Dotado friends leaned against the doors. Their faces looked familiar, but I hadn't bothered to get to know any of them.

I craned my neck to see past him. Shadowed figures lined the floor, but I couldn't make out any features. Only a few lamps had been lit.

"Cosme, please. Let me through." I stepped around Cosme.

He clasped my shoulders. "I'll escort you to your room." He whistled to a tired-eyed Sir Lucas. "Can you transport us up?"

Lucas grabbed ahold of Cosme's forearm with a limp smile tugging up one of his cheeks. "Ye—"

"That's all right. Laude and I can walk," I said. Something unsettled my heart. Had it been other people's twists of emotions knocking into my chest? I pulled Laude's hand and stomped through the main corridor and to the base of a wide stairwell.

Upon seeing the many stairs we'd need to ascend, I thought my knees might buckle. A long breath slipped between my lips. I climbed.

Each step pounded in a new fear. What if Mamá did not approve of Zichri? Even worse, Papá might ban me from seeing him again. What if Zichri's father held us responsible for Zichri's injuries? What if Zichri was considered a traitor? The Himzos did lose the battle.

Laude and I trudged the second set of stairs. My mind raced with ways to convince Papá to approve of a betrothal between Zichri and me. It seemed easier for us to run away, living out our dreams in the woods, with no politics—no worries. We'd be free to make our own choices. That would never happen living in Giddel. What if Zichri asked me to move to Himzo? I could never do that either.

Corridor lamps shone on the giant doors to my room, and each of my muscles relaxed. My body knew what to expect upon entering. Laude pushed open the glistening wood.

The balcony doors let in a cool breeze. Laude tapped the wick of my bedside lamp, sparking a flame to life. My canopy bed was in the same place as always, but it somehow felt too big. I had been here earlier today, but my entire life had shifted even more since then.

Laude laid out a simple chemise.

"Where will you sleep tonight?" I peeled off my slippers.

"I'll find a place to lay my head. After sleeping in hammocks in the woods, I'm sure I can handle sleeping in a palace, Princess." The playful ring to her voice lightened the tightness coiling inside of me.

"Please, stay in my room tonight. You can sleep in my bed. It's much too large after so many nights in a hammock." I lifted my index finger when she began to protest. "I will not take no for an answer. Plus, you need to tell me what happened during the battle."

Laude couldn't resist an invitation to talk and talk she did. I changed for the night and lent Laude a chemise. As we wiped our feet and braided our hair, I listened to every agonizing detail about how the servants launched attacks using the secret tunnels. She went on and on and on. I considered practicing my gifting while she spoke, but that would intrude on her privacy. And really, everyone should be allowed some privacy within their own skin.

We finally slid under the duvet and sunk into the silken bedcovers. Laude put out the lamp flame. Darkness covered us while a churning sensation circled within my chest, sending a riptide of emotion throughout every part of me. Laude's voice hummed on like a melody to comfort an achy soul.

But even she couldn't keep me from reliving all that had transpired:

The blank stares of soldiers fallen over marble floors. Lux's smirk before he attempted to murder Zichri. My hands from whipping out my panic and launching Lux through a window.

Laude yawned. "Goodnight. Don't let the nightmares give you a fright."

"Goodnight, Laude," I said breathlessly.

Laude had broken me out of my thoughts, and I grasped for happier memories. Even picturing Zichri's handsome smile couldn't stop my jaw from quivering. I needed peace that could calm the storm raging from the ache at my temples to a throb on my little toe.

So I did the only thing I could think to do.

"If it isn't too much to ask, could you, Ancient One, help me rest?" I whispered. The words didn't have the right feel in my mouth. Almost like I bit into a hollow chocolate when I expected something more. "Why did you give me my gift? I didn't deserve it. Look at what I did to Lux." Quick tears slid down my temples. "But if I would have done nothing, Zichri would be dead. Am I an awful person?"

The weighty shroud over me lifted the more I spoke until finally, I drifted to sleep.

CHAPTER 46

I AWOKE TO BULKS of forest green fabric, and golden swirls stretched overhead. I was home. This was my bed canopy. My sore body screamed for me to stay in place.

Dull light bathed the gold duvet since we had forgotten to pull the bed curtains shut. A strong gust of wind chilled my skin, and the balcony door tapped the wall with each new breeze. I yanked up my covers. Next to me, Laude's wild curls splayed all over the pillow. I wished I could sleep so deeply.

Myla entered and tiptoed across the bedroom. "Princess Beatriz, are you ready to start the day?" She closed the balcony doors, but they continued to rattle.

"Does Mamá call?" I croaked.

"Ahhh, I wondered where Laude found rest." A pinched expression crossed her face. "Yes, your father called an assembly. She also wanted you to know that Zichri awoke."

I threw the covers off my body. "Help me get dressed."

Myla lifted her chin high. "Wake Laude." A grimace touched every line on her face. "I have much to attend to."

Anger boiled in my stomach. "I asked you, Myla. She will not work today because she needs her rest."

"As you wish, your Highness." Myla scowled but buttoned the back of my dress and braided my hair. I ignored her foul manners since all I wanted to do was get ready as fast as possible.

I flew down the stairs. The outer layer of my red dress floated behind me. Soldiers, servants, and townspeople continued to buzz around the cavernous atrium: cleaning, fixing, and gathering waste. A broad-shouldered man shouted, "Should we remove the wicked prince from the post?"

I flinched. They were referring to Lux. I headed out the palace entrance against the current of people, feeling like a fish swimming upstream. The bustle of voices mixed into the background. I should have gone straight to Zichri, but I couldn't help myself. Seeing might give me a sense of finality to this whole nightmare. Sweet memories with Lux building sandcastles and playing pranks swam into my mind. Did he ever really care about me?

A crowd gathered at the stakes. Cosme had placed them outside the palace when he went on a decorating frenzy. I stepped from under the entrance portico.

Blood dripped from Lux's impaled body. I turned my gaze away, but the image branded to my memory. His stiff arms. The agonizing grimace. My heart hammered against my breastbone.

I cupped my hands over my mouth, gasping.

I did that to him.

Running back in, I rammed into servants and soldiers trying to get away from the horror outside. I slammed into someone's back and tipped backward. An arm caught me before I hit the ground.

"Princess, do you need me to call for help?" The man squinted with concern. He wore a ruffled shirt like all the royal servants.

"No, I merely got a fright." My voice trembled. "Please, have someone take down the prince's body from the stake."

"Of course, Your Highness." He dipped his head and escorted me through the crowd before relaying the message to another servant.

I felt disoriented and began wiping my palms on my gown. My hands felt filthy after seeing what they had done.

Why had I come down? Zichri. I jogged toward the infirmary, leaving the servant behind.

Upon entering, the frizzy-haired nurse lifted her head from

attending a soldier near the entrance. "Good morning, Princess. Your beloved prince waits for you."

A curtain surrounding a patient blocked my view of Zichri. Palms sweaty, I wrung them on my skirt, unsure how this would go. I turned down the row of beds near the back wall. Zichri fixed his sight on me, and I swallowed hard. He had the same effect as always. At least some things didn't change.

In a hoarse voice, Zichri said, "Good morning, love. I hope I didn't dream everything from yesterday. Some details are hazy."

I sat next to him, stiffer than I'd imagined. The sight of Lux's mangled body took something from me. "What do you hope to be true?"

He reached for my hand. "That you love me."

"Yes. I said that." I let out a shaky breath.

"What's wrong?" He grazed his thumb along my knuckles. "Something disturbs you. I hope it's not me."

"No, no ... I just saw Lux's body. I have never killed a person before. And though you saw the darker side of him, I had considered him a friend since childhood."

Zichri wrapped his fingers around my tiny hand but said nothing for some time. Moisture trailed along my nose, onto my lips, and dripped from my chin.

The buzz of people talking, walking, and tending the injured continued all around. I kept my head low until the tears stopped. Zichri quirked a sympathetic smile, still holding my hand.

"Princess?" Laude's voice came from behind me. "Your father is set to address Giddel from the balcony soon. Lady Myla sent me to retrieve you."

Zichri met my gaze, and my stomach did a flop. I didn't want to move. "Duty calls." I rose and knocked into Laude.

But she didn't move. Her sight fixed on a spot close to the exit. I followed her gaze and found Jaime watching Laude. He stepped forward and rammed into a nurse, toppling her tray. He then rushed to help the nurse and piled the equipment back onto her tray. Laude covered her mouth with a dainty hand, failing to hide a nervous giggle. I gently squeezed her elbow, settling a riptide within her soul to peaceful waters.

She smiled at me. "Thank you, Princess. I think I needed that."

"How much time do we have?"

"An hour or so, I suppose. If you don't bathe." She bounced on her toes with excitement. "And if you don't change gowns."

"Meet me upstairs when you're done talking to Jaime." I fluttered my lashes to tease her.

"Oh Princess, I've never been so happy." She pranced toward Jaime.

He wrapped his arms around her like he'd never let go. "This," he said. "This makes yesterday worth it."

The plump nurse came by with an unveiled stare.

"Could she not show some sense of decorum?" I snapped, loud enough for the nurse to hear.

Zichri squeezed my hand. "Don't lash out. I had said something to her, and she asked me a question."

"Is that so?"

Zichri smoothed his face with his dark brown eyes wide. He blinked a few times, and a deep crease formed between his eyebrows.

I playfully slapped his shoulder. "You're acting secretive."

"It might not be the right time." He rubbed his thumb over my knuckles.

A biri-biri-bum started in my chest. I pinned him down with a look. "Zichri?"

"As I understand it, you were in search of a suitor, and it was your choice who you would marry." Zichri's eyes glimmered.

I tried to smother a grin but tittered when he lifted my chin. Stray tears slipped down my cheeks without my permission.

"Is that a yes? Will you have me as your betrothed?"

I nodded, unable to clear my throat. Though he lay on an infirmary bed and my home was in shambles, this moment was perfect. I could never have imagined this. He chose me, and I chose him. The match was one of love. I was sure we could make our match politically advantageous, but that did not matter. All the details about how we would live didn't matter as long as we fought for the love between us.

CHAPTER 47

THE WIND WHIPPED OVER the balcony at the palace. I tucked my rather large flyaways behind my ears, darting a glance at Laude. A grin touched every line on her face, and her unruly curls danced like flames through the air. Though our appearances could have been better, I didn't regret spending more time by Zichri's side earlier that day.

I rubbed my palms along my emerald dress and rubbed at the golden embroidered hibiscus lining the hem of my top skirt. The golden bottom layer shone in the midday sun with an intensity sure to be seen on every rooftop in the town below.

Giddelians flew the emerald flag with the golden hibiscus through the winding streets. Guiterna melodies collided with so many musicians playing different traditional ballads. Guiros made their rat-ta-tat-tat. Tambourines vibrated like the players skimmed the surface with their thumbs over and over again. Girls danced on balconies, and boys reenacted the fighting at their mothers' sides. I took a step forward and craned my neck. Even within the palace grounds, Giddelian soldiers stood shoulder to shoulder, awaiting their king.

Papá stepped through the doorway and met my gaze. I stepped back. He winked an amber-green eye at me and swaggered a few paces to the balustrade. His emerald robe brushed the stone floors while white furs with black dots encircled his shoulders. He held his back erect and placed a hand on the hilt of his sword.

Mamá appeared beside me, holding herself rod straight and

wearing the same dignified pout I always sought to emulate. Cosme rushed to Mamá's side with Sir Lucas and three more of the Dotado fellows. Behind them, Milo, Jaime, Gonzalo, and Blas lined up, hands clasped in front of them and feet a handbreadth apart, like they'd practiced this stance many times before.

I dropped my chin. What did this mean that Papá and Cosme invited our Himzo friends to a place of honor?

A short man rushed around the onlookers on the balcony and neared Papá. He placed a glowing palm up in front of Papá's chest, ready to amplify his voice.

"Good people of Giddel, yesterday our courage was tested. Kingdoms we loved and kingdoms we hated joined together to bring us to our knees." Papá raised a brow in my direction. "Those of you we thought weak proved strong. Those of us who thought themselves strong proved their courage." He glanced at Cosme. "The Dotados suspected forces worked against us, and I slacked in doing my due diligence to investigate. For that, I am sorry." His breath caught. "Those we lost will be mourned. Our one comfort, Prince Lux of Pedroz, was brought down by six unlikely heroes. Princess Beatriz of Giddel and her five Himzo friends." Papá gestured toward me and then toward the Himzos.

Applause abounded.

"Bravo!"

"Viva Princess Beatriz!"

A blush crept up my neck. I worked hard to steel my emotions so that the praise wouldn't bloat my ego ... So I would never be accused of being selfish again.

Papá signaled with a finger, and the applause and praise quieted. "I promise to you all, I will work to settle an agreement to benefit Giddel and Himzo. We will test the loyalties of the kingdoms around the Agata Sea. We will bring unity to this region once again."

The strength in Papá's voice bolstered my confidence in a future where Himzo and Giddel could finally be at peace. Nevertheless, that peace may not have meant allowing his beloved daughter to become the bride of a Himzo prince.

I twirled red, green, and blue braided ribbon in between my fingers while sitting on my balcony settee. Laude had started teaching me how to braid, but Myla interrupted us. Somehow, Myla guilted Laude into working, even against my wishes. I should be happy, though. Myla had forgotten her threat to whip her.

My door latch clicked, and footsteps padded toward me. My mother's formal expression launched me to my feet.

"I knew you'd come soon," I said as I brushed my palms down the emerald silk on my dress, unsure where to begin. Ask about Laude? Or that nagging question? It's strange how Mamá, who once seemed so familiar, could feel like a stranger. I took a breath and cleared my throat. "Laude's mamá was married. Could Laude marry?"

Mamá's brows furrowed like she expected a different question. "Laude's mother is a story for a different day. And no. Laude cannot marry in her current position." Her expression broke into a warm smile. "But that can change." Her reassuring tone bolstered my courage.

I released my breath, satisfied. "You said that your gift was weak. But you annihilated the Pedrozians and Himzos without even touching them."

Mamá leaned an arm against the white doorframe and looked over my balcony. The sun dropped over the horizon, painting the most dazzling pink-tinted sky. She stepped toward me, full of her usual grace. Flipping out the tail of her emerald gown, she took a seat on the settee next to my ribbons. "Come sit. You pry. I can feel you drawing out information."

"Really? Lu ... Someone said the same thing." I mimicked her delicate way of sitting. "What does it feel like?"

Mamá grabbed my forearm and dragged her hand over my palm, forcing it open. "It's like a tug. Your Papá described it like someone snatching his tunic from his back." She watched my expression, waiting for a response.

"I presume I need to work on being gentler." Flipping my braided hair to one side, I twirled the loose ends.

"Sit up. It's unbecoming for you to slouch." Mamá folded her hands in her lap as if my perfect posture would make this conversation easier. "That brings me to the matter of your gifting. Didn't your whyzer teach you how to use it?"

I flinched. "I don't even know exactly when I received it or what it is." It may have happened upon entering Giddel, or it could have been when Zichri caught up to us on the road.

"Let me understand this. You went to Valle de los Fantasmas?" She checked for my nod. "You met with your whyzer, and he didn't give you instructions?"

The shock in her voice echoed through me. I rolled my shoulders back, trying to find the most succinct explanation. "He refused to give me the gift and sent me away. We left the valley. Laude and I snuck into the Himzo encampment and raced back with the information. When I arrived at Giddel, I had the gift." I watched Mamá blink more than usual before adding, "Why is that so shocking? How did you get your gift?"

She pursed her lips, agitated at the sharp turn in the conversation. This conversation was supposed to be about me, but I needed to know why she led me to believe she had a weak gift. She had always said that the whyzer arrived when she was five and her sister was three. He ate dinner with the family, said some special incantation over the girls, and they each received a gift. That explanation now seemed too short. Somewhere she learned to do harm rather than heal.

"Mamá, how did you learn to use your gift so well?"

"You mean, how did I learn to kill with ease?" She lowered her head.

"I thought you only could heal small wounds. Do you blame me for wondering?" I made sure to keep perfect posture, as not to distract her from talking.

Just when I thought to cut the silence, Mamá said, "After your grandpa passed, we had no money. Our home fell into disrepair, and we couldn't afford the luxuries to which we were accustomed. A man with gnarled hands arrived, saying he'd pay me to use my gift." Mamá laughed humorlessly. "At the time, Mamá had trained me in the basics of healing, but I could barely do even that. Our whyzer had spent more time with your Aunt Isabelia. I was ten years old and thought the visitor wanted me to fix his hands. Mamá let the man in and heard what he had to say."

I considered for a moment, rubbing the hairs that prickled on my arms as she spoke.

She turned her face to the sea. "From ten years old to sixteen, I learned a different use for my gift and made no progress in healing. Our family got paid very well, but I could barely lift my chin from how embarrassed I was of who I had become. I met your Papá, and everything changed for the better."

"That doesn't explain why you call yourself weak." I lowered to the floor, sitting on my haunches and placing my chin on Mamá's lap.

She dipped her head further down. "It's easy learning to destroy, but not to put back together. Many healers worked with me on more challenging tasks. Until Zichri, I thought I had made no gains. He was so close to death." She patted my hands and lifted her glistening eyes. "You have a deep affection toward the Himzo prince, don't you?"

I gulped. How I hated laying out my heart. "Yes. He saved my life in more ways than one."

"I understand."

"You do? In what way?"

"Your Papá in his own way helped me see how I'd become a slave to money. Before he ever saw *me* in court, he caught me impersonating an heiress in the middle of a lucrative job—I was stealing a map to find powerful relics. He had an idea of what I was up to but allowed me the freedom to move about." She spun a finger in the air to emphasize her point. Papá could have taken control of her muscles.

She continued, "I thought him a fool at the time, but his kindness made me curious. He asked me a question that changed my life."

"What did he ask you?" I shifted my legs to the side. They had fallen asleep under my weight.

A smile lifted at the corners of her mouth like she savored a sweet memory. "He asked if I was satisfied. It may seem silly to you, but I'd been wrestling with that exact question. I didn't understand the cost to me every time I was offered a large sum of coins."

"Did you answer Papá?"

"I did." She pushed back stray hairs from my face. "I told him to erase the last six years of my life and give me a new start. Your Papá can be many things, but his wisest moments come when he forgets himself, his ego."

"What did he do next?"

"He invited me to court, saying all could change if I only asked. I thought it was an invitation to marry him. It turns out he wanted to show me what it meant to acknowledge the Ancient One. I had felt unworthy to speak to any such deity, and I *was*... unworthy. But Papá said that the invitation stood so long as I stopped selling my gift—really my soul."

Laude pranced in. "Princess, I'm back. Did you want me to show you the regular braid or the... Oh, I'm so sorry." She dropped a curtsy. "Your Majesty."

Mamá stood slowly. She smirked and patted Laude's back. "I'm so happy you two bonded so well on your trip. It makes my heart sing. Your precious mother would be glad. I must go." She strode out of the room.

"I dare not say this, but does something seem off about your mother?" Laude's concern etched on her forehead, and it stirred a giggle within my chest.

CHAPTER 48

DAYS PASSED. I VISITED Zichri at his bedside each spare moment. The thing between us—whatever it was—blossomed like my moonlight lilies in the garden. For that, I was thankful. The details of how our relationship would work loomed over our heads, but we laughed it off, coming up with the most fanciful ideas. Zichri said we'd live on an island until our fathers worked out the details of the treaty. I'd feed him strange fruits, and he'd hunt purple beasts that hide in caves.

The day before, Zichri walked through the infirmary. The way he sucked in his breath from time to time hinted that he may have put on a brave face to hide his pain. Healers swooped in to help Zichri after each lap around the room. Today, he stretched and did a set of exercises while I sat on a stool near his bed.

As he combated the limits of his body, I also fought against my new ability. Even as I watched Zichri's progress, invisible connections tethered me to others. That healer who touched Zichri's thigh to relax the muscle was bored. The soldier sleeping across the room twisted with guilt. A dozen more links formed. I steeled myself from emotion, focusing on the sunlight pouring in through the tall windows. Using my gift felt like an intrusion into others' lives. The truth was Lux's contorted body blazed through my memory as a reminder and warning. Why would I ever want to use my gift again?

Zichri walked over to my seat and offered his arm. "Ready for our garden walk?" He had insisted on getting outdoors.

I looped an arm through his as we walked over the grassy paths that crisscrossed the palace grounds. The sun kissed the green-purple encircling a pink gash on Zichri's cheek. I grazed the satin roses, enjoying the feel when I pricked a finger on a thorn. A warm drop of blood swelled on my fingertip.

"Are you still nervous about our meeting with your father?" Zichri examined my throbbing finger.

I lifted my chin high. "There's no reason to be nervous." I lied, putting on my most dignified smile.

"You like to avoid this topic. I enjoy the daydreaming, but we need to discuss where we'd live. And the possibility of our—"

"Don't say it."

"Of our—"

"Don't." The what-ifs tormented me at night, and our daydreams revived my soul. Why ruin a perfectly good walk? I tugged on his arm to continue along the path where servants repaired trampled grounds.

Laude dug her fingers into the soil, planting flowers with all the other servants. The gardens closest to the sea had been ravaged by all the fighting. I waved at her, hoping a distraction would shift the lingering question still in Zichri's intense gaze. Gonzalo, Blas, and Jaime carried a rough spun sheet piled with black soil. They'd volunteered to help with some new project around the palace each day. Somehow, they managed to always work on the same projects in which Laude got assigned.

Zichri patted my hand, calling my attention back to him. "Beatriz, I want us to have a plan in place. It would be a shame if I agree to something you are opposed to." He massaged his forehead at seeing me picking flowers. "Please listen."

"I am listening." Placing one hand on his shoulder and the other in his palm, I sang, "The days of our kingdoms shall never go in want, with ..." I lengthened the last word so he could join in with me. When he did not, I sighed and said, "We still have yet to dance again."

The hard lines on his face softened, and Zichri chuckled. I took it as him resigning to my wishes, and it pleased me. He led me into a spin. My dress skirt floated around my body, refreshing me with a tiny breeze. I wanted to lock this moment in a bottle. Then I'd drink from it anytime I needed a perfect moment to wash away pain or hardship.

Papá sat next to Mamá on a plush loveseat. I didn't know why my parents chose the parlor room for this conversation, but I was happy to be part of it.

Cosme lounged on the couch across from them, levitating his two daggers. Catching Cosme's daggers by the handles, I rolled my eyes at how he flexed his gifting. "Could you please put these away? We don't want Zichri to get the wrong impression."

Cosme removed his suit jacket, revealing more daggers sheathed in the belts crossing the front of his chest. "You can never be too careful with Himzos for friends."

Vexed, I dropped into a seat. There was no reasoning with Cosme. Zichri, Gonzalo, Blas, and Jaime would arrive soon, so I held back my tongue.

Laude entered the parlor with a pitcher and glasses of cool lime water, just like I asked her to do. I winked at her, letting her know to continue with our plan.

"Your Majesty, would you like me to bring out a shrimp cocktail?" Laude kept her head bowed in a most reverent way. She and I knew how Papá could not resist his favorite dish. It was always a good idea to make Papá as content as possible before asking big questions.

"Yes, that will do." A hint of a smile passed beneath his mustache.

As Laude strode out, Zichri and the men walked in. Jaime misjudged the spacing in the doorway and collided with Laude. She flushed, giving Jaime a flirtatious grin that was hard not to notice.

"My humble apologies, miss." Jaime dipped his head and continued to follow Zichri in. He glanced back, stealing an extra glimpse at Laude.

Cosme flared his nose. "See what I mean?" He must have been speaking about a previous conversation between our parents and him.

Thankfully, Mamá and Papá ignored him. Mamá held up her chin, smiling confidently. Papá lifted his thick brows, tenderly squeezing her hand, showing more affection than I'd seen in a long time. Near-death experiences do have a way of revealing how important people are to us. One nod of Mamá's head and Papá got to his feet in respect toward our guests. The rest of us followed though Cosme grunted in disapproval.

Zichri bowed his head, almost touching his gruff chin to his simple white tunic. A respectful greeting rolled off his tongue. He stood in front of the plush armchair between Papá and me. I willed him to look at me, but he fixed his gaze in Papá and Mamá's direction, as was proper.

"We'd like to thank you both as king and queen and a father and mother for saving our daughter," Papá spoke in his formal tone of voice.

Zichri dipped his head in thanks. The door swung open, and Laude strode across the room with a tray overflowing with shrimp tails in bulbous cups. Another maid snuck in behind her with plates and cups, and a third maid slipped in with a pitcher of lime water.

Jaime stood behind Zichri, hands clasped at his back, smiling and watching Laude set a dish on a side table next to each seat. I hoped for their sake that Papá approved of Zichri and me. Though most personal maids don't marry, I was confident Laude wouldn't be my maid for long. Papá sat.

We all took our seats. I couldn't take it anymore. I wanted to scream, but I clutched a chunk of my woolen skirt instead.

Papá savored a shrimp while Laude poured him a glass of lime water. I tried not to appear too excited about priming Papá's good disposition, but I caught Mamá arching a brow at me. How did she always see through me?

The other maids scuffled out the door.

Zichri took a glass of pulpy liquid from Laude. "Your daughter is extraordinary. I'd give my life for her again if the chance presented itself."

"We have two matters to discuss." Papá straightened up, wasting no time. "Because of our gratitude, we traditionally grant a token of our appreciation."

My heart pounded. I had no idea how Zichri would ask for my hand or how Papá would respond. How I wished to use my gifting to search everyone's hearts. But I decided not to use my gift for personal gain.

Laude trickled lime water into my glass.

"If you will permit, I would like a formal betrothal with your daughter." Zichri stared unflinchingly at my parents.

Papá nodded to Mamá. I'd seen this a million times before. He gave Mamá the official response to Zichri's request. Mamá shot me a knowing look. They must have discussed this beforehand.

Mamá turned her gaze to Zichri. "Prince Zichri of Himzo, I was opposed to this notion up until this morning when I spoke with the Ancient One. I allowed myself to listen and let go of my anxious thoughts. We have no objection to your request but our law ..." Mamá's melodic voice rang in my ears.

But our law. What could that mean? I wanted to stand in opposition, but Mamá's training whispered through my mind. *One should always listen carefully before saying a word.* So I clasped my clammy hands together over my lap, begging in silence for the law to be reasonable.

Papá shifted in his seat. "That leads us to the second matter of business. Our law prohibits the union of unallied kingdoms with anyone on our royal court."

Cosme perked up in his seat. Laude passed me my glass, and I held it to my lips, attempting to sip. The water sloshed from the way I trembled, making it impossible to drink.

"But," Papá continued, "if you could arrange for a peace treaty between Himzo and Giddel, my daughter may choose whether or not she will have you as a future husband."

I straightened my back, ready to shout *yes!*

Cosme hunched and tossed a shrimp into his mouth.

Laude handed me a small plate and a tiny fork to spear shrimp onto my plate. She strolled over to pour lime water for Cosme.

"I can arrange it, but I will need time." Zichri raked his fingers through his hair. No hint of joy crossed his face. Why did he look almost sullen?

"You may have up to a year. Giddel is a generous kingdom, but we do not take an attack lightly. If you do not produce the treaty, Giddel has no choice but to send its full force against your kingdom."

Cosme shifted in his seat, and a creak echoed through the room. Tension pressed around me like a palpable force. Laude kept her head down and shook her head as if realizing she was supposed to be pouring Mamá her drink.

At that moment, Zichri could have been chiseled from stone, showing no sign of emotion. "I understand. I have but one request. Once I attain the treaty, will you allow for a short engagement?" He glanced in my direction for the first time since the conversation began. His dark chocolate eyes gleamed from the sunlight pouring in through the windows.

If he could produce a treaty quickly, I could be a married woman before my eighteenth birthday. I pressed my lips together to stop from smiling too wide.

Mamá patted Papá's knee. "If that is Beatriz's wish, you may marry whenever she sees fit."

Papá rose to his feet, reaching out an arm. Zichri shot up, fitting his shoulder under Papá's hand. Like a mirror image, Zichri placed a hand on Papá's shoulder, settling the agreement in one simple gesture.

Servants led four steeds to the palace portico. Zichri held my hand, grazing his thumb in my palm.

"You could leave in a few weeks." I squared up to him. "The healers say you will do better with some rest."

He gazed down at me with a sympathetic smile.

The moment Papá explained what was required for us to marry, anxiety leaked out his skin, without me having to reach for it. He wouldn't say what ailed him.

Drawing my knuckles to his lips, he assured me, "I will be back for you. If I tarry, I will send word. Your father leaves the direct road open."

"When did you speak to Papá?" I considered yesterday when he spent the entire day with me and the day before when we met with my family. That was odd of Papá to have spoken to him twice in one day when he had so much work because of the political fallout.

Zichri smirked. "Your brother shared some choice words."

"Please say he hid the daggers."

"No. They were pointed at my neck." He chuckled.

I clenched my fists. Cosme had no business threatening Zichri.

"Don't get so upset. I would have done the same thing for my sister. Why do you think Milo is under my command?"

"Well, that's different than putting a dagger to Milo's neck."

"It's worse. We found all sorts of cruel rituals to start in order for him to be accepted into our group." He drew me in closer. "Enough about that."

Inhaling deeply, I smelled castile soap on his skin.

"Don't worry," he traced my jawline, "I'll get my regular forest aroma on the road."

I smacked his chest, flustered that he always caught me smelling him. Holding back a giggle and tears, I whispered, "You come back soon, Zichri of Himzo."

"Like I said, I will no matter what." He leaned in, pressing his warm lips to my forehead. "I dreamt you kissed me."

"I did." My throat tightened.

"When I come back, we will finish that kiss." He stepped toward the horses.

Blas and Gonzalo had already mounted and were bantering. Laude embraced Jaime in a way that made me believe I'd need to pry them apart. But one tap on the shoulder from Zichri and the two separated. Laude swooped to my side. A breeze undid some of my hair, and I tucked it behind my ear. I petted the steeds, speaking peace to each one—anything to help them ride safely.

The mares clomped the stone and trotted away. Zichri promised to come back, and he was a man of his word. I waved as they made it under the giant arch at the front gate. Sadness flooded within me, though I had almost all that I wanted. My gift. Respect. And now the hope of a betrothal to a man I loved. How could I be anything but happy? I lifted my chin high and stretched a practiced smile across my face, watching the horses disappear into the city.

THE END

ACKNOWLEDGMENTS

FIRST, I'D LIKE TO thank God for His goodness toward me and for taking me on this writing journey. I always enjoyed a good story but never dreamed I'd write my own novel.

Before I started writing, I always read the acknowledgments and wondered at the long list of people mentioned. Now I understand why there are always so many names.

Thank you, Hope Bolinger, for believing in this story and reigniting my attention toward it. I finished this manuscript years ago and left it in the figurative drawer for a long time. It went through many, many drafts. After a while, I didn't believe it would ever be published. It was a breath of fresh air to have someone else love my characters like I love them.

Thank you, Rylie Fine, for helping me finetune this story and finish it into what it is today.

The next set of people that whipped this story into shape were an unknown set of judges in the Genesis contest. I had the privilege of making it to the semifinals. They gave me feedback that would shape this book.

My critique groups and my beta readers also have strengthened this story. Whenever I read the scenes, I can see and hear their feedback. Thank you, Storyteller Squad, Susan Miura, Jenna Carlson, Chandra Blumberg, Delores Yamnitz, Carolyn Ridler, and many others.

Also, I'd like to thank Lydia Craft for giving me her notes on this manuscript. This book needed Lydia's keen eye on its pages.

My family has been an endless source of encouragement. My mom is the first person who ever gets to read my stories. Her encouragement and love for books keeps me writing. Even though my husband is not a fiction reader, he has kept me from quitting and has been supportive through the entire process.

Lastly, I'd love to give a shout out to my amazing street team who helped me release my book baby into the wild.

Thank you, everyone, who has followed me on this publishing journey. Your support and friendship have made all the difference in getting this book into your hands.

If you enjoyed this book, will you consider sharing the message with others?

Let us know your thoughts. You can let the author know by visiting or sharing a photo of the cover on our social media pages or leaving a review at a retailer's site. All of it helps us get the message out!

Email: info@ironstreammedia.com

    @ironstreammedia

---

Brookstone Publishing Group, Harambee Press, Iron Stream, Iron Stream Fiction, Iron Stream Kids, and Life Bible Study are imprints of Iron Stream Media, which derives its name from Proverbs 27:17, "As iron sharpens iron, so one person sharpens another." This sharpening describes the process of discipleship, one to another. With this in mind, Iron Stream Media provides a variety of solutions for churches, ministry leaders, and nonprofits ranging from in-depth Bible study curriculum and Christian book publishing to custom publishing and consultative services.

For more information on ISM and its imprints, please visit IronStreamMedia.com